CROWN OF CHAOS
THE KNIGHTS OF ALANA
BOOK III

AARON HODGES

Edited by Genevieve Lerner
Proofread by Sara Houston
Illustration by Joemel Requeza
Map by Michael Hodges

ABOUT THE AUTHOR

Aaron Hodges was born in 1989 in the small town of Whakatane, New Zealand. He studied for five years at the University of Auckland, completing a Bachelors of Science in Biology and Geography, and a Masters of Environmental Engineering. After working as an environmental consultant for two years, he grew tired of office work and decided to quit his job in 2014 and see the world. One year later, he published his first novel - Stormwielder.

FOLLOW AARON HODGES…

And receive TWO FREE novels and a short story!

https://aaronhodgesauthor.com/newsletter

ALSO BY AARON HODGES

The Sword of Light

Book 1: Stormwielder

Book 2: Firestorm

Book 3: Soul Blade

The Legend of the Gods

Book 1: Oathbreaker

Book 2: Shield of Winter

Book 3: Dawn of War

The Knights of Alana

Book 1: Daughter of Fate

Book 2: Queen of Vengeance

Book 3: Crown of Chaos

The Evolution Gene

Book 1: Reborn

Book 2: Havoc

Book 3: Carnage

Descendants of the Fall

Book 1: Warbringer

Book 2: Wrath of the Forgotten

Book 3: Age of Gods

Book 4: Dreams of Fury

The Alfurian Chronicles

Book 1: Defiant

Book 2: Guardian

Book 3: Conquest

The Swords of Heaven and Hell

Book 1: <u>Darkstrider</u>

The Four Circles

Book 1: Help! My Wizard Mentor Had A Heart Attack And Now
I'm Being Chased By A Horde Of Giant Spiders!

The Untamed Isles

The Path Awakens

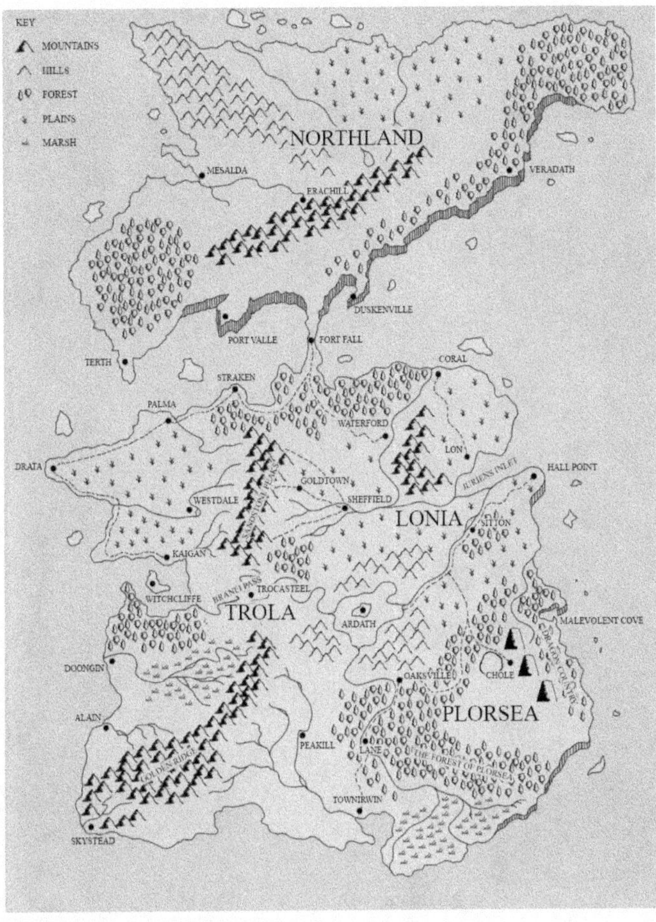

KEY
MOUNTAINS
HILLS
FOREST
PLAINS
MARSH
NORTHLAND
MESALDA
ERACHILL
VERADATH
DUSKENVILLE
PORT VALLE
FORT FALL
CORAL
TERTH
STRAKEN
PALMA
WATERFORD
LON
DRATA
HALL POINT
GOLDTOWN
BURIENS INLET
WESTDALE
SHEFFIELD
LONIA
SITTON
KAIGAN
WITCHCLIFFE
BRANG PASS
TROCASTEEL
MALEVOLENT COVE
TROLA
ARDATH
DRAGON COAST
DOONGIN
OAKSVILLE
CHOLE
ALAIN
PLORSEA
GOLDEN RIDGE
PEAKILL
LANE
THE FOREST OF PLORSEA
TOWNIRWIN
SKYSTEAD

PROLOGUE

The first hints of dawn had just touched the horizon when Braidon stepped into the courtyard of the Castle. Walking slowly, he crossed to the old stone stairwell and started up. It was some thirty feet before he reached the ramparts of the defensive wall. A fresh breeze greeted him, but even there the tang of smoke clung to the air.

It had taken them most of the night to gain control of the fire. In the end, half the Castle had been gutted, but that was nothing compared to the loss of lives. A lump lodged in Braidon's throat as he recalled the men, women, and children who had been trapped in the pantheon. They had never stood a chance, not after Dominic and his men had lit the fire, after they'd barred the doors to trap them inside…

Braidon's stomach twisted and it took an effort of will to keep from throwing up. The fire had burned so hot that there had been little left by the end. Where just hours before there had been a hundred souls, filled with life and love and hope, only ash remained. Dead because of Braidon's folly.

Silently, Braidon slammed his fist down on the granite crenulations. Why had he trusted Dominic? He should have realised the man's evil, should have seen the darkness in his heart. But Dominic had been there in the moment of Braidon's greatest weakness. And so the king had put his faith in the man.

Braidon would regret that decision for the rest of his life.

Shuddering, Braidon turned his eyes inwards, to that void that was his inner mind. Once his magic had burned there, a gift granted to him by the Gods. But that power was long gone, departed with their death some thirty years ago. And for thirty years the void had been empty, an infinite darkness at his core.

Now though, a fresh power burned there, the multi-coloured glow of a hundred lives. A shiver slid down Braidon's spine as his mind touched the energies. They lit his veins aflame, filling him with renewed vigour, giving him confidence that he could take on the world. He shuddered at the sensation, at the strangeness of it all.

In an instant of despair, Braidon had reached for the flames and tried to extinguish them with the power of his own life force. It had been a futile act. The strength of one man, however brave or noble, could not quench such an inferno.

But in doing so, Braidon had sensed something else—the energies of the dead, the power of the departing souls. He had seen an opportunity then, a chance to make something of their loss. Here was the power he had prayed for, the strength he needed to defeat his vile wife. So he had gathered the power to him, had drawn in the life forces of the dying members of the Order, and made them his own.

The light was growing now, the sun creeping up over the

rooftops of Chole. The Dying City stretched out all around him, the outer walls a half-mile away at their nearest point. They were strong walls of granite and iron, walls that had never fallen, not even to the Dark Magicker Archon. They would serve him well in the coming war. He might not yet have the strength in arms to carry the fight to Marianne, but neither did she have the numbers to attack him here.

And even should she take the walls, the city would fight her to its dying breath. They had seen the darkness of the Order of Alana, the cult that had lifted Marianne to queen. Their Knights had threatened to burn the Temple of the Earth, to purge the city of those they deemed blasphemers. Only Braidon's interference had kept the temple and its priests safe.

Now he had taken their Castle, the centre of the Order's power in Chole. With Marianne's followers purged from the city, he would make their fortress his own. There was nowhere else stronger in Chole. He would be safe here, protected until the time came to face his wife. It would buy him time to plan the revolt, to train his army and plot the queen's eventual downfall.

Boom.

Braidon's thoughts were interrupted as the doors to the keep swung open in the courtyard. Shaking himself free of thoughts of the future, he looked down at the new arrivals. Men and women emerged from the keep in twos and threes, heads down, their whispers carrying up to where Braidon stood unnoticed.

Yesterday, Braidon had offered all who'd followed him a position in his army. Though their losses had been heavy and even the survivors were battered and bruised, most had accepted. Afterwards there had been some celebration, but most of his new recruits had been muted, still processing the violence and raw grief of battle. Soon they had taken to their beds—lying down wherever they could find space in the parts of the castle untouched by the fire.

He had bid them return to the courtyard at first light, and now it looked that most were gathered below.

All but Dominic and those men who had joined him in burning the pantheon.

As though summoned by his thought, the doors of the keep creaked open again, and the betrayers filed out one by one, their arms bound behind their backs and mouths gagged with cloth. Two guards led the way across the courtyard, forcing the crowd to part before them, while his King's Guard, Kryssa, brought up the rear with a third soldier.

Their eyes met as Braidon started back down the staircase. Kryssa's face was gaunt, her eyes dark with shadow. She had taken the loss in the pantheon even harder than Braidon, after driving off the Elder that had been protecting them. It had been the right thing to do—the man had slain hundreds to grant himself power—but there was little Braidon could say to sage her guilt.

They met in the centre of the courtyard. Kryssa stood a few inches below Braidon's own five feet and nine inches. She'd retired from his King's Guard over a decade ago, but with the rest of his Guard decimated by Marianne's treachery, Kryssa had been forced out of retirement. Fortunately for Braidon, she had lost none of her edge. She was now his most steadfast lieutenant—though he knew she longed to go in search of her missing daughter, Pela.

The thought reminded Braidon of his own son, Calybe, taken hostage by his wife in Ardath. He could not attack the city so long as Marianne held the boy, though such thoughts were a long way off yet. First he needed an army.

Transferring his gaze to the condemned men, Braidon was touched by doubt. He could not afford to lose a single loyal soldier, not with the war to come. And Dominic had proven his loyalty without question. He and the others had made a terrible mistake, but…

Swallowing, Braidon caught Kryssa's eyes on him, and knew he could not turn back now. The energies of a hundred innocent lives flowed in his veins, lost because of the hatred in the hearts of these men. However desperate his cause, Braidon must hold to the laws of the land.

He nodded to Kryssa, and as one they turned to the makeshift gibbet that sat in the corner of the courtyard. Six nooses had been tied and hung from wooden poles over-hanging the courtyard, while matching barrels waited beneath. Kryssa and her guards led Dominic and his fellows across the courtyard and forced them onto the barrels at sword point, then looped the nooses around their necks.

Whispers spread around Braidon as his followers realised what was happening. Several cast angry glances in the king's direction, but most watched in silence, though he did not miss the sorrow in their eyes. Braidon felt it too. There had already been so much loss, so much destruction —and for what? To fight for a crown he had never wanted, to defend a nation that had rejected him time and time again?

For a second he was tempted to turn and walk away from it all, to leave his crown and Chole and Plorsea behind.

It will all be yours one day, son, his father's voice whispered from the depths of his memory. *It has been my life's goal to make this land safe for you and our people.*

Braidon shuddered. The Tsar had been evil at the end, but once he had loved his children, had cared for his people. It had been his ambition to free the Three Nations of magic, to bring balance to the world. That had been Braidon's destiny, to usher in the peace his father had always dreamed of.

Instead, his rule had invited only chaos. But he knew the reason now. His wife, Marianne, had been scheming behind his back all along, plotting his downfall. Now she wished to rule, to hold herself up as the rightful queen.

No, he could not walk away now, could not leave the world to chaos. Marianne was mad, would plunge Plorsea into another war and allow her Knights to roam freely, hunting the faithful of the Old Gods. Braidon had no choice—Marianne must be destroyed for what she had done to his nation.

For what she had done to *him.*

Shivering, Braidon forced himself back to the present. Dominic and his five fellows stood awaiting their fate and the whispers of the crowd were growing. The mood was muted, the ecstasy of their victory lost with the morning's gloom. It was time to end this, and fast.

"The six of you have been found guilty of mass murder," Braidon called, stepping up before the condemned men.

Of them all, he knew only Dominic. The former guard had risked his life to protect Braidon, had sheltered him at great risk. Braidon had promised Dominic the world for his aid, but now he stood staring down at his king in terror, and he would receive only death.

"The act was witnessed and admitted," Braidon continued at last, "and so I am left with no choice—"

"My liege!"

Braidon spun as a woman's voice called from across the courtyard. There was a commotion amidst the crowd before Dominic's wife, Janylle, pushed her way to the fore. Her eyes were wide and stained red, and there was a panicked look on her face. She stumbled up to Braidon, tears streaming down her cheeks. Several men made to stop her, but Braidon waved them back.

"Please, don't do this!" Janylle gasped. "Dominic gave up everything to serve you. Please, you are the king! Grant him pardon, and he will be your loyal soldier until the end of his days."

A shiver ran down Braidon's spine as he looked at Janylle, remembering the conversation that had passed between them just a day before. She had feared losing her husband in Braidon's war, that he would die fighting in some distant battle. But she could never have suspected *this*, that her husband would meet his end by Braidon's own hand.

But then, no one could have predicted what would happen next.

"He murdered innocent men and women, Janylle," he croaked, his voice close to breaking. "He murdered *children*. I cannot pardon that."

He made to turn away, but Janylle lurched forward and grabbed his arm. "Bastard!" she screamed. Braidon tried to break free, but there was no hiding from her words. "So this is how you repay loyalty? We sheltered you, protected you! Now you turn your back, defend the lives of those devils from the Order over your own people?"

"I'm sorry, Janylle—"

"Damn your sorries," she spat. "Those so-called innocents were followers of Alana. They would have betrayed you to their precious queen the second she reached our gates. My husband did you a favour, ridding you of them. But you were never strong enough to make the tough choices. Now he pays the price for your weakness."

Braidon scowled. He'd heard enough of the woman's ramblings. At his gesture, several of his newly appointed guards dragged Janylle away. Her screams continued long after she was gone though, ringing in his ears, in his thoughts, and Braidon couldn't help but wonder at their truth.

Shivering, he looked up at Dominic. The fear had vanished from the man's eyes, and now his face was screwed up, contorted by a terrible rage. Braidon swallowed and cast a glance over his shoulder, but Janylle was long gone.

Gritting his teeth, he lifted a hand and six guards took their places behind the condemned. Ice spread through Braidon's stomach as they looked to him for the final signal. He wanted to be anywhere but the shadowed courtyard, but he was as trapped in his fate as Dominic was his own. There could be no going back.

Braidon dropped his hand, and the barrels were kicked out from beneath the prisoners' feet.

❧   I   ❧

An entire day passed after their fight with the Knight before Pela found the strength to walk again. Even then, her entire body ached, making every step an agony. It hurt just to speak, let alone eat or drink, and so she and Ruebyn passed the time in silence. Yet with the Knight's companions still somewhere in the mountains, neither dared wait long, and as the sun dawned on the second day, they started off around the lake.

At her stumbling pace, it took long hours to traverse the steep slopes and reach the pass leading down into Trola. Only when she stood between the towering mountain peaks and looked down into Trola did Pela finally feel relief, that they had truly escaped their pursuers. She wouldn't let herself think about what lay ahead, about the fate that awaited if the Trolans found them.

By the time they reached the foothills, the last of their food was gone and they were forced to scavenge for whatever scraps they could find. Thankfully the western slopes of the Sandstone Mountains were covered by lush forest, and they were able to forage for late berries and tubers dug from the roots of trees.

Without a bow, they could not bring down any of the game they spotted amidst the undergrowth. But a dozen streams crisscrossed the landscape, and in one isolated pool, Pela found a fat trout trapped by the falling autumn currents.

The contrast to Lonia was a welcome change. On the other side of the mountains, the land had been dry, the earth parched but for a few glacier-fed rivers, and the vegetation had been thin and unwelcoming. Now as they reached the lower slopes, tall saplings of pine and firs rose around them, providing shelter from the mountain winds.

"A hundred years ago, great forests covered most of Trola," Ruebyn explained one morning as they made their way down a steeply sloping hillside. "But they were almost all cut down—or burned—to make way for farmland. These trees are young, though. I guess their new king is allowing the forests to regrow."

Pela wasn't particularly interested in Trola's history with forests and farming, but she nodded anyway and offered a smile to show she had heard. With nothing else to add though, the conversation quickly petered out, turning to an uncomfortable silence.

A distance had grown between them in the last few days. Pela had been unable to recover the closeness they'd shared the night of the storm. They hadn't spoken about what had happened between them that night, and now she felt too much time had passed, that she no longer knew what it had meant.

So instead, she focused her thoughts on what lay before them. For decades, Trola's borders had been closed to Lonia and Plorsea, entrance forbidden on penalty of death. Desperation had forced her westward, but now Pela was no longer sure she'd made the right choice.

The iron collar around her throat was a constant presence, the dull black gem at its centre an ugly reminder of her time in the darkness, her captivity. It was the collar that had forced her down this path. It marked her as a slave. Any Lonian citizen who saw her would know what she was. There was only one punishment for an escaped slave —death.

Trola had been her only choice for freedom, but Ruebyn could have chosen another path. He had been her overseer in the mines, and while their hunters thought him culpable for her escape, he had no collar to mark him as a fugitive. He could have returned to Lonia unrecognised, could have lived out his life in peace.

Five days after their desperate battle with the Knight, they finally emerged from the fledgling forest into open farmland. There the going became gentler, the rolling hills giving way easily to their worn-down boots.

That day they saw no sign of any other living soul, except when Pela noticed a flock of sheep in the distance. They'd diverted from their course in case the shepherd was nearby, and when darkness fell, they'd lit no fire.

The next morning Pela woke before the sunrise, feeling strangely alert, ready to begin the day. Ruebyn still lay asleep nearby, his eyelids fluttering in the grips of some dream. His brown hair, once cropped short, was now long enough to hang across his face. Several twigs and leaves had taken up residence in it during the night. She found herself smiling at the sight, and she gently brushed them away.

A groan sounded from Ruebyn's throat and he twisted

on the ground, his brow creasing with a frown. Then his eyes snapped open and she saw a look of panic there. He flinched away from her and half-scrambled to his feet.

"The Knight!" he gasped, spinning around as though he expected the steel-clad warrior to come upon them at any moment. Then his senses finally seemed to return. Staggering to a stop, he cast a sheepish glance at Pela. "Sorry, bad dream."

Pela shivered, remembering her own nightmares, how the Knight still hunted her there. So many terrible things had happened since their escape, but the image of his mottled face as he leaned over her, the twisted nose and bulging veins and loathing in his eyes…she would never forget that face as long as she lived.

"It's okay," she said softly, even as her hand drifted unconsciously to her throat, where the Knight had tried to throttle the life from her. "He'd dead. We never have to worry about that monster again."

Ruebyn stared at her for a long moment before sinking back to the ground. "Ay," he whispered. "Thank the Saviour he lost his footing and fell."

Pela frowned at his wording. "What are you talking about?" she asked, arching an eyebrow.

They had said nothing about that brief, violent battle in the past few days. Neither of them wanted to relive those frantic moments, those brief seconds during which they had been mere inches from death.

"You must have missed it, you were barely conscious. I was trying to reach you, but he was too quick. He had you by the throat, but the stones were loose, and he stumbled backwards, went over the edge before he could recover."

Pela's frown deepened and she shook her head. "That's…not how it happened."

In those last moments as the Knight tried to strangle her, Pela had found a final spark of strength within her. Pinned beneath his weight, she had been unable to fight against him, but in her desperation Pela had taken that last ounce of energy and hurled it at the Knight with her mind.

"I…threw him from me," she murmured, her eyes on the ground. "I don't know how. It was like I could use my own life force against him, as if I could project my strength beyond my own body." She looked up at Ruebyn as she finished, unable to offer a better explanation.

He raised one bushy eyebrow. "That's not possible."

"Why not?"

"Because what you're describing would be magic," he replied, wearing a slightly bemused grin. "And magic died with the…Old Gods."

Pela scowled. "It wasn't magic, it was…a part of me."

Ruebyn sighed. "Pela, you were barely alive when I reached you," he said. "Is it possible you imagined it?"

He held out a consoling hand, but she slapped it away and leapt to her feet. "No, it's not."

"Fine, then show me," Ruebyn replied, sounding weary.

"What?"

"Show me this power of yours," he said patiently. "If you could use it on the edge of death, it should be easy to summon now."

Pela flashed him a glare, but after a moment's hesitation, she closed her eyes and turned her back on him. Drawing in a breath, she tried to squash her irritation. She had felt the power flickering within her the last few days, burning hotter as she recovered her strength, but she had not tried to reach for it.

Now she drew on her mother's teaching, seeking to sink into the meditative trance where she had first noticed the strange power. Her mother, Kryssa, had taught it to her as a child, passing down the knowledge from her own adopted mother, Selina. As she had grown older, Pela hadn't given the technique much thought, though she'd continued to practice during their weekly visits to the old temple.

Pela cursed inwardly as she realised her mind had become distracted. Letting out a sharp exhalation, she focused again on her task. Meditation was meant to calm, to bring clarity of thought, but Pela was unused to being watched while she practiced. She could hear the heavy breathing of Ruebyn behind her, could sense his impatience, and it tugged at her concentration.

Finally, she swore and swung around. "Damn you!" she snapped.

He leapt away, eyes wide and hands raised in front of him, but Pela ignored him. Sweeping her scant belongings into the worn backpack and clipping their only dagger to her belt, she started off across the hillside. She was too angry to look back and check whether Ruebyn followed.

It was so like him to disbelieve, to question her words. He believed in nothing but what his damned teachers back in Lon had taught him. Even his precious Saviour preached the importance of the physical, the need to push back against the magic the Three Gods had once instilled in the land. The spiritual was anathema to the Order of Alana and their followers.

Yet Pela knew what she had felt—just as she knew that even without the Gods, there were other powers at large in the land. On the shores of Malevolent Cove, the queen had wielded some strange new magic against Pela and her friends, *commanding* them. Only her uncle Devon had been able to resist—and he had died for it.

She couldn't help but think it was all connected. Another memory flickered into her mind, of her pickaxe plunging through sheer rock, back in the mines beneath the Lonian mountains. She had been meditating then as well; had she unwittingly tapped into her own power? The thought twisted her stomach into knots—her friend Siden had been killed in the landslide that followed. If that was true, his blood was on her hands.

Suddenly cold, Pela forced her attention to the path ahead. They were still moving through hilly country, though with the forest behind them, it was easy to see the way now. Taking her bearings against the sun, she continued southward. If they were lucky, they could keep to these backcountry trails and avoid the Trolan people entirely. The Brunei pass was somewhere to the south—it would take them to Plorsea, and safety.

"Where is everybody?" Ruebyn asked after they had been walking for an hour.

Pela's head jerked up. She had not looked at him since their fight, but now she slowed, allowing him to catch up. He offered a sheepish grin as they drew level, as if to admit he had been a fool earlier.

"What do you mean?" she asked, deciding it best to let the issue of her power drop.

"Look around," he said, indicating their surroundings. "This is good land, but these fields are untended. See here." He pointed to where a cluster of saplings grew near the trail. "The forest is returning, even here. Why would they let that happen?"

Pela shrugged. "Maybe they prefer the trees." Then she started to laugh. "Besides, we should be thankful! We're not meant to be here, remember?"

Ruebyn shook his head. "It's weird, I'm telling you."

"Ruebyn, you worry too much," she said, flicking him a sidelong glance. But when he only frowned and said nothing, she let out a sigh. "Look, we're still a long way from the coast, right? Weren't most of Trola's cities close to the ocean?"

"Yeah but there were still *people* in the countryside, surely?"

Realising he would not be convinced, Pela suppressed a sigh and they settled back into silence. She couldn't help but feel as though something had been lost between them these last few days. Gone was the closeness they had found in the mountain cave. She longed for the warmth of his company, the heat that had burned in her chest at his embrace, and yet…

Cheeks flushed, Pela shook her head to dislodge the memories. The day was quickly growing warm and while it was a welcome relief after the chill nights in the mountains, she unbuttoned her coat to cool herself. The ground was soft beneath her feet and for a time she was forced to concentrate on each footstep, lest her already crumbling boots disintegrate altogether.

But eventually her thoughts drifted once more. Despite herself, Ruebyn's earlier words still irked Pela. In her mind, somewhere in that awful fight with the Knight, she had been changed. Just a few short months ago, she would never have even thought about challenging such a warrior. Yet somehow she had found the courage and ability to stand against him. And this time there had been no hero to come to her rescue, no Devon or Caledan or her own mother to save her.

And she had won. Through magic or skill or sheer determination, she had bested him. It had changed her in ways she still could not comprehend.

And yet in a few short words, Ruebyn had denied her that victory.

"There!"

Pela jerked to a stop as Ruebyn suddenly let out a shout. Swinging around, she saw him pointing to the way ahead. Her gaze followed his finger, out across the rolling fields. A shiver passed through Pela as she saw the village lying in their path, nestled at the top of a nearby hill. Slate rooftops shone in the noonday sun, sloping down to brick walls that stood to either side of a dirt road.

She glanced at Ruebyn. "I hope you're happy," she muttered.

But Ruebyn wasn't smiling. His eyes were still fixed on the distant town. A frown wrinkled his face and without saying anything, he started forward again.

"Hey!" she cried, snatching his arm and dragging him back. "What are you doing?"

His hazel eyes turned to look at her. "I don't think anyone's home."

2

"*D*amnit!*"*

The scream greeted Caledan as he stepped into Marianne's apartment. He ducked as a bottle of wine went hurtling past him to shatter in the corridor. Quickly he closed the door behind him before anyone else noticed the queen's outburst. Whatever had brought about Marianne's sudden change of mood, the whole citadel didn't need to be alerted to her distress.

The queen herself stood before her desk, the contents of which were scattered about the room in various states of destruction. The sofa had been flipped on its side and the wooden chair to which he'd once been bound lay in pieces against the far wall. It looked as though a small tornado had swept through the apartment.

"Something the matter?" he asked, struggling to conceal his surprise. Marianne was usually so controlled. He hadn't seen her in such a state since…Malevolent Cove. He shuddered at the memory and quickly cast it aside.

Marianne spun at his voice. Surprise showed on her face

at the sight of him standing amidst the wreckage. Her auburn hair was frizzed and shadows of fatigue hung beneath her sapphire eyes. Clenching her fists, she took a step towards him.

"What?" she snapped.

Caledan raised an eyebrow. "That was a Lonian red, if I'm not mistaken," he said, gesturing to the shattered bottle that lay behind the closed doors. "Your favourite, and hard to come by nowadays."

The breath hissed between Marianne's teeth as she exhaled, her eyes flickering closed. Caledan waited as the queen gathered herself, and was not surprised to see that her rage had vanished when she looked at him again.

"I apologise, my Champion," she said formally. "You should not have had to bear witness to such an…outburst."

Composed once more, she gestured at the sofa. As though gripped by the hands of a giant, it rose from the ground and righted itself. Marianne took a seat and nodded for him to join her. Used to her displays of magic by now, Caledan said nothing. But after her earlier rage, he still hesitated.

"I have had a…setback," Marianne admitted.

Letting out a breath, Caledan crossed to the couch and sat. No sooner had he done so did Marianne leap back to her feet. He watched in confusion as she paced back and forth in front of the sofa.

"What…was the setback?" he asked.

"Servo has taken Lon!" the queen exclaimed, swinging on him. "I don't understand how. The council and the Lonian army are loyal to *me*. Not all the Knights in the land could have retaken the capital for the Order!"

"Perhaps it is a falsehood?" Caledan mused. "How did you receive this news?"

Marianne strode to her desk and searched amongst the papers that had fallen alongside it until she came up with the one she wanted. She thrust the letter at him as though it were poison. He took it and set it aside without reading.

"Tell me," he said quietly.

Marianne stared at him, nostrils flaring, eyes wild. Her calm demeanour had cracked again, and he sensed this was about more than just the Lonian capital. He had never seen the queen so flustered, not even when Servo himself had threatened her son. In the two weeks since they'd driven the Elder from the citadel, Caledan had all but forgotten the man. Their attention had been focused on Braidon, on how to deal with the former king's uprising in Chole.

"It doesn't say much," Marianne said, slumping down beside him. Her eyes took on a haunted look. "And what it does say makes no sense. The Lonian army turned on itself. It was open war on the streets of Lon. Servo arrived amidst the chaos with several thousand militants—untrained civilians mostly—along with his Knights. After that, Lon fell within a day. Now they cheer his name in the streets."

"What does it matter if they cheer for that monster?" Caledan asked. "The people of Plorsea love you."

"Ay, I bought their love with peace," Marianne said, looking away, "but what will become of their love when a Lonian army marches south? When Servo burns their villages and pillages their crops? I will become like my damned husband, loathed for my failures."

"You will never become like Braidon," Caledan replied with a smile. "The man is a coward, but you have the power to stop this war before it ever begins. When the time comes, we will sweep Servo from the streets of Lon, just as you did for Ardath."

Marianne sighed. "There is more."

"What?"

Her eyes shimmered as she stared into the distance. "You asked me once where my power came from."

"You never gave a straight answer," he murmured, "but...I surmised that the Elders had found a way to feed their magic with death."

"That is...the essentials of the exchange," Marianne agreed, the faintest of smiles touching her cheeks. "Though Servo and his ilk think of it as a gift from the Saviour, a way of cleansing the unfaithful from this world, of using their lives to fight against the return of the False Gods." She snorted. "Garbage, I now realise. The Elders, like all men, were greedy for power."

Caledan frowned. "But you stopped the cleansing. And I have never seen you take a life, except..." *For Devon*, he thought, though he left the sentence unfinished.

The queen's eyes fell to the floor. "Yes, that was my first taste, my initiation into the circle of Elders—though I had learned to use my own life force to perform small miracles before that."

"Then how...do you perform your magic now? Surely the power you took in Malevolent Cove..."

"Was consumed long ago," Marianne agreed. "Thankfully, I have more imagination than all the Elders combined. When I first learned of their powers, I had my engineers in Lon begin work on a secret project, one that would allow me to harness the energies of many, from all across Lonia."

"I see," Caledan commented, though her explanation had not told him much.

Marianne gave a throaty laugh. "I can see the specifics do not interest you overly much, My Champion," she said. "So I will get to the point. My engineers and I created new collars for the Lonian slaves, ones that would capture their life force upon their deaths and channel them back to me, through this." She pulled back the sleeve of her silk dress, revealing the silver bracelet on her wrist.

"But how does this have anything to do with Servo?" Caledan asked.

"Not only has Servo taken Lon, he has taken my power with it. He must have gotten the truth from the council, and had their engineers tune the collars to him."

Now Caledan saw the fear in the queen's eyes, realised what she was saying. Servo had stolen the source of her power, would use it now for himself. And with the power of Lonia at his back…

"But…you were using your power just now," he said as the thought came to him.

"Yes, and I was fool to do so," Marianne cursed. "The energies of all those who died before Servo stole control of the collars still rest within me. But there will be no more, not unless I resume the cleansings, and I will not countenance any more bloodshed. Not after risking so much to free ourselves of that evil."

"I'm glad to hear it," Caledan replied with feeling. He rose and strode past her desk onto the marble balcony. Footsteps followed as Marianne joined him, and he gestured out over the glistening rooftops. "As will they."

The queen said nothing, only slumped against the banister. Her eyes were fixed on some distant point, and he wondered if she were already regretting her declaration. Marianne was a woman driven, and she had already shown her willingness to do whatever it took to have victory. If that meant sacrificing a few more lives…

"From now on I must conserve my power for the confrontation with Servo," she said, then swore. "I knew it was a mistake to let him slip through my grasp. Had I gone after him, there would only be Braidon to deal with."

"Had you gone after him, both myself and your son would be dead," Caledan reminded her softly, placing a hand on her shoulder.

It had been Caledan's task to protect the boy while Marianne confronted the Elder Servo. But he had been alone against five armed men. In the end, he had slain four of his foes, but the last had mortally wounded him. Marianne had arrived just in time to stop the Knight and heal Caledan's injuries with her magic.

"You're right, I know you're right," she whispered, and he saw the shiver go through her, saw the haunted look in her eyes. "I am forever in your debt for that day."

"You paid that debt when you brought me back from the brink of death."

It was true. There in that room, waking from what he'd thought to be the sleep of death, Caledan had truly become Marianne's champion. She had given up the last of her strength to save him, had slipped into unconsciousness even. He would never forget her sacrifice. Not even the news of Braidon's uprising could shake his loyalty. Braidon had had his chance to rule, and had failed on every front. Marianne's day had dawned now.

The queen smiled at his words. "Don't be absurd. You gave your life in service to me. The debt remains, My Champion." She moved closer on the balcony, so that her body pressed up against his. "You have only to ask, and it will be repaid."

Caledan shivered at the offer in the queen's sapphire eyes, suddenly unsure of himself. He was not a stranger to strong woman, but Marianne was beyond anything he had ever imagined—powerful, elegant, beautiful. She could crush him at a whim, or lift him up to heights unimagined.

He swallowed, thinking again of her fear, the challenges to come. Servo was a threat they could not ignore, and unlike Braidon, he was likely to act sooner rather than later. Caledan needed to be alert. He had seen men who became entangled in thoughts of love. They inevitably died, their senses distracted, their decisions compromised. Without her power, Marianne was vulnerable.

Nodding his thanks, Caledan stepped away from her slightly and returned his gaze to the city. The distant waters of the lake shone in the setting sun. Laughter came from the queen as she reclined against the bannister, though Caledan sensed a note of disappointment beneath her mirth.

"So, My Champion," she said, "how shall we defeat my enemies?"

3

The *thuds* of swords striking shields met Kryssa's ears as she left the Castle and entered the courtyard. A week had passed since the burning, but the air within the stone walls still stank of smoke, a constant reminder of the evil that had taken place there. So it was with relief that she felt the sunshine on her face, breathed the fresh air. Unfortunately, the sight that greeted her did little to lift her mood.

Over five hundred men and women filled the courtyard. For the last week, she and Braidon had chosen sergeants from amongst their ranks, and grouped the remaining soldiers into regiments of fifty. Each sergeant was to command a regiment when the war finally came, though Kryssa remained doubtful of many. There were a few veterans from the civil war, but for the most part they were young souls, eager but inexperienced in battle.

But they were still better than the majority of Braidon's recruits. Most of those gathered had hardly seen a sword before this week, and no more than a handful showed any real promise. Given six months, Kryssa might have forged them into a half-decent force, but they didn't have months. They didn't even have weeks. A Lonian army was marching south, and word from the capital was that Marianne would soon ride out to meet them.

And now Braidon needed her for something else, some secret quest that would take them from the city for at least a night. In truth, the thought of leaving Chole—and the Castle—was a relief. It might have been the strongest fortress in the city, but there was hostility about the place, as though the very stones screamed out against their presence. Or perhaps that was just her own guilt.

Yet despite her relief, Kryssa couldn't help but think she was needed more in the city. Morale was already low amongst the recruits after the hanging, and to leave them in the hands of the untrained sergeants was to invite disaster. Even as she watched the chaotic training taking place in the yard, one of the recruits slipped and fell. Within seconds a sergeant was at his side, screaming for him to get back up.

Irritated, Kryssa started towards them, ready to give the sergeant a few choice words about leadership, but at that moment the clatter of horse hooves carried from across the courtyard. She looked around as the king emerged from the stables leading two horses.

"Kryssa!" he called, and she was forced to turn her back on the beleaguered recruit.

She watched as he approached, her mind turning again to this secret mission. What could possibly be so important that they needed to leave Chole now, when so much relied on their holding the city? What if Marianne stole a march on them while they were away? Or worse, the Order?

"So where are we heading?" Kryssa asked when he joined her.

Braidon only grinned and offered her a set of reins. "I'll tell you at the city gates," was all he said before mounting up.

Cursing inwardly, Kryssa leapt into the saddle and directed her horse after him. At least the king looked to be in a better mood today. The strain of the past week had taken its toll on the man, adding a stoop to his shoulders and leaching the life from his face. Despite their success at taking the city, he knew they still stood little chance against the forces Marianne could muster. The army marching from Lonia had been a terrible blow for Braidon. This was the first time she'd seen him smile since receiving the news.

They passed quickly through the city, Braidon taking the lead through the broader avenues that would take them to the southern gates. They stopped only once as they passed the central plaza, where a demonstration was just beginning.

Braidon dragged his horse to a halt as the voices echoed from the stone walls.

"Murderer…traitor…coward…king…"

A vice clenched around Kryssa's chest as she realised they were talking about Braidon. She glanced at the king, seeing the smile vanish from his lips, his fists tightening around the leather reins. As he was dressed in nondescript clothing, the crowd had not noticed the king's presence. Even so, Kryssa edged her mount forward, placing herself between Braidon and the protest.

"Ignore them," she hissed under her breath.

"It's Janylle," Braidon replied, his voice cold.

Kryssa twisted in the saddle, her gaze sweeping out across the square to where the crowd had gathered around the silent fountain. A woman stood above them beside a statue of King Thomas, the man that had saved Chole from Archon's army. A shiver passed through her as the woman threw back her hood, revealing the wife of Dominic.

"The king had betrayed us!" Her voice carried over the jeers of the crowd, her face twisted with hatred. "He says he will protect us from his queen, but it is a lie. When she comes, our king will greet her with open arms! Then our temple will burn, and the Knights of Alana will take us…"

A roar rose from her followers, and Kryssa did not hear what else she had to say. She didn't need to. Glancing at Braidon, she saw the rage in his eyes, and the hurt that lurked beneath. Janylle had been their friend, but that had been before…

"Come on," she said, urging her horse forward. "Let her rage, they are only words."

Braidon did not reply, but after a moment he obeyed, turning his horse and riding from the plaza.

The sun was still low on the horizon when they finally reached the gates. They found them open and the first few wagons already trundling into the city, overseen by the fresh faces of the day guards.

"Okay," Kryssa said as they passed beneath the heavy blocks of stone and out onto the plains of Chole. "Speak."

"What?" Braidon asked, sounding distant. Then he shook himself and his eyes focused on her. "Oh, you want to know where we're going?"

"It's easier to protect you when I know what's coming."

The king let out a long sigh. "Sorry," he said. "After Marianne…its difficult to trust anyone."

"What about your talented new sergeants?" Kryssa asked, her voice dripping sarcasm.

"Not the most promising of recruits, are they?" Braidon

asked, but despite the words, his voice gained some humour. "Not to worry—if my plan comes to fruition, they won't matter come tomorrow."

"Oh?" Kryssa said as they started off across the open plains.

Braidon grinned. "Just you wait and see," he replied, and before she could ask any more questions, he kicked his horse into a gallop.

They alternated between trotting and walking their horses through the rest of the morning, and all the while Kryssa grew more irritated by Braidon's silence. They had left the road hours ago and the land around them was rugged, the bush untouched by man's axes. Twisted trees dotted the landscape, offering scant shade against the sun. While they'd seen the end of summer, the days were still hot on the plains, the air still.

Only as the sun started its inevitable journey towards the western horizon did Braidon finally break the silence.

"It's good to be on the road again," he said, eyes on the snow-capped peaks rising to the west. "Sometimes…sometimes I wish this could be my life again. Some of my best memories are from traveling the backroads of Onslow Forest with Devon." His voice cracked at the mention of her father. "If only…"

Kryssa said nothing. She and Derryn had made much the same decision when they'd first discovered she was pregnant, retiring from the King's Guard and moving to Skystead. But the decision had not been difficult for either of them. They'd known someone else would step up to take their place.

Braidon did not have that luxury. If he abandoned his duties, there would be no one left to stand against

Marianne, no one to oppose the darkness of the Order.

"If only…" Braidon said again into her silence. "But then who would avenge Devon and my King's Guard? Who would rally Plorsea against Marianne and her Lonian allies? Who would protect the people against the Knights of Alana?"

Kryssa sighed. "I don't envy you, Braidon."

Braidon chuckled. "Forgive me my self-pity, Kryssa," he said, offering a sad smile. "It gets the better of me sometimes, when I see people like Janylle, when I remember how my decisions have hurt people. But I've always known this was my fate, to rule Plorsea. Still, sometimes it's nice to dream."

"Of course," she replied with a grin. "So is that the purpose of this trip, then? A quick ride down memory lane, before you lead the forces of good against the dark queen?"

Now Braidon really laughed, his mirth echoing out through the browning trees. "Sadly, no," he replied, looking more relaxed than he had in weeks. "There is reason behind my madness, I'm afraid. We're out here looking for the tribes of Chole. They aided me in the last war, against Lonia. I'm hoping they will do the same again."

"And how do you expect to find them out here?" Kryssa asked, her good humour evaporating. The tribes were an unknown quality, and while they might have once allied with Braidon, there was no guarantee they would do so again. "These plains stretch for a hundred miles in every direction."

"Don't worry, we're on the right track," Braidon said, though he did not look her in the eye. "I've been experimenting with this new power. I found their trail yesterday. We must be drawing near by now."

Kryssa's heartbeat doubled as her eyes flicked to their surroundings. Silently, she cursed Braidon for a fool. The people he sought were nomadic and wild, and many tales considered them little better than the Baronians from whom they were said to have descended. She still remembered their mounted units from the war, how they had carved through the Lonian foot soldiers. It would be a mistake to cross them, and by trespassing on their land uninvited, Braidon risked doing just that.

The scrub had grown up around them now, alternating between thick bushes spotted with long thorns and open patches of grass. Movement came from nearby and she spun in the saddle, her hand dropping to the dagger on her belt. A cow lifted its head to stare at the passing horses, before returning to its meal.

Braidon chuckled. "You worry too much, Kryssa."

She snorted and loosened her sword in its scabbard. "That's my job as your King's Guard," she said. "You should have told me about this sooner."

"You would only have argued against it."

"I would have suggested you bring more soldiers," she snapped.

"As I said, I don't trust them. I can't have word getting back to Marianne of my plans," he argued. "And anyway, how many would you have brought? A dozen? A hundred? The tribes number in the thousands, too many, however many of our recruits stood with us. No, it's better just the two of us. At least now they will not see us as a threat."

Kryssa ground her teeth. "You still should have told me."

"Fine," Braidon surrendered. "Next time I go wandering into the dragon's den, I'll give you fair warning."

"Don't get me started on those beasts," Kryssa remarked with a shudder. She still hadn't gotten over the trauma of their flight from Dragon Country.

Braidon grinned. They were riding through another patch of scrub and Kryssa scanned the way ahead. The light was fading now and she could see little in the shadows beneath the wiry trees. The sound of breaking branches came from nearby, followed by movement. Kryssa's sword leapt into her hand, but it was only another cow. It pushed through the bushes, the thorns unable to pierce its thick hide, and stumbled into the narrow track they were following.

"This is ridiculous," Kryssa snapped as they were forced to stop, their way barred by the beast. "What are cattle doing in this sort of country—"

She broke off as the answer came to her, and sword still in hand she kicked her horse forward into Braidon's. A hiss came followed as an arrow slashed the air where she had been. Her horse screamed as a second rushed from the bushes and struck its hide, and then it was rearing up beneath her, feet lashing the air.

Kryssa tumbled from the saddle and crashed to the earth. She rolled to the side as the horse slammed back down, its hooves mere inches from her face. Before she could regain her feet, the beast fled back the way they had come, its screams echoing in her ears.

Scrambling for her sword, Kryssa leapt to her feet and swung around, searching for the enemy. Braidon was still trying to recover control of his own mount. The beast bucked beneath him, its screams echoing through the fading light and making him an easy target. Cursing, she staggered forward to help him.

Laughter brought her up short as men and women appeared from the shrub with bows bent. A dozen steel-tipped arrows pointed at Kryssa's chest. She froze, raising her hands, while the cries from Braidon's horse faded as he got the beast back under control. A curse exploded from the king as he finally noticed their assailants.

Teeth clenched, Kryssa edged towards Braidon, seeking to shelter the king from their arrows. If he was lucky, the mount might carry him clear and back to Chole. She, however…

Movement came from amongst the hunters as an older woman pushed her way to the fore. White streaked her brown hair and her face was wrinkled, but she still moved with the confidence of youth, as though unconcerned by her advancing years.

"Put down the sword, girl," she said. Her teeth flashed in a wild grin as she looked from Braidon to Kryssa. "Unless you have a desire to become a human pincushion."

Kryssa risked a glance at Braidon. He gave the slightest nod. Exhaling loudly through her nostrils, Kryssa lowered the blade and the woman laughed again.

"So the man is in charge. How quaint. What foolish desires have brought you to our lands, vagabond?" the woman asked.

"These are *my* lands," Braidon grunted. "Unless you have forgotten your treaty with the Plorsean crown, Loyla?"

It took a moment for the significance of Braidon's words to sink in. Frowning, the woman took a step closer, her pale eyes sweeping Braidon up and down before widening in recognition.

"King Braidon," she murmured. "Death does not suit you, *Your Majesty;* you look…poorly."

Braidon scowled and gestured at his horse, requesting permission to dismount. The woman he'd named Loyla nodded and signalled her warriors to lower their weapons. Kryssa breathed a sigh of relief as the steel points were put away. With a scuffling of leather, Braidon leapt from the saddle and approached the nomadic leader.

"Can't say I've missed your honesty, Loyla," he said, wearing a grim smile, "nor your hospitality. I don't suppose some of your people would be so good as to chase down my Guard's horse?"

Loyla chuckled. "It'll be halfway back to Chole by now." Her gaze turned to Kryssa. "My apologies…?"

"Kryssa."

"Kryssa," Loyla confirmed with a nod. "I will have my people provide you another horse." Her attention switched back to Braidon. "Our camp is not far. I assume you wish to talk, unless Your Majesty has taken to enjoying long rides in the countryside?"

Braidon scowled. "I *was* rather enjoying it, until your people showed up." Then he laughed. "What happened to giving a warning shot?"

"Since men in iron suits began waging war against our people, we've become somewhat less forgiving of interlopers," Loyla replied.

"When did this begin?" the king asked.

"A little over a year ago. They started crossing our country, taking the mountain paths towards Dragon Country. Didn't take well to company. They killed several of our hunting parties before we learned to avoid them—or kill them on sight."

A cursed exploded from the king. "That news would have been useful a year ago."

"You think I did not send word to Ardath?" Loyla replied mildly, though Kryssa caught the shimmering in her eyes, the silent rage. "I never received a response. I assumed you were too busy with that pretty wife of yours to concern yourself with such a trivial matter."

"Marianne," Braidon muttered under his breath, then louder: "My apologies, Loyla. I would have acted, had your letter ever reached me. I fear there is much you do not know."

"I can imagine," Loyla said dryly, glancing from Braidon to Kryssa. "But night is approaching. Let us continue this conversation in our camp. We have not seen the Knights for several months now, but there are still dark creatures that stalk these plains at night."

4

"There's no smoke," Ruebyn whispered.

Pela frowned, looking at the town again—though it could hardly be called that. There were no more than a dozen of the stone buildings, clustered around a hilltop that would give the occupants clear views in all directions. Squinting, she saw that Ruebyn was right about the smoke.

"It's barely autumn," Pela shot back, though even as she said it, she wondered about the cooking fires or iron stones that would surely be burning at this time.

She drew in a breath, seeking the telltale scents of humanity—smoke and dust and cooking meat, the musk of animals kept in close quarters. But all she could smell was the crispness of the crushed grass beneath their feet.

A breeze blew down the valley, whistling through the rooftops of the village. The hackles lifted on her neck as she realised the buildings were utterly silent. From where they stood, surely they would hear sounds of civilisation, the buzz of voices and the hammering of tools, the squeal of wagon wheels or the screaming of a child.

But there was nothing.

Suddenly uneasy, she glanced at Ruebyn again. "I think you're right."

He nodded, but his face remained grim. "What do we do?"

"I don't know."

Pela shivered, thinking again of Ruebyn's earlier words. Trola's borders had been closed for decades. The rest of the world had assumed it was to rebuild after their liberation from the Tsar…but after so much time, anything might have happened.

"I say we go in," Ruebyn whispered, as though afraid now they might be overhead.

Fear touched Pela, and unconsciously she dropped a hand to the hilt of her dagger. "Why?"

"We have to find out what's going on," he replied.

He straightened his shoulders and glanced at her, but when she said nothing, he started along the path again. After a moment's hesitation, Pela followed, though she was still unsure if they were making the right choice.

By the time they reached the village, there was no longer any doubt that the place had been empty for a long time. Abandoned by their former owners, many of the houses were showing signs of dilapidation. While the stone walls still stood, roofing tiles now lay scattered across the dirt street or in piles amongst the ruins.

The first door they encountered was slumped in its frame, and fell backwards at a touch. Pela coughed as dust swept up around them, but shielding her eyes, she stepped inside. Light spilled in from a hole in the ceiling to illuminate the room. The house's occupants had obviously departed in a hurry, for their belongings had been left behind—pots and pans and furniture, half-rotten books and children's toys. A fine layer of dust covered everything and there was a heavy stench of decay. It was clear the place had gone untouched by human hands for years.

Pela retreated into the street. "What happened here?" she whispered to Ruebyn.

There were no bodies, but she couldn't shake the feeling that something terrible had happened. The whole village felt like a tomb, a place for the dead.

"What happened to Trola?" Ruebyn countered.

Pela scowled, rebelling against her earlier thoughts. "One village is not a nation."

"We've seen no sign of life since we crossed the mountains," he argued. His gaze travelled eastward, where the hills still stretched up to snow-capped peaks. "I don't like it. I think…maybe we should go back."

"Back?" Pela felt as though he had struck her. "*Back?*"

"There's something wrong here, Pe—"

"I can't go back!" she shrieked, lifting her chin to emphasise the slave collar. "Or had you forgotten *this?* Have you forgotten what they'll do to me?" She stalked towards him until they stood face-to-face. "Remind me, overseer," she hissed, her voice like ice. "Remind me the fate your precious handbook sets out for runaway slaves."

"I…I…" he stammered, then shook his head.

"*Tell me!*" she shrieked, grabbing him by the shirt and shaking him.

Ruebyn's eyes were wide as he stared at her, but finally

he bowed his head. His answer came in a whisper. "They would break your legs and leave you in the mountains for the scavengers to find."

Pulling him closer, Pela placed her lips at his ear. "*I'm never going back*," she hissed, then pushed him away from her.

He staggered several steps before righting himself. "I didn't mean it like that," he said, looking hurt. "I…there are people that would help us, even in Lonia. You told me Elder Lewis tried—"

"And failed," Pela spoke over the top of him. "Do whatever you like, Ruebyn. I don't care. I'm staying right here. Whatever surprises Trola holds, they can't be worse than your Godsforsaken nation."

She was shaking now, her mind racing over every hurt, every awful thing that had happened to her over the last few months. She thought again of Genevieve, dying alone in the snowstorm so that they could escape. How could Ruebyn even think about returning after that? Suddenly she couldn't believe she'd ever slept with the foolish boy, had ever considered him anything more than a useless coward.

Turning her back, she marched down the street, intending to leave Ruebyn behind with whatever ghosts still haunted the awful village.

But as she neared the edge of the stone houses, a distant thunder carried to her ears. She paused, glancing at the sky, but there was hardly a cloud overhead. Frowning, she looked back at Ruebyn, but he only shot her a look of utter confusion.

Pela rushed to the edge of the village. A beaten dirt road stretched away to the south, what must have been left of this part of the Gods Road from ages past. She followed its winding path down the valley, through the overgrown fields and patches of trees. In the distance, sunlight flashed, reflecting off metal.

Her heart raced as she finally saw the horsemen. They were approaching from the south, riding at a steady trot that would see them reach the village in minutes. A cloud of dust rose obscured any details, but Pela made out flashes of Trolan blue. Whirling, she rushed back into the village.

"Hide!" she snapped at Ruebyn, and ducked into the nearest building.

Darkness embraced her, along with the icy cold of a space that had been untouched by fire or sunlight in years. Stones crunched beneath her boots—the roof here remained intact, but parts of the ceiling had begun to crumble, leaving a fine layer of dust and mortar on the ground.

Glancing back, Pela searched for Ruebyn and realised too late he had not followed her. He still stood frozen in the middle of the street. There was a frown on his face, as though he was still trying to work out how he could have been wrong about Trola's fate. She cursed beneath her breath and ducked back to the empty doorframe. The rattle of hooves grew louder as she leaned out—the riders would be upon them at any moment.

"Ruebyn!" she screamed. "Get out of the street!"

His eyes widened and he swung to look at her, then back at the houses on the other side of the street. Those houses were closer, and without further hesitation he ducked into one of them, vanishing from view.

A second later the rumble of hooves grew to a roar as the riders entered the single lane through the village. Pela shrank back from the doorway, seeking to disappear amongst the darkness. Her heart hammered against her ribcage, so loud in her ears she was sure the riders must hear it. A terrible fear touched her then, that the men had already seen them, that they had come to this village to hunt them down.

Standing in the darkness, Pela waited for the shouts of discovery to come. Her breath came in ragged gasps as she watched the door. The thunder of horse hooves slowed, then came to a stop outside. The whisper of voices followed, carried in from the street by a breath of wind. But standing in the corridor deep within the house, she could not see what they were doing.

Unable to take the suspense, Pela slipped into a room on her right, hoping for a view onto the street. When outside, she'd noticed that every window in the town had its shutters drawn. She should be able to spy on the street through the gaps without the horsemen noticing—or so she prayed.

The room in which she found herself was plain and unadorned, its simple furnishings covered by the same fine layer of dust as the rest of the house. A shiver passed through Pela as she saw the small bed tucked into a corner. The covers were still made, while on the floor a toy carriage lovingly carved from wood lay abandoned by whatever child had once lived there.

Shivering at the memories locked within the room, Pela skirted the toys and crept to the window. A shadow passed across the shutters and she ducked midstride, breath held. Through the cracks she saw a mounted man ride past.

"Men, dismount!"

The voice was so loud it seemed to rattle the shutters. Pela pressed herself up against the wall, suddenly terrified of being seen. It was clear from the man's tone that these were military men—soldiers, possibly sent to patrol the border against trespassers. Thankfully, her room was entirely in shadow, and it would have been all but impossible for them to glimpse her through the tiny cracks in the shutters.

The thump of boots against dirt came from outside, followed by groaning and the distant buzz of conversation. Pela let out a long breath and edged up alongside the window. Silently, she pressed her eye to the shutters.

Her heart sank. Finally she had a clear view of what they faced. At least a dozen men stood in the street. There was no question now that they were soldiers. Each wore plate mail armour and full-faced helmets, the steel stained dark blue, and all were armed with longswords. Kite-shaped shields hung from the saddles of their horses.

"Ten minutes break, then we continue," the last man to dismount shouted as he stepped down onto the street.

Sighs of relief came from the other soldiers as they removed their helmets. Several rummaged in their saddlebags, coming up with strips of jerky and honey cakes. The food was handed out, along with skins of water. Pela's stomach rumbled as she watched, and she struggled to suppress her hunger. She and Ruebyn had found little to eat since leaving the forest.

When the food was done, the men drifted apart. Their casual manner had eased Pela's fears, but now her chest constricted as several soldiers wandered close to her hiding place. Their leader stretched his arms above his head and yawned. As they drew closer, she noticed the intricate patterns inscribed into the breastplates, accentuated with several jet-black gems. Matching stones had been inset into the hilts of the blades they wore on their waists.

They were drawing closer to her hiding place now, close enough they might glimpse her through the blinds. She edged back, taking care not to move too suddenly and draw their attention. But as she placed her foot down, it landed on the wooden wagon. The toy slipped beneath her boot, throwing her off-balance.

Pela bit back a cry as she stumbled sideways, her arms windmilling in a desperate attempt to keep upright. Thankfully there was nothing else to trip over, and in two steps she recovered her balance. Freezing in place, she stared at the shuttered windows, blood pounding in her ears.

"Wha' was that?"

Her stomach twisted in a knot as the voice carried in from the street. A shadow flickered beyond the shutters as a soldier approach. His shape filled the window as he pressed an eye to a crack. Pela hardly dared to breathe. Scrunching her eyes closed, she willed herself to disappear, to vanish from the sight of her enemies.

"Can't see nothin'," the voice spoke again in the thick accent of the west. It was shockingly loud in the tiny room, and Pela had to keep herself from flinching. "Prob'ly some damn cat."

Pela's breath hissed between her teeth as the man stepped back. Her legs trembling, she sank to the floor, hardly able to believe her luck. These men truly were confident they were alone—or they would have searched the building.

"*Hey!*" Pela's heart dropped into her stomach as a familiar voice carried through the blinds. "Whatchu idiots doing in my place?"

No, no, no!

It was Ruebyn, making some terrible attempt at a Trolan accent. Leaping to her feet, she rushed to the window in time to see the soldiers forming up. Steel flashed as they drew their blades and advanced on the solitary figure standing on the other side of the street. Ruebyn yelped and tried to retreat, but they had him surrounded in seconds, swords extended, ready to impale him.

"Wait!" he gasped, raising his hands. "Don't, I'm unarmed."

Pela closed her eyes and repressed a moan. What was he thinking? He had already dropped the horrible accent. It was clear as day to anyone who heard him speak that he came from an eastern nation. Her hand dropped to the hilt of her dagger, but she could not fight so many. She swallowed, the collar pressing hard against her throat.

"What are you doing here?" the captain of the soldiers snapped, advancing until the tip of his sword rested on Ruebyn's chest.

"I...I...I seek asylum!"

"Asylum?" the man asked, and his voice revealed his disbelief.

"Yes. I am hunted..."

A stunned silence answered Ruebyn's words, before laughter broke out across the street. Ruebyn leapt back in fright, but the leader kept pace, his sword pressing forward, and now it drew blood. A scream came from Ruebyn as he tripped and went crashing to the ground. Pela snapped a hand to her mouth to keep from crying out as outside the captain raised a hand. The laughter died as quickly as it had begun.

"I would say you are caught, Lonian," the captain said,

a cruel grin on his face. "Tell me, have they forgotten our laws in the east? I would not have thought it needed reminding that our nation is closed to foreign scum!"

Ruebyn's mouth opened and closed, but no words came out and the soldiers laughed again. Pela swallowed, a tremor running down her spine. They were going to kill Ruebyn and there was nothing she could do to stop them. And once he was dead, they would search the village to make sure he was alone.

Slowly she drew the dagger from its sheath. Her hand shook as she rose and stepped back into the hallway. Light beckoned from the front door, drawing her back out into the street. Focused on her friend, the soldiers didn't notice her approach until she was just a few steps away.

"Hey!" a man shouted as he glanced back and finally saw her.

The others responded instantly, whirling to face her with weapons raised.

"Leave him alone," she said quietly, raising the dagger.

The men stared at her for half a moment, before their laughter rolled out across the street again. A cold fury lit in Pela's chest. Instinctively, she reached within herself, seeking her calm centre, the burning flame at her core. This time it came easily, flaring to life in her mind's eyes, filling her with warmth, with power. She bared her teeth.

"I said *leave him alone!*" she cried, putting all her anger and energy into the words.

A tremor went through the men. Steel rattled as they wavered, then one by one stepped to the side, swords dropping to their sides. Pela stood gaping as Ruebyn sat up, a frown creasing his face. Her heart beating hard against her chest, Pela rushed forward and dragged him to his feet.

She glanced at the men, but they made no move to stop them.

"Wha…what?" Ruebyn mumbled, looking groggy. Blood stained his tunic where the soldier had sliced his chest.

Pela shook her head, and stars danced across her vision. Blinking them away, she tried to walk back down the row of men, to draw Ruebyn away from them, but her legs felt suddenly weak. She gasped as they gave way and she sank to one knee. A collective cry came from around them as the soldiers returned to life.

"So." The captain's voice was cold now as he advanced on them. "The people of the east have discovered power. No matter." He lifted his sword above her head. "It will not save you from the *morbus*."

"Please," Pela gasped, scrambling back, "where is your mercy?"

The captain drew back his lips, revealing sickly yellow teeth. "To set foot in Trolan lands is death," he said cruelly. "*This* is our mercy—now hold them!"

Men leapt forward at his command. Pela lashed out with the dagger, but the blade scraped uselessly against a steel breastplate before it was knocked from her grasp. Iron hands pinned her arm behind her back and pressed her face into the dirt. She could no longer see Ruebyn, but from the sounds of his struggles, he wasn't faring any better.

The thump of boots approached, and screaming, Pela tried again to break free. But her assailant bore down on her, his weight unmoveable, and she slumped back to the ground gasping. Desperately, she reached for that unspoken power, but in her terror, she could not find it.

"Ready them," the captain growled.

"Bastards!" Pela shrieked as a rough hand pulled her silver hair to the side, exposing her neck. "Cowards!"

A cry came from overhead and Pela closed her eyes, expecting the end.

"What is this?" the captain whispered.

She shuddered as a hand touched the back of her neck. Looking up, she found the captain leaning in close, his eyes on the back of her head—no, *on her collar*. There was a frown on his face, as though he were seeing something he could not quite believe.

Then Pela noticed her dagger, lying forgotten on the ground, just a foot from her face. She stretched out her arm, slowly so as not to draw attention, though her heart was racing and she knew at any second the captain must return to his task.

Her fingers were just on the hilt when the captain cried out as though bitten. Suddenly his hands were in her hair and he was dragging her up, spinning her around. She gasped, shocked at the violence, and threw out her fist. But the blow was poorly aimed and her hand careened from his breastplate.

"Who is your master?" the captain snapped, ignoring her attack. When Pela only stared at him blankly, he grasped her by the collar and shook her: "*Who is your master?*"

"What are you talking about?" Pela gasped, fighting to break his hold.

Releasing Pela's collar, he kicked her legs out from under her, sending her crumbling to the ground. Red flashed across her vision as her head struck the earth. Groaning, she crawled several paces away from the captain before turning to stare at him. Ruebyn lay nearby, still pinned by one of the soldiers. The others stood watching on, amused grins on their faces.

"You're monsters!" she cried.

"Ay," the captain replied, then turned to his men. "Mercy will have to wait. Bind them. Our lord must see what we have found."

$\mathfrak{H}$ 5 $\mathfrak{H}$

Sitting with his legs crossed beneath him, Braidon looked at Loyla and wondered what he needed to do to win the woman's support. It was dim inside the tent, lit only by a single lantern, while the swirling smoke from the incense burning in each corner made the air thick and difficult to breathe.

It galled Braidon to think that Loyla's call for aid had gone unnoticed. Had Marianne kept the message from him, or had it been someone else in the capital, some aide who thought the plight of the nomadic people unworthy of his attention? He might never know, but it was unworthy of the crown to have ignored them after everything they had done in the war against Lonia.

Even so, that did not excuse Loyla's treatment of him. She had said nothing to him since reaching the camp, and now sat making conversation with Kryssa. The two were talking about the sword his Guard wore, how it had been her husband's, apparently, before passing to her daughter and then finally to her. Kryssa still planned to give it back to Pela one day.

"Loyla," Braidon said suddenly, unable to keep the impatience from his voice. Despite the touching nature of the story, he was in no mood to be ignored, particularly not after being set upon earlier. "I am sorry, but time is short. Already I have been gone too long from Chole."

Kryssa chuckled dryly at that, until a glance from Braidon silenced her. Calming himself, he looked again at the nomadic leader.

"I came in person to ask for your aid, as a matter of respect," he murmured. "Had I known you would get along with Kryssa so well, I might have reconsidered the use of my time."

"Prickly, isn't he?" Loyla said to Kryssa with a smile, before addressing Braidon: "Forgive me, Your Majesty, and thank you for honouring us so. Now, on behalf of what fresh squabble do you wish my people to spill their blood? I had heard your wife now sits on the Plorsean throne—can I take it this involves something of a lover's quarrel?"

Braidon scowled. "Marianne is the reason the Knights have been harrying your people."

"Is that so?" Loyla mused, her eyebrows lifting into her fringe. "Yet the Knights have not bothered us for some time, and rumours from the capital speak of the queen driving them from the city."

"Don't be fooled; Marianne is good at manipulating the truth," Braidon snapped. "Make no mistake, it was she who invited the Knights into our lands."

"Braidon speaks the truth," Kryssa offered. "The queen stood with the Order in Malevolent Cove. She used their profane rituals to grant herself power. If she has driven the

Knights of Alana from Ardath, it is for her own ends, not yours or our own."

Loyla stared at Kryssa for a long while before turning back to Braidon. "You have a loyal ally in this one," she said softly. "You speak of your wife's evil, but what is it *you* want, Your Majesty?"

Braidon frowned. "I want peace for my nation."

"Perhaps," the woman murmured, "or perhaps you only want power for yourself."

"What?" Braidon started. "I have dedicated my entire life to Plorsea, to righting the wrongs of my father. I have done nothing but fight for this nation these last thirty years. Through war and betrayal, I have done my duty. And still you question my motives?"

Loyla's eyes drilled into him. "I do."

Braidon could hardly believe what he was hearing. He wanted to shout at the woman, to scream at her for her accusations, for spitting in the face of his honour—but he sensed that was what she was waiting for. Instead, he sucked in a breath and slowly exhaled.

"Under Marianne's brief reign as queen, the Knights of Alana have marched unchecked in the streets of our cities, slaughtering hundreds on the altar of their Saviour. A Lonian army marches on our nation, and she waves the flag of greeting. Make no mistake, Loyla, there is a darkness coming. And like my grandmother, Enala, before me, I am the only one left to stand against it."

Silence answered his words. Kryssa sat beside him, looking from the nomadic leader to Braidon, her brow creased with concern. Braidon ignored her, his whole attention fixed on Loyla, as though by willpower alone he might force her to agree, to do her duty to her king and nation.

"Perhaps you are right," Loyla said finally, her words so soft they could barely be heard. "Perhaps there is a darkness that must be opposed. But are you the man to lead us, Braidon? I had faith in you once, in younger days, when you fought against Ashoka to keep us free. But now…the years have lessened you, Braidon."

"What must I do to prove myself to you?" Braidon asked, his tone rising in notches. He was exhausted, so tired of fighting for a nation, a people, that did not care. Recalling his conversation earlier in the day with Kryssa, he wondered again whether he should just walk away, if he should turn his back and ride off into the mountains.

A smile crossed the woman's face as she rose. "Come," she said, gesturing towards the tent flap.

Braidon let out a heavy sigh and followed her into the night with Kryssa. A thousand stars shone down from overhead, while in the distance the crescent moon was just peeking above the horizon. They were camped out on the plains, away from the tangled scrub they had been traversing earlier. Braidon's horse was tethered nearby, alongside a new mount for Kryssa, but Loyla did not lead them there.

Instead, she made her way through the cow-skin tents towards a distant whispering. Turning his gaze ahead, Braidon sought the source of the voices and saw the glow of flames. Silhouettes moved in the darkness as they stepped from the tents out into the open, where a bonfire was burning brightly.

Men and women packed the space, but they retreated at the sight of Braidon, forming a wide circle around the bonfire.

Frowning, Braidon turned to Loyla. "What is this all about?"

She smiled. "You asked what you must do to prove yourself. So I will tell you. Prove you are still the Braidon of old, that the flame of your ancestors still burns in your heart. My champion awaits."

With the words, she gestured at the fire. A shadow stepped from behind the bonfire, a hulking presence in the twilight. Braidon swallowed as he looked the warrior up and down, taking in the barrel chest and trunk-like arms. He was at least as big as Devon had been in his prime, and almost a foot taller.

"This is him?" A grin twisted the giant's face as he appraised Braidon. "He does not look like much of a king, mother."

Braidon turned back to Loyla. "You would have me fight your own son?"

Loyla chuckled. "Are you afraid, Your Majesty?"

Scowling, Braidon faced the giant and drew his short sword. Steel rasped against leather as his opponent removed a massive scimitar from a sheath on his back. Firelight glittered on the curved blade and Braidon widened his stance, readying himself for the power the giant would put behind his strikes. Suddenly he was glad for the sparring sessions he'd had with Kryssa back in Dragon Country.

"Loyla, are you sure this is necessary?" Kryssa asked, advancing half a step to put herself between Braidon and the giant.

"Get out of the way, Kryssa," Braidon snarled.

Taking his sword in both hands, he reached for the power burning in his core. Braidon was done playing Loyla's games, done with the disrespect, with the constant questioning of his every decision. He was the rightful King of Plorsea, damnit. He'd never wanted it, never asked for it, but the kingship had been thrust upon him all the same. No one had ever acknowledged that sacrifice.

His every muscle was lit aflame as the energies of those lost in the pantheon leapt to his summons, feeding him fresh strength. Lifting his blade, Braidon saluted the giant. He would not kill the man—to do so was guaranteed to lose Loyla's support—but he would show the woman exactly who she was dealing with, that he would not be questioned.

Still grinning, the giant started towards him, scimitar raised in preparation to strike. Still feeding the power to his arms and legs, to his ears and eyes, Braidon let him approach. When the first blow finally came, it seemed to Braidon as though his foe moved in slow motion, the giant blade lifting high and swiping ponderously for his skull.

Ducking low, Braidon easily avoided the blow. The blade hissed over his head, rippling the parting of Braidon's hair, before he straightened and smiled at the giant. His foe stumbled forward a step and then leapt backwards out of range—though Braidon had not so much as lifted his blade. A frown touched the man's face as he struggled to comprehend exactly how the king had bested him.

Braidon smiled and spread his hands. "What happened, sir? Are you having trouble with your balance?"

The giant scowled. Hefting his blade, he approached again—though cautiously this time. Still Braidon let him come on unchallenged. Holding his short sword casually at his side, he adopted a bored expression. Enraged, the giant stabbed at Braidon's chest with a roar.

Braidon skipped sideways to avoid the blow. His sword flashed up then down, connecting with the giant's blade close to the hilt. Sparks flashed as the impact drove the scimitar from the giant's hands and sent it skittering across the stony ground.

"Clumsy, clumsy," Braidon *tsk*ed, kicking the blade back to the giant. "Did your mother not teach you how to hold a sword?"

The giant swore and swept up his weapon. "How did you do that?" he hissed.

Braidon grinned. The man's bulk dwarfed him and the power behind his blows would have been enough to cut Braidon in two. But after two encounters, the advantage was entirely Braidon's. There was fear on the giant's face now, as he came to the realisation Braidon's skill might be beyond his abilities.

Then the man's face set, his fear vanishing behind an iron mask, and he started forward again. Braidon was impressed—this was a man unused to being challenged. Yet now, when faced with certain defeat, he did not skulk or turn away.

But it would change nothing. This time as the giant rushed forward, Braidon leapt to meet him. The shift in tactic caught his foe by surprise, and the man's eyes widened to find Braidon suddenly within range of his blade. Howling, he swung down with all his might. Braidon's short sword slashed up, catching the narrow blade of the scimitar with a shriek of grating metal.

Despite the power surging through his veins, Braidon grunted at the weight behind the blow. Under normal circumstances, his blade might have shattered, leaving the giant's scimitar embedded in his skull. But as the weapons came together, Braidon fed his energies into the blade, reinforcing the steel and adding strength to his own arm.

And so the giant's blow was stopped dead, caught upon the hilt of Braidon's short sword. The man gaped down at the king, unable to believe his own eyes. Smiling, Braidon took full advantage.

Twisting his sword sideways, Braidon caught the scimitar's hilt and sent it crashing to the ground. The giant staggered back emptyhanded, still stunned from the sudden turn of events, and Braidon leapt after him. His short sword slashed out, opening a cut in the giant's chest and igniting cries of fear from the crowd.

Lashing out with his boot, Braidon caught his foe in the chest, hurling him from his feet. Blood pounded in his skull as he advanced on the man, short sword gripped tightly in one hand. The giant lay crumpled on the ground, a hissing noise coming from his throat as he struggled to breathe. Fear showed in his eyes as he saw Braidon approaching. Still winded, he scrambled back, one arm raised as though to fend off a blow.

Braidon slammed his foot down onto the man's chest, pinning him to the ground. Another cry came from the audience as Braidon lifted his blade, pointing it at the giant's heart. He hardly heard their fear over the roaring in his ears, the fire burning in his core.

"Wait!"

A voice cut through the screams. Braidon looked up, finding Loyla standing nearby. He stared at her coldly, sword still poised to strike.

"You would have me show mercy?" he asked quietly. "I thought you had need of a strong king? One with the power to face Marianne? *She* certainly will have no mercy, when she comes for you."

"You have shown us your power, Your Majesty," she said

quietly. "There is no need to prove your cruelty. Let my boy go."

The giant was still squirming beneath Braidon's boot, but despite his bulk he could not dislodge the king's weight. Braidon tasted disgust as he glanced at the man, that he had allowed Loyla to shame him so, to fight for her loyalty.

He still clutched the short sword tightly in one hand, its leather grip digging into his flesh. The tip trembled as he shifted it to the warrior's throat. The man stilled at the touch of cold steel, and he could not keep the terror from his eyes now.

Smiling, Braidon returned the blade to its sheath and faced Loyla. The giant warrior scrambled back to his feet and fled to his mother's side.

"You are satisfied?" Braidon asked in a whisper.

"Ay, I have seen enough," she replied softly. "You will get no aid from us, Braidon."

"*What?*" Braidon exploded, so stunned he could only stand and stare at the woman.

"Loyla, please," Kryssa put in, extending a hand in entreaty. "You cannot—"

"I will not ally myself with one who has drunken the lives of others," Loyla hissed, her eyes shining in the light of the bonfire.

"What are you talking about?" his King's Guard asked. A frown creased her forehead as she looked from the woman to her king. "Braidon, what is she saying?"

Feeling inexplicably ashamed, Braidon allowed his gaze to fall to the ground—before his rage came rushing back. His head snapped up. "They did not die by my hand, nor by my orders," he said to Loyla, before glancing at Kryssa. "I did what I had to…when the fire was raging."

The colour drained from Kryssa's face at his words. "The pantheon?" she whispered. "You took their life force, when they died? You couldn't have…"

"They were already gone, Kryssa," Braidon said, then swung on Loyla. The woman had pushed and prodded him, had sought to test his resolve, but now it was she who shirked her duties.

"I am your rightful king," he growled. "It is your duty to answer my call, to march beneath my banner."

"Ay," Loyla replied, "and yet still I refuse you."

And with that, she turned and walked away into the night. One by one her people followed, their silhouettes fading into the darkness, even as the bonfire raged on behind Braidon.

Braidon stood staring after them, too stunned to intervene, to call her back. How could she do this to him? He had proven his strength, shown that his will was the equal of Marianne's. And still she abandoned him.

Finally there was no one left but Kryssa. Their eyes met and for the merest of seconds he saw the horror there, the disgust at what he had done. It was gone in a second, replaced by a mask of polished silver.

"I am sorry, Your Majesty," she said in a wooden voice, barely audible above the crackling of flames. "Shall we return to Chole?"

Sadness touched Braidon as he felt the distance between them. Gone was the camaraderie they had shared since Dragon Country, the openness. The last of his anger faded, replaced by despair, and he nodded silently. Together they returned to their horses and climbed into the saddles.

They rode from the camp in silence. Braidon was still reeling from his rejection, from the utter failure of his mission. He might still have gone after Loyla, might have argued and fought and forced her to accept his authority, but there was little point. Her people would fight him at every turn if he tried.

Only as the darkness of the night embraced them did Braidon finally see the truth. If he was to defeat Marianne and free his nation from the grips of the Order, he must do it himself. There was no one left in the world he could trust, not even Kryssa.

He was alone.

6

The rain was falling hard in camp by the time Caledan lifted the canvas flap to Marianne's command tent. The journey downriver from Ardath had been long and fraught with difficulties, the vast array of fishing vessels and ferries struggling to keep together on the swiftly flowing currents. The rain had not helped, as the river swelled to the point of topping its banks. The brown waters had surged around the vessels, promising death to any who fell overboard, and Caledan was thankful none had been lost on the journey.

Most of the king's galleys had been destroyed along with the King's Guard and the only real ship left now was the strange vessel Marianne had used to sail from Malevolent Cove. But she had sent that ship south with her son, Calybe, in case the worst happened in the coming battle.

So their whole force of two thousand had been ferried downriver in a host of trading galleys and fishing ship, barges, and anything else that could survive the journey. The fleet had set out at sunrise, taking the better part of a day to travel downriver through the foothills that surrounded Lake Ardath.

Finally reaching the plains of Plorsea, they had set ashore on the eastern banks of the Jurrien River. Word had already reached them of Servo's army—his force was said to be some five thousand strong. Gladly, they had yet to cross the Jurrien, and Caledan had sent scouts ranging west to ensure they were not come upon unawares.

He could do less about the sheer size of the Elder's force. Not for the first time, Caledan found himself cursing Braidon. The former king had gutted Plorsea's standing army, reducing it to little more than his King's Guard and a handful of militias dotted around the nation. There was no true fighting force left in Plorsea, and Caledan had struggled just to gather their two thousand. Most were raw recruits with little fighting experience, more to make up numbers than of any real use. If it came to open battle, he would rely mostly on a core force of some five hundred veterans and sellswords to hold the army together.

Their one advantage was the Jurrien River. Further downstream, the Forest of Sitton blocked passage of ships from Lonia. Servo could have taken his force the long way down the eastern coast and up the River Lane, but instead had opted to march overland. No doubt he'd expected them to wait for him in Ardath, safe in the city fortress while his army ravaged the land.

But with Marianne's power source in his control, the Elder's power would only grow with time. Marianne had had no choice but to confront him. Now he would be forced to ford the Jurrien and face her in battle, or risk their army cutting off his supply lines and harrying him from the rear.

It was a bold plan and might have been enough to win

the war, if not for Servo's overwhelming numbers. They might hold the banks of the Jurrien against the bulk of his force, but Servo had enough men to send forces up and downriver. There they could cross unopposed and circle back to attack the Plorsean army from the rear.

"Come in, My Champion," Marianne's voice called from inside the tent. "You're letting in a breeze."

Shaking off his worries, Caledan let the canvas flap fall closed behind him. Inside, the tent was lit by several lanterns, though Marianne was the only one present at that hour. Once they might have found an inn on the banks of the Jurrien, but they had long since closed with the loss of the river's trading route.

Outside, the rain poured down and despite the coal brazier in the corner, the air was cold in the tent. Marianne did not seem bothered though. She sat on the other side of the room in a wooden folding chair, a glass of wine in one hand and a smile on her lips. Over the last week she had pushed herself hard to ready her nation for war, organising supplies and speaking to the people, rallying their morale when word reached the capital of the approaching army.

Caledan had barely slept since the day Marianne had told him of her power, and even less after she had named him as her general. He was a sellsword and had fought in many battles, but he was no strategist. Marianne had given him the command because there was no one else she could trust, but he did not know how to win this battle.

Since their departure though, a sense of peace seemed to have come over the queen, as though the last week had removed a great burden from her shoulders, rather than adding to it. Tomorrow would determine not only the fate of her queenship, but that of her own life and her son. Yet she sat in her chair as though she held not a care in the world.

"Take a seat, and a glass, Caledan," she said, nodding to the bottle on the table beside her. "You look as though you could use the rest."

"There is still much to do, Marianne," he murmured. He did not sit, but he took her lead in dropping the formalities. "We need to decide a strategy, some way of defeating Servo."

Marianne leaned back in the chair, her sapphire eyes appraising him. "His forces are on the opposite banks of the river," she said finally. "They have commandeered several barges that are used to ferry goods along this strip of the river. Tomorrow, when the flood waters have receded, they will try to cross. We will do our best to stop them. Now, will you join me for a drink, Caledan?"

He stood staring at her for a long moment, unable to understand how she had received such intelligence before his scouts had returned. In the end, he decided it was best to let the subject drop. Exhaling, he poured himself a glass, and placing a chair close to the brazier, sat.

"Stopping them will be easier said than done," he said finally. "Servo has more men, and if he has gathered enough power…"

Almost unconsciously, Marianne lifted a hand to the bracelet on her wrist, before dropping it back to her side. "Relax, Caledan," she replied, though her voice had tightened. Drawing in a breath, she continued in a calmer tone: "We have done all we can. Tomorrow, we will find out if it was enough."

"Very well," Caledan consented, though there were still half a hundred things he wanted to discuss. Instead, he sipped at his wine, then made a face. "Whiskey would have been better."

"I'm afraid it was all destroyed after my husband's… departure," Marianne said with a grin.

"I take it you'd rather not discuss how you're going to deal with him, either?"

The queen chuckled. "You are persistent, sellsword."

Caledan took another sip. It was a red from the vineyards of northern Lonia, something of a taboo he would have thought, considering who they were going to fight tomorrow. But he supposed Lonia was still Marianne's home, whatever her adopted nation. Perhaps that was why she did not want to talk about the morning.

"Do you still miss it?" he asked, then when she only raised her eyebrows, elaborated: "Lonia? I can't imagine what it must be like, marching against the people who raised you."

Marianne did not look up from her glass, but he saw her eyebrows lift in reaction to his question. "You know, you're far more astute than I would have given you credit for, sellsword."

"Understanding one's foe is half the battle," Caledan replied.

"Are we still foes then, Caledan?" Marianne murmured, glancing at him now. The hint of a smile touched her lips. "I had hoped for more loyalty from my Champion."

"You know I am yours, Marianne," Caledan said. He locked eyes with her until the queen was forced to look away, then laughed. "But I doubt my behaviour surprises you as much as you would like me to believe."

"Oh?" the queen asked, arching one eyebrow.

"You've always been one step ahead of everyone else, Marianne," he answered. "You would not have chosen me to protect Calybe unless you had seen something more in me, something beyond a mere sellsword."

"You've caught me," Marianne laughed. "After our… encounter in Malevolent Cove, I had my people enquire about all of those who had escaped. You kept your secret well, but there were those who knew of your hatred for Braidon. Yet you had carried the man to safety from the amphitheatre. It was a puzzle I could not solve until you sat here before me, and told me of the hammerman's request. I knew then you were the man I needed."

"I am flattered, My Queen," Caledan said with a smile, "but you are diverting from the conversation."

Rich laughter pealed through the tent. "So I am!" she replied. "Very well, Caledan, you have seen me. I do not long for our battle on the morrow. I love my people, for it was never them who betrayed me. Servo has misled them, claiming I am an enemy of the Order, of Lonia. But it is he who has corrupted the teachings of the Saviour, who would so callously throw away their lives, all for his own gains."

"He must be stopped," Caledan murmured, "or his corruption can only spread."

"He must," Marianne agreed. She took another sip of wine, then gave a sharp shake of her head, as though she had tasted something sour. "But why must it always be *my* people who bleed? When the Tsar ruled the Three Nations, it was Lonian soldiers who formed his vanguard, though they were as much enslaved to his power as the Trolans they faced. Even in ages past, it was Lonia who bore the brunt of

Archon's wrath. Now they will bleed again, following a leader who cares naught for them."

"I do not know what to tell you, Marianne," Caledan replied, "only that I believe in you. And that tomorrow I will stand at your side and do my best to keep you safe."

"I am glad," Marianne said quietly, then sighed. "I am sorry for my melancholy, Caledan. I told you we should not discuss such matters tonight." She rose to her feet and stepped around the brazier, stumbling slightly as she did so. Caledan's eyes were drawn to the bottle of wine, and he realised she had drunk most of it before his arrival. She knelt awkwardly beside where he sat and placed a hand on his knee. "But I will reward you for your service, my Champion."

Caledan swallowed at the queen's proximity. Her eyes were wide, her face flushed red, and for a second he was struck by a desire to take her in his arms and kiss her, to tell her everything would be okay. Almost as quickly the thought was gone, replaced by a wave of doubt.

Would things be okay? Tomorrow they would face bloody battle on the waters of the Jurrien. With her powers limited, Marianne would be relying on him to protect her from harm while she faced off against Servo. He could not afford any distractions.

So again he pulled away from her. Carefully her removed her slim hand from his lap. "I am sorry, Marianne," he croaked, his mouth suddenly dry. "I cannot accept…such a gift…not with the battle on the morrow…"

"What?" For the merest of seconds, shock showed in Marianne's eyes. It was gone in an instant, and suddenly she was standing, her face a mask once more. "I did not mean that kind of gift," she growled, her voice like ice.

Caledan's mouth dropped open, but no words came out. Mortified, he stared at the queen, wishing he could sink into the floor.

"Your sword," she snapped, holding out her hand. "Give it to me."

"I…" Caledan closed his eyes, unable to face her rage.

He had failed her. Now he must face the consequences. He stood and unclipped his sword belt before handing her the weapon. She took the sheathed blade without a word and drew it into the lantern light. He did not flinch away as she held it in her hand.

But Marianne made no move to strike him down. Instead, a calm settled over her face as she closed her eyes. Her hand began to glow, as though she held some multi-coloured light between her fingers, and slowly that light danced its way up the blade. Swirling and flickering, it spread until the whole blade was aglow.

Then slowly, reluctantly, the light seeped into the sword, until nothing remained of the power Marianne had summoned. Wordlessly, she sheathed the blade and handed it back to Caledan.

"Carry the blade into battle tomorrow, sellsword," she said coldly. "If you are truly faithful, perhaps it will offer you some small measure of protection."

Stunned, Caledan looked from the sword to Marianne. "I…thank you—"

"That will be all, sellsword," Marianne spoke over him. "Leave me now, I have much to think about."

At that she turned away, dismissing him with a glance. Caledan stared at her back, then swinging the belt around his waist, he started for the tent flaps. But at the entrance he hesitated, glancing back. Marianne stood beside the brazier, her eyes on the coals. For a second he was struck again by the impulse to go to her, to wrap her in his arms and pull her close.

Then she glanced back and saw him still standing there. Flames appeared in her eyes, a silent rage that promised retribution. Spinning, Caledan fled the tent in silence.

$\mathfrak{K}$ 7 $\mathfrak{K}$

The ride to Kalgan took three days, during which Pela and Ruebyn were watched day and night. The soldiers had freed up two packhorses to carry them, though without proper stirrups, riding the beasts was impossibly uncomfortable. Their hands had also been bound, and with the horses being led by the soldiers, they'd no control over the pace at which they rode. By the first night, Pela had felt as though her entire body was one giant bruise.

The following days had not improved from there. Pela had soon come to realise that Ruebyn had been right— Trola was empty. For three days they saw only empty fields and ghost towns, a land abandoned by its people. Even as the road had widened and the way grew clearer, the countryside remained bare.

Only as they neared the capital had people finally appeared. The first had been a lonely vagabond, wandering slowly down the side of the road. His eyes had been fixed to the ground and he did not look up as the soldiers rode past. The next was the same, while a third carried a hand wagon loaded with dishevelled-looking onions. They'd overtaken him just an hour before the city, and the soldiers had been unhappy by the delayed caused while he shifted his wagon from the centre of the road.

In the silence on the road, she and Ruebyn had not been able to talk about what had happened in the village. But that had not stopped her anger from brewing. She still could not believe he had acted so foolishly, had revealed himself, and for what? Some half thought out plan to save her?

Her anger was made all the worse now she knew they could easily have avoided detection in the Trolan country-side. Their path would have been clear, if only Ruebyn had not given them away.

Now they were at the end of their journey, Pela wondered what fate awaited them in the ancient city. Kalgan had stood as the capital of Trola for a thousand years—even during the reign of the Tsar, when he had razed it to the ground. Its walls rose before them like moun-tain cliffs, so high she could hardly believe they had ever been taken. Guards stood at the gate, dressed in the same blue armour as their captors, and Pela and Ruebyn were ushered through without delay.

The city itself was a strange place, its buildings squat and unadorned, as though their creators had feared to make them beautiful lest the Tsar return again to burn them. A heavy silence hung over the place, and for the first few minutes Pela feared the city as dead as the rest of Trola. But as their party progressed through the grid-like streets, she saw hints of life—a wagon rumbling by the next intersec-tion, a flicker of movement in a nearby building. The door to one house stood open, and peering inside, Pela saw stairs leading down.

She remembered then a tale her uncle had told her once, that after the Tsar's invasion Kalgan had built down, rather than up. Beneath the streets were half a hundred tunnels and chambers, a civilisation hidden from the world above. Who knew how many souls still survived beneath their feet?

Nearing the city centre, Kalgan's streets finally began to fill, though its people still walked with their heads bowed, avoiding eye contact with the soldiers. Those who could went hurriedly about their business, while the beggars and occasional street vendor did their best to avert their gazes from the armed men. Most wore little better than rags, the fabric worn and dirt-streaked, though despite their obvious poverty they all displayed at least one piece of jewellery— bracelets or necklaces, or for many, a plain circlet of brass or copper. Each was inset with the same black gems sported by the armour and weapons of the soldiers.

But it was their eyes that haunted Pela most. Though they were quick to look away, she could not miss their despair, the misery of all they passed. Trola had suffered during the Tsar's reign, but with his fall they had been free to prosper. What then had happened, that Trola's crops went untended while its people starved?

"Look," Ruebyn whispered as they turned a corner.

Pela would have stumbled to a stop if she'd had the ability. Instead, her horse continued its slow plodding towards the glimmering marble walls at the end of the street. They rose some hundred and fifty feet above their head—the towers beyond even higher—a stunning citadel of marble and gold, utterly out of place amidst the squat buildings of Kalgan.

"They really rebuilt it," Ruebyn whispered.

Pela could only nod as she carefully closed her mouth. Before the Tsar had invaded, all of Kalgan must have looked like the citadel. It was said to have been badly damaged by the dragon fire that had ravaged the city, but its renewal had been one of Trola's first projects after they'd won their freedom, to restore the pride of a broken nation. But that had been before the borders had closed, and no one in the east knew whether the work had been finished.

Without magic, Pela could hardly imagine how such a feat was possible. The marble blocks must have weighed tonnes, and the spiral towers looked so delicate that a strong breeze should have blown them down. Built of marble and granite and gold, it was a glorious and terrifying foil to the poverty that surrounded them, a reminder of all Trola had once been—and had since lost.

"It looks just like the history books," Ruebyn said as they approached.

Finally shaking free of her shock, Pela flashed him a glare. "I wouldn't know."

"It's said the original citadel predated the False Gods," he went on, unaware of her anger, "that ancient powers were imbued into its very walls." He fell silent, glancing at their captors, but now that they were close to the end of their journey, the soldiers seemed to have relaxed. "The Sword of Light, from your own legends, hung in its gardens before anyone learned how it could be used."

Pela lifted her head at that. He was right—she knew that tale. "The Trolan King, Thomas, came for it when Archon's forces first invaded the Three Nations," she murmured, then frowned. "No, that cannot be right—he was fighting on the frontlines, and the war only ever made it as far as Plorsea."

Ruebyn offered a telling smile. "You're right," he

replied. "The stories say King Thomas led the final battle in Chole, but that The Way transported him to the citadel in time to defeat the Dark Magicker."

"The Way?" Pela frowned. Her grandmother had told the story many times when she'd been a child, but that was long ago, and the details were fuzzy.

"It was said to be a magical portal between Plorsea and Trola, left over from the Great Wars. Supposedly it was a place of safety, used for peace negotiations, but it became corrupted during the time of Archon." Ruebyn chuckled. "Personally, I've always thought it proof that the stories are no more than that. Magic was never powerful enough for such a feat."

Rolling her eyes, Pela tried to rub the circulation back into her wrists where the cords had cut deep. "I thought you might have learned to open your eyes by now," she said. "There are powers not even your engineers can explain, Ruebyn. Or do you think the soldiers stood aside willingly when I came to rescue you?"

Ruebyn fell silent at that, though Pela sensed he was far from convinced. Even so, she let the subject drop as they moved into the shadow of the citadel walls. Oaken gates groaned as they swung open and darkness embraced Pela as the horses carried them into the gate tunnel. A shiver passed through her as she sensed a change in the air. Frowning, she studied the ancient stones, but they looked no different than the outside. A moment later they were returned to the light, and the world was normal again...

...if what greeted them on the other side could be called normal. In place of the slums they had left behind, a brilliant lawn of lush grass spread out before them. Gardens of gold and red and violet flowers grew here and there, while vines and creepers covered the inner walls of the keep.

There were people too, merchants and nobles it seemed, from the cut of their clothes. They wandered amongst the gardens in pairs, arm in arm as they spoke in soft voices, their lives as disconnected from the poverty outside as a desert cat from the ocean.

Pela could only stare as they rode past. After her time in the mines beneath Lonia, she knew well the pain of the poor, the agony of working until her hands bled and still not earning enough food to sustain herself. Those outside might not have been slaves, but they were still trapped by their poverty, made servants to the rich who wandered these gardens.

Anger touched her then, a wild rage at everything she had suffered, born of her frustration, of the days of silence.

"What is wrong with you?" she shouted, tugging hard at her bindings, trying to redirect her horse at the nearest couple. "How can you just stand here talking while there are people outside starving?"

The nearest couple looked around at the commotion. Their eyebrows lifted half an inch when they saw her, as though surprised that an outsider had spoken to them. They stared at Pela for a long moment, the slightest of frowns denting their brows. Then a look of disinterest came over their faces, their eyes turning blank, and they turned their backs and wandered away.

"Bastards!" Pela screamed after them. "You don't even care!"

She had expected the soldiers to react, but the man holding her reins merely edged his horse onwards, drawing her along with him. Pela swung on him, using every curse word she'd learned in the mines, but he remained impassive. The mood of the soldiers had grown sombre upon entering the citadel and even the captain rode with his eyes fixed straight ahead.

Finally the soldiers reached the inner keep and dismounted. The captain himself cut Pela's bindings loose. She stepped down clumsily, but her legs numb from the morning's ride and she would have fallen had he not caught her by the collar. Dragging her up, he brandished a knife.

"You will be silent before the king," he hissed, "or I'll remove your tongue before our little appointment."

Pela swallowed an angry retort when she saw the darkness in his eyes. Instead, she nodded and clamped her jaw shut. The captain smiled grimly and led her inside, while the man she had come to know as his second-in-command brought Ruebyn. The others remained outside with the horses. Pela saw no guards here—had seen none since entering the citadel, in fact. She supposed they weren't needed. Everyone the nobles might fear was kept outside by the massive walls.

They walked quickly through the marble corridors, their way lit by the warm glow of lanterns. Great tapestries covered the walls, though these surely could not have been the originals. Those would have been destroyed when the Tsar's Red Dragons had burned the city.

A shiver ran through Pela as she noticed the tapestries hanging at the end of the hall. One depicted a narrow canyon, bordered by snow-capped peaks. A great battle was taking place between the cliffs, as soldiers of red and blue hurled themselves at one another. In the centre of the red-caped soldiers, one man stood shrouded in darkness, a terrifying warhammer held high above his head. Yellow eyes glowed in the shadow of his face, as though the warrior were possessed by the devil himself.

On the other wall was a matching tapestry, this time of the rolling hills in northern Trola. Here the red-cloaked army swarmed up towards a last bastion of resistance—an army of blue and green, led by the golden figure of the Northland Queen and the man Betran, who would later become the Trolan King, at least before the borders had closed. And there again was the hammerman, though now a pure light shone upon him.

Devon.

Pela had once been ignorant of her uncle's past, but no longer. The tapestries depicted the two battles that had marked his great life—the first where he had led the Tsar's forces to victory against the Trolans, the second years later, when he had stood with the resistance and put right the mistakes of his past.

Boom.

She jumped as a crash echoed down the corridors, but it was only a set of iron doors opening ahead. The captain and his second gestured them onward, and Pela fell into step beside Ruebyn. Servants pressed their shoulders to the doors as the four of them passed inside, and a second *boom* followed as they were sealed inside.

Coming to a stop, Pela was surprised to find herself in a sparsely furnished room. Gone were the grand tapestries and golden fittings. Even the walls were looking worn, the stone stained with moisture. At the opposite end of the room several men and women sat speaking at a wooden table, their whispers echoing from the high ceilings. The voices died away as a dozen eyes turned to face the entrance.

"Captain Shand," an old man at the head of the table rasped, coming slowly to his feet. Pela started as she saw the copper crown upon his brow, inset by a single black gem. "What brings you to the citadel? I had thought you stationed in the northern regions."

The captain released Pela and stepped forward, bowing low. "We were, Your Majesty," he said as he straightened, "but we found these two wandering in a village in the foothills."

"Ah, such beautiful country," the king murmured, settling himself back into his seat. "I have not visited in many years, hardly once since the great battle. I must plan a return…one day…" He trailed off, his eyes taking on a distant look.

There was a moment's pause as the captain waited for him to continue. When the king remained silent, he cleared his throat. "Your Majesty?"

"What?" The king sat up suddenly, shaking his head. "Oh yes, my apologies, Shand. You found them where? I thought all the villages in those parts had been decimated."

"They are not Trolan," Shand announced. "They crossed the border from Lonia."

A collective gasp came from the table as the men and women there turned to one another, speaking quickly. Pela's heart pounded hard in her chest as she watched them, wondering what they would say, how they would pass judgement.

Finally she could bear it no longer. The captain had left her unattended, and gathering herself, she leapt past him. "We seek asylum—" she shouted, before something hard slammed into her from behind.

Stars flashed across her vision as she struck the ground,

the weight of the captain driving the breath from her lungs. Gasping, she tried to roll away, but then his hands were in her hair, forcing her face into the cold marble tiles.

"Stay down, you little witch," he snarled.

Straining to breathe with his weight on her back, Pela replied in a series of hissing sounds that might have been agreement. The pressure relented a little, and after a few more gasping mouthfuls, she managed to draw a full breath. She turned her head as a muffled cry came from across the room, and saw Ruebyn struggling with the second soldier.

"Pela!" he managed, before the captain's second cuffed him in the side of the head and he slumped into his captor's arms.

"Shand!" the king's voice echoed from the ceiling, louder now but still seemingly frail. The soldiers froze, looking up as the monarch continued. "What is the meaning of this violence?"

"Forgive me, Your Majesty," Shand grunted. Taking hold of Pela's hair, he stood, dragging her up with him. "As I was saying, these two came from beyond the mountains. We do not know who sent them, but I believe they could be a threat."

"Release them—now," the king said, his voice taking on a dangerous tone.

The captain obeyed immediately, releasing Pela so quickly she almost fell and dropping to one knee.

"Forgive me, Your Majesty," he replied. "I only meant to protect you."

"I will have no violence in my throne room, Captain Shand," the king murmured, his voice so low now he could hardly be heard.

Pela shuddered at the look he gave the captain, but

seeing her opportunity, she gathered her courage and faced the king.

"Your Majesty," she said, bowing low. "As I was saying, we come seeking asylum."

"Asylum?" he asked, then waited until Pela nodded before continuing. His eyes were sad as he looked at her, as though her fate were already sealed. "I see. Did you not know it is forbidden to enter Trola—on pain of death?"

"Y…yes, sir," Pela stuttered, put off by the man's demeanour. Would he so easily condemn them without ever hearing their story? "But…we were desperate!"

"There are many desperate souls in our world," the king said, his eyes turning distant once more. "So much war, so much death and destruction. Oh, how my people have suffered these past fifty years." Then his eyes focused on her once more. "Tell me, girl, do you know my name?"

Pela shook her head, not daring to speak, though she prayed to the Gods this was the man who had once fought beside her uncle.

A smile crossed his face. "I am called Betran, he who fought alongside the Northland Queen in the battle for our freedom." There was a touch of pride in his voice, though it hardly seemed to lift him from his melancholy. "It fell upon my shoulders to lead Trola from the ruin left by the Tsar's reign."

"Betran?" Pela whispered. Her heart soared and she was hardly able to believe her luck. "My name is Pela, and this is Ruebyn. You knew my uncle, Devon!"

Now it was the king's turn to show surprise. A spark lit in his eyes as he looked at her, burning through the sadness. "You are related to the hammerman?" he whispered. "I thought him long dead. Perhaps there are heroes yet in this world."

"I am sorry," Pela said, and watched the spark fade, "he died not long ago." She forced a smile, and when she spoke the words were strained. "But his memory lives on in all of us."

The king made a gesture, as though to dismiss her words. "I am sorry for your loss, my dear," he said. "Though I am more sorry you have so carelessly thrown away your own lives."

"What?" Pela hissed, the blood pounding in her ears. She took a step towards the king, one hand extended in entreaty. "Please, surely you can make an exception, after everything Devon did for your land."

"An exception?" the king asked. He stared at her for a long while, then slowly he shook his head. "You do not know, do you?"

"Know what?" Pela asked. When the king still said nothing, her voice rose to a shout. "*Know what?*"

"I suppose word did not reach your lands," he replied. His eyes drilled into Pela. "Closing our borders was an act of desperation. It was the only way to stop the *morbus*."

"What is the *morbus?*" she asked, though in her heart she already knew.

"A plague, my dear. One unlike any the Three Nations has ever seen."

❦   8   ❧

Kryssa and Braidon rode all night to reach Chole just as the sun began to stain the horizon red. In all that time, they'd said not a word. Kryssa was still reeling from the revelation in the camp, that Braidon had taken the energies of the dying as the pantheon burned. She knew that the king had had nothing to do with the slaughter, and yet…just the thought of what he'd done made her skin crawl.

The guards were just pushing the gates open to admit the first travellers of the morning as the two rode up. Kryssa was flagging, her strength consumed by her preoccupation with Braidon's new power, by the endless ride, and a desperate lack of sleep. Yet the king still seemed fresh, as though such trivial matters no longer affected him. Indeed, they might not, with the life forces he had gathered…

"Sir!" one of the guards called as Braidon edged his horse forward, sounding surprised. "Your Majesty—your sergeants, they've been looking for you!"

A look of irritation crossed Braidon's face at being recognised, but was quickly concealed. "I was called away on an urgent matter," he replied from the saddle. "Was there a message?"

"Ah…" The guard trailed off, glancing at his companion before continuing. "No, but…I imagine it was to do with the riots, sir!"

"Riots?" Kryssa asked, concerned. She edged her horse up alongside Braidon. "What's happened?"

"Well, maybe not riots," the guard replied. "There was a protest, outside the…err, *your* Castle, sir. They refused to leave. There was some…confusion about what to do about them."

"And what *did* my illustrious sergeants decide?" Braidon asked coldly.

"They…they led a few regiments out the gates and sent them packing."

Braidon swore. Giving his horse a kick, he set off at a gallop. Kryssa followed just a few feet behind, her heart racing. What had Braidon's men been thinking? They needed the city on their side, not on the verge of an up rise. How could such a disaster have unfolded in just a few days?

The streets were empty as they raced through the city, and there was no sign of Janylle or her followers. A shiver ran down Kryssa's spine as she wondered whether the woman had been involved in the protest. Her eyes fixed on Braidon's back and she wondered what he would do.

There was no sign of disturbance in the streets outside the Castle either, but as they approached, men appeared atop the ramparts. Kryssa pulled back on her reins as several crossbows were pointed in their direction.

"Halt!" a voice bellowed down. "Who goes there?"

"Your king," Braidon snapped. Unlike Kryssa, he had not slowed his approach. "Now open the bloody gates."

There was a moment of confusion atop the walls, until someone apparently recognised Braidon. The rattling of chains was followed by the creaking of steel hinges, and the wooden gates cracked open. Braidon rode through without so much as a glance back, and Kryssa hurried after him before the recruits locked her out.

Inside the walls, she was surprised to find a regiment standing at arms. Braidon had already dismounted and was now striding through their ranks, bellowing for his sergeants. Her heart racing, Kryssa looked around for an attendant or stablehand, but there were none in sight. The gates slammed closed behind her, and cursing, she leapt from the saddle and ran after the king.

"Braidon!" Kryssa gasped, but the king did not turn back.

She didn't catch him until the inner corridors of the Castle. Even then he did not spare her a glance, and they strode down the hallways in silence, making for the room Braidon had designated as his war chambers. An aide met them as they approached the final corner, puffing hard. He had been a minor noble before, working as a tax collector. In need of every spare hand he could get, Braidon had raised the man up to help with the organisation of the Castle.

"Sir," the man gasped. "Where have you been?"

"Gather my sergeants," Braidon snapped, ignoring the question. "I want them in the war chambers, now."

The aide recoiled at Braidon's abrupt tone. The king was always polite with his assistants, but he was gripped by a terrible rage now, one that brooked no argument. After a second's hesitation the aide nodded and raced off down the corridor.

A few minutes later, Kryssa found herself alone in the war chamber with Braidon. Though the name sparked images of grandeur, of a space filled with maps and strategy papers, the room itself was nothing of the sort. Containing only a long wooden table and a dozen chairs, it had been someone's sleeping chambers before Braidon's occupation. The bed had been removed and the windows shuttered to keep unwanted intruders from entering, but otherwise the space hadn't been changed.

Finally able to catch her breath, Kryssa sank into one of the chairs. Braidon's aide still had not returned and the space was unlit, the gloom casting shadows into the corners of the room. Winter was a long way off, but a chill clung to the stones of the Castle, as though the ghosts of the dead still haunted its passageways. Kryssa cast a glance at Braidon, wondering what it must be like to hold the lives of so many innocents within him.

Shuddering, Kryssa quickly returned to her feet. There was a wood stove in the corner, probably used by its previous occupant for heating during the winter, and she crossed to it. Pulling open the iron door, she was pleased to find a small stack of wood already in place. She lit the stove with her flint and returned to her chair.

All the while, Braidon paced back and forth across the room, his jaw clamped closed. She watched him from the corner of her eye, still wondering what he would do, what had happened. The king could not afford such unrest in his city, not with Marianne due to join with the Lonian forces in a matter of days. With an army beneath her command, it would only be a matter of time before they stood outside Chole's gates.

One by one, the various men and women Braidon had

elected as his sergeants filed in. Each cast one glance from the pacing king to Kryssa, then took their seats in silence. Kryssa nodded to a few, but taking her cue from Braidon, she said nothing. The only sounds were the padding of the king's boots, the gentle crackling of the fire.

"How many died?" Braidon announced when all ten of his sergeants had gathered, his eyes sweeping over them. When no one replied, he strode to the head of the table. "I asked: *how many died?*"

Several of his sergeants flinched as the king's shout echoed from the walls. Kryssa held her breath, waiting to see which of her fellows would take the lead. Movement finally came from the end of the table as a woman climbed to her feet. Kryssa thought she recognised the face, but she'd not yet taken the time to memorise all of their sergeant's names.

"Two recruits, Your Majesty," the woman murmured, her eyes fixed to the tabletop. "Of the crowd…we aren't sure. The dead and wounded were dragged away by their fellow protestors."

"Estimate," Braidon grated.

The woman swallowed visibly. "Ten? Twenty? No more than that, we believe."

"And was it you, Sergeant Macy, who gave the order to attack unarmed civilians?" Braidon asked, his voice like ice.

The sergeant drew herself up. "No, sir," she replied in a wooden voice. "It was decided amongst all of us, in your absence."

Kryssa winced. There was no missing the rebuke in the woman's words, the implication that Braidon had failed his people in their moment of need. The king stared at the sergeant, his eyes hard, and when he spoke, his voice was like granite:

"Sit down, Sergeant Macy." Wood grated against stone as the woman practically fell into her chair. Teeth bared, Braidon continued. "From now on, no action is to be taken against the population of this city without direct orders from myself or Lieutenant Kryssa." He let out a long breath, seeming to calm somewhat. "Make no mistake, what happened is a tragedy, but we must press on. Any day now, Marianne will meet with the Lonian army. We must be ready when they come. How goes the training of our recruits?"

The sergeants exchanged nervous glances. Several looked to Macy again, but apparently the woman had decided she'd said enough. Finally one of the men rose. "There have been…setbacks, Your Majesty."

For the merest of seconds, Braidon's eyes slid closed. "Yes?" he asked, as though he already knew what was coming.

"A number of the recruits have…quit. The rest continue their training, but morale is low, especially after yesterday. Some are questioning…" He trailed off, glancing at his companions as though seeking their support before continuing. "Questioning your commitment to destroy the Order."

Placing his palms against the table, Braidon leaned forward, his gaze locked on his subordinate. "And what do you think, Sergeant?"

"I believe Your Majesty knows best!" the man shouted.

"And what about the rest of you?" Braidon snarled, swinging on the table. Not one of them could meet his gaze, and after a moment the king turned away. Arms clasped behind his back, his next words barely rose above a whisper. "Get out, all of you."

The sergeants went. Only Kryssa remained in her seat, waiting until the rest had gone before rising and approaching the king. Her heart was still palpitating in her chest, and she couldn't help but question whether Braidon had done enough. A dozen civilians were dead, and he'd given his sergeants little more than a reprimand…

"Braidon…?" she whispered, rising to her feet.

"What?" he snapped.

She recoiled at the fire in his eyes, but Braidon made no move towards her, and after a moment the flames faded. His shoulders slumped and he stumbled to the table. Sinking into a chair, he laid his head in his hands. Kryssa stood staring at him for a long while, then crossed and took the seat beside him.

"What am I going to do, Kryssa?" Braidon croaked, lifting his head to look at her. "It's all falling apart."

Despite her disgust at what he'd done, Kryssa felt pity for the king as she saw the despair he had been trying so hard to conceal. For a moment out on the plains, Braidon had been himself again, free of responsibility and the burden of leadership, but now its weight hung heavy on his shoulders. Drawing in a breath, she reached out and gripped him by the shoulder.

"We keep fighting," she said, making a conscious effort to squash her own qualms. "We struggle on, for what's right, for our freedom."

"What's the point?" Braidon asked bitterly. He made a gesture, as though to include the whole city. "They've all abandoned me. Why should I fight for them now? Why *shouldn't* I just abandon them to Marianne's tender care?"

"Because you're their king," Kryssa whispered. "Because the blood of heroes flows in your veins. Because you're all we have, Braidon."

A sad smile twisted the king's lips. "Now that's a depressing thought." Groaning, he pushed himself up. Shadows lined his face and red streaked his eyes. The exhaustion of the road seemed to have finally caught up with him. "I'm sorry I didn't tell you," he murmured. "About the…pantheon."

Swallowing, Kryssa supressed a shudder. "Get some sleep, Braidon," was all she said.

The king waved a hand. "I'll sleep when I'm dead." Even so, he closed his eyes for half a moment, as though to gather himself. "Come on then, there's much to do if we're to save these fools from my dear wife."

Kryssa rose and made to follow him, but the king only managed two steps before a new arrival stepped into the doorway. Movement came from the corridor as other figures pressed forward, and Kryssa frowned, wondering who wanted to speak with the king now.

"Who—" Braidon started, coming to a stop, but before he could finish the figure threw back her hood.

Janylle stood in the doorway, her face a mask of hatred. She clutched a dagger in one pale fist.

"I said you'd pay, Braidon!"

$\approx$ 9 $\approx$

Pela sat in silence at the dining table. Her eyes were on the servants carefully carving a haunch of ham nearby, but her thoughts were far away, her mind occupied with that one, terrifying word.

Plague.

The word had hardly been spoken in living memory, but since the demise of magic, it had become an unspoken fear amongst the peoples of Lonia and Plorsea. In the past, healers from the Earth Temple had used their magic freely in times of illness. But without magic…there was only the knowledge of doctors to defend against disease.

The morbus.

That was what they had called it, the reason why the fields and villages of Trola stood empty. It had swept the living from the land, had decimated the already crumbling nation. No wonder they had closed their borders, why they had not dared send a single rider to carry word to the east.

She and Ruebyn had stumbled right into the middle of it, had more than likely exposed themselves when they'd entered the village. The king had not seen how the sickness spread, but…Pela had seen their doom in his eyes. There was a burning sensation beginning in the back of her throat, and she wondered if that might be the first symptom.

But no one had told them anything more, only bustled them from the throne room to a private chamber where they'd been ordered to bathe and change clothes. Pela had scrubbed herself until her skin was raw, but she feared it would do her no good. Then they had sat, alone on their single beds, and waited to be summoned for they knew not what.

Now she could only stare as the servants placed a steaming plate of roast ham and vegetables before her. She had hardly eaten anything in days—the soldiers had fed them the barest of rations—but she was not hungry now. Her stomach was a churning mess of emotion, and she was on the verge of throwing up.

Ruebyn sat beside her, his eyes just as distant. He hadn't spoken a word as they waited for the king's summons, hadn't even looked at her. She could sense his anger, knew what he was thinking—that this was all her fault. If only she had listened to him, if they had turned back when he'd sounded his warning, they might have never come to Trola.

But despite her fear, despite the king's words, Pela was not ready to surrender. Surely there had to be a cure—how else had people survived, however few?

The king himself sat at the head of the table, fingers steepled as he watched the servants prepare the last plate and set it before him. Another man sat to the king's left. They still had not been introduced, but it seemed to Pela that the man was watching her from beneath his long black hair.

Finally the servants were finished, and with quick bows to the king, they turned and departed through a pair of mahogany doors.

"Very well," the king announced, turning to them. "Thank you for joining us for a meal, young Pela and Ruebyn. This is Rayan, my son. I must apologise for my earlier melancholy. You can understand, the pain I have felt, watching my nation suffer so." He let out a sigh, before a smile broke across his face. "But we must make good on the gifts we are given. It pains me to hear of Devon's fate, but I am honoured to welcome his niece to my halls. Now, let us eat!"

So saying, he picked up his knife and fork and began to cut the tender meat. Pela could only stare, unable to comprehend the strangeness of it all. Just a few hours ago, this man had proclaimed them both doomed; now he sat eating with them, as though this were any normal supper. A tremor shook Pela as she watched him lift a morsel of ham to his mouth.

"No!" The cry tore from her without thought.

Steel rattled on porcelain as the king's fork slipped from his fingers and fell back to the plate. Mouth still open, he turned to stare at her, followed by the gazes of the others. She stared back, her own lips parted, unable to believe what she'd done. But there was no taking the word back now.

"I…" She swallowed, flicking a glance at Ruebyn before continuing. "Please, we need to know, what's going to happen to us?"

A smile returned to the king's face as he picked up the piece of ham that had fallen on the table and placed it in his mouth. He chewed it slowly, his eyes boring into hers.

"I had thought you might enjoy some food before

speaking of such grim tidings," he said finally, after he swallowed. "You spoke of some strife, before you reached Trola. Are you not hungry?"

"Please!" It was Ruebyn's turn to burst out. His hands were gripping the table so hard they'd turned white. "Please tell us!"

The king offered a sigh. "Very well," he said, knitting his fingers together. "It seems I may have spoken too hastily when I announced your fate earlier."

A warm tingling sensation spread across Pela's skull. There was hope! She wanted to scream for joy, to demand to know what had changed, but she found that words had quite abandoned her.

"What do you mean?" Ruebyn asked, his voice tight with expectation.

The king turned to his son. "Rayan, would you be so kind as to check, before their hope grows too great?" He turned back to them as his son rose. "Rayan is one of our chief engineers in the citadel," he explained.

Pela felt as though she'd been punched in the gut. The king's words had left her in utter confusion, and she could only watch as Rayan walked around the table and knelt beside her. He was older than her own eighteen years, closer to thirty than twenty. But he wore a kindly smile as he gestured to her neck.

"May I?" he asked in a quiet voice.

Blinking, she looked from him to the king. "What?"

"Your necklace," Rayan continued. "May I see it?"

"My…necklace?" Pela asked. Then the warmth fled her face as she realised what he meant. "It's…not a necklace," she whispered. "It's a slaver's collar."

"Oh!" he said, pulling back slightly. A frown creased his brow. "I'm sorry, we did not know."

"It's okay," she said, swallowing her mortification. "I… what did you want to know about it?"

"I'm not sure yet," Rayan replied.

He made another gesture, and she nodded that he could take a closer look. A shiver ran down her spine as his long fingers stroked the steel, turning the collar back and forth. Absently, he brushed a lock of black hair from his face, and she saw now that his eyes were the darkest green, almost as dark as his hair. His eyes narrowed as he came across the black gem set into her collar, before he finally rose and returned to his seat.

"Well?" the king asked.

A hesitant smile appeared on Rayan's face as he looked at her. "It is a primitive design, but it contains the right elements."

"What does that mean?" Pela croaked.

"The *morbus* has no cure," the king replied. "But working with our doctors, the citadel's engineers did find a way to defend against the infection."

"A long time ago, we realised that not all of the Gods' magic died with them," Rayan continued for the king. "Some crystals have retained the magic of the Earth Goddess. Black opals in particular have the power to heal. Captain Shand recognised the crystal on your collar when you were found. That is why they did not…" He trailed off, then abruptly returned to his earlier train of thought. "The crystal is the same as what we have worn these past decades to protect against the plague's spread."

At that, Rayan pulled an amulet out from beneath his shirt. Hung from a chain of steel links, it held a black gem far larger than the others Pela had seen, but now she looked at it closely, she realised it was true. It was the same as the one set into her slave collar. Relief swept through her—followed by a terrible despair as she realised what this meant for Ruebyn.

She turned and stretched out a hand to him, trying to relay her remorse, but he flinched away from her. His eyes fixed on Rayan, and when he spoke, his voice was like iron.

"What does this mean for me?"

The king and his son exchanged a glance. "Yes…" Rayan said finally, drawing a fine silver chain from his pocket. "You may wear this," he said, sliding it across the table, "it may save you yet."

Pela watched as Ruebyn scooped the chain into his palm. "Its power comes from the Goddess?" he croaked.

"That is our belief," Rayan replied.

"Ruebyn…" Pela whispered. The Saviour forbid the use of magic to enhance oneself, but surely in times of such desperation…

Ruebyn scrunched his fist into a ball around the necklace, and she could see the pain in his face. Finally he exhaled, and with a nod, he slid it over his head. He seemed to relax somewhat, his shoulders straightening almost imperceptibly.

"I pray the opal works," Rayan murmured, "but I fear it is already too late."

"Surely not?" Ruebyn whispered, the fear returning to his face. "We have seen none of the infected since we arrived here. Even a plague needs a means of dissemination."

A smile touched Rayan's face. "You are a learned man, Ruebyn," he said, "but I fear your people have never seen anything like the *morbus*. Our doctors believe it spreads through the very air, that it can survive in a room for decades undisturbed. Every soul in the village you entered fell to the plague. Just by stepping foot in their houses, you likely doomed yourself."

Ice ran down Pela's spine as she looked at Ruebyn. His face had turned a deathly pale and his whole body was shaking.

"I'm so sorry, Ruebyn," she whispered.

His eyes flicked in her direction and she saw the accusation there, the reminder that this was all her fault, for refusing to listen when he'd said they should turn back, that something was wrong. But after a moment, Ruebyn's eyes returned to his plate. Woodenly, he picked up the utensils and began to eat, ignoring the rest of them.

A long silence stretched out, during which the king and his son started on their food as well. Pela did not so much as touch her fork. Her entire insides were churning, so tangled up she couldn't even stomach the idea of food. What had she done, leading them here? She had been so confident they could face whatever they found in Trola, but she had never expected this…

"And what of our eastern neighbours?" the king spoke finally, adapting an overly cheerful tone. "What has become of Plorsea and Lonia after all this time?"

"War," Pela said after a long while. "After you closed the borders, a decade-long war broke out between Lonia and Plorsea. It only ended eight years ago, when a peace treaty was brokered between King Ashoka and Braidon."

"Braidon!" the king exclaimed. "I met him during the revolution—charming young man. Shame about his sister, though I never got to meet her. Must have been quite the woman, to have old Devon traipsing across the Three Nations looking for her." He paused, a look of sadness crossing his face as he glanced at Rayan, then back to Pela. "I don't suppose you would tell me how the hammerman died?"

"I'm sure the girl does not want to recount her uncle's death, Father," Rayan interjected, a scowl marking his forehead.

Pela swallowed. It was true; Devon's death was still too raw, too recent. But the icy silence coming from Ruebyn was worse. She would do anything to break it, to distract herself from the reminder of her failure.

"It…was a few months ago," she began softly. "On the beach of Malevolent Cove. My mother and I had been taken by…" She glanced at Ruebyn before continuing. "By the Order of Alana."

"Oh!" The king's face showed his surprise. "That must be quite the story in itself."

Nodding, Pela went on with Devon's story. "A woman… I'm not sure what to call her, Braidon's estranged wife? Though she calls herself Queen of Plorsea and Lonia now. She was with the Order, wanted to kill us. Devon…delayed her while the rest of us escaped."

"And so ends the life of one of our greatest heroes," Betran murmured, his voice returning to its usual melancholy. "Alas, it seems that all the greats have now passed from this world."

"Not all," Pela replied. "Braidon lives because of Devon's sacrifice. He will stand against Marianne and the Order."

"So it seems another war is brooding," the king murmured. He had abandoned his food and was staring into the distance again. "The Three Nations remain divided. It will never end."

"It has ended for Trola," Rayan offered. His eyes were soft as he turned to Pela. "If your people knew the pain my nation has suffered, perhaps they would not be so quick to throw away their lives in such petty struggles."

"Then why the soldiers?" Ruebyn cut in sharply, dropping his cutlery onto the plate. The sound rang into the sudden silence as he scanned the table. "Your men certainly didn't seem fond of peace when they tried to execute us, nor when we were brought before you in the throne room."

"I am sorry for that," the king replied, "but we do what we must to ensure our nation's safety. Anyone in our land found without the protection of a black opal is to be executed, to protect against further…upheaval."

"That's barbaric," Ruebyn replied.

"It is mercy," Rayan said sadly. "You do not yet know… the pain of the infected."

"That is their choice!" Ruebyn spat back. "Who are you to take it from them?"

"I am their king!" Betran snapped suddenly. He half rose from his seat, but went no further. Drawing in a deep breath, he lowered himself back down. His eyes shone as he looked at Ruebyn. "I do what I must, to protect the ones I love. Without the black opals, our people would have ceased to be."

"So you raised an army to ensure no one could question your power." Braidon snorted. "That doesn't sound like peace to me."

"It was not just for the opals," Rayan murmured. "After the plague, much of Trola became a lawless place. Without soldiers, without guards, bandits ruled the land. There was no safety for the survivors. Soldiers such as Captain Shand are helping us to reclaim our lands, so that we might prosper once more."

"Nor do I forget the lessons of our history," the king added. "That is why I built the fortress across the Brunei Pass, to ensure our fate will never again be controlled by a foreign Tsar."

Uncomfortable with Ruebyn's accusations, Pela flicked him a warning glance, but he only glared back at her. She swallowed, and felt the cold of her collar pressing against her throat. A shiver passed through her. The thing might have saved her life, and yet…

"I…" she started, then trailed off, thinking of Ruebyn's likely fate. But it was too much, the constant reminder of her torment, her bondage to the mines. "Do you…do you have any way to remove my collar?" she whispered.

A smile appeared on Rayan's face and her heart lifted. "Of course," he said. "A blacksmith can come in the morning. I believe I have an opal necklace that would serve as a replacement against the *morbus*."

"Thank you!" Pela gasped. Her eyes teared up at the thought of finally being rid of the thing. She touched a finger to the cold steel, hardly daring to believe. "Thank you so much."

"Had we known, I would have had it removed immediately," the king said with a laugh. "How unfortunate that it is not some new fashion trend in the east, or we might have finally been safe to open our borders."

"Or perhaps they already know about the opals," Rayan mused.

Ruebyn snorted. "Unlikely—none of my teachers ever mentioned them. Though I cannot imagine why they gave such precious things to *slaves*." His voice was bitter as he looked at Pela, and she looked away, unable to face his rage. "I—" he tried to continue, but was interrupted by a hacking cough.

Pela spun back as Ruebyn bent in two over his dinner plate, palms pressed tight to the table. Another coughing fit shook him, an awful wheezing that rose from the depths of his chest. Specks of red splattered the porcelain plate as he coughed on and on, until finally, gasping, he collapsed back in his chair. Air rattled in his throat as he struggled to catch his breath. There was terror in his eyes when he looked at her.

"Pela!" he gasped.

10

"I said you'd pay, Braidon," Janylle snarled.

"Janylle, don't!" Kryssa shouted.

But the woman was already drawing back her hand, the dagger shimmering in the lantern light. Abandoning any hope of reasoning with her, Kryssa kicked her chair, sending it skating backwards across the room. Braidon stood frozen, eyes wide, too shocked to react to Janylle's threat.

Kryssa cried out as the blade hissed across the room, throwing out an arm. Instinctively, she reached within for the power at her core. Her life force leapt to her aid and went from her in a rush, surging out to meet the blade. There was a shriek of twisting metal, then the blade went hurtling sideways to bury itself in the back of a chair.

Relief swept through Kryssa a second before the exhaustion. Her energy spent by the spell, she sagged against the table. Across the room, Janylle and her supporters stood frozen, but their shock did not last long. One of those behind Janylle lifted a sword and roared.

Gathering herself, Kryssa straightened and dragged her sword from its sheath.

Face pale, Braidon still stood staring at Janylle as though she were some ghost from his past. Snarling, Kryssa shoved him aside and leapt to meet his foes. Steel rang out as her blade met the swordsman's, then spinning, she twisted her weapon and drove it into the man's stomach. Caught off-guard, he crumpled in two as the death blow struck.

Satisfied, Kryssa tried to tear her sword loose, but the man collapsed to the floor, dragging her weapon with him. She cursed and leapt back as Janylle's other followers entered the fray, dodging a clumsy blow that had been aimed at her head.

"Kill the witch too," Janylle snarled, picking up the sword of her fallen follower. "She's no better than her master."

Kryssa raised her hands and started to back away. She did not dare glance around to see what Braidon was doing. Unarmed and badly outnumbered, she scanned her foes, trying to figure which would attack first.

"Janylle, don't do this," she said, trying to stall. "Think about what you're doing. Dominic—"

"*Don't you dare say his name!*" Janylle screamed, waving her blade wildly in Kryssa's direction.

The rest of her followers filed in from the corridor. They were five in all, and she and Braidon didn't have a blade between them. They were hopelessly outmatched, and from the look on Janylle's face, the woman knew it too.

"How could you do it?" Janylle whispered, edging forward. "After everything we did to help you, how could you string him up like that?" A tremor shook the woman as she raised her sword. "I would expect such cruelty from a man like Braidon, but you, Kryssa? How could you help him do such a thing to a fellow soldier?"

Kryssa's stomach twisted at the accusation in her words, but she did not back down. "You know what he did—"

"Be damned!" Janylle screamed over the top of her. Baring her teeth, she thrust out with her blade, forcing Kryssa back. "You'll die slow for what you did to my sweet—"

"Enough!"

Kryssa jumped as Braidon's voice thundered inside the room. Janylle and her men took a collective step back, their faces showing shock. Braidon advanced, his eyes aglow. The hackles on Kryssa's neck prickled as she sensed the power radiating from Braidon, and now she remembered the energies he had collected. The assassins outnumbered him five to one, yet within Braidon carried the power of a hundred lives.

But Janylle did not know that.

"How dare you command me?" the woman spat, her face now a mottled shade of red. She raised her sword and pointed it at Braidon's chest like a spear.

"Tonight you have betrayed your nation, Janylle," Braidon continued, ignoring her threat, "but all of you have not yet thrown away your lives. Put down your arms and surrender to the king's justice, and you might yet keep them."

Janylle laughed. "Your words are dirt, King, nothing but lies. You would hang us before the day is done. No, you are unarmed and outnumbered. So I think we'll finish what we came here to do."

Raising the sword, she started forward, the others at her side. Fists clenched, Kryssa made to step up alongside

Braidon, but instead felt an invisible presence holding her back. She lashed out at the barrier, screaming at the king, but he did not seem to notice. His eyes were fixed on the assassins, though he seemed no more concerned by them than a cat by a mouse.

Only when his foes came within striking range did Braidon move. As the first assassin rushed him, the king raised his hand. The man ran on, stabbing low for Braidon's stomach—but as the point flashed down there came a hideous *shriek*, and the blade shattered as though it had struck solid rock. The shards flashed backwards as though propelled by a catapult, impaling the assassin's chest.

Braidon watched calmly as the man staggered to a stop. His eyes fell to the terrible wounds, the slivers of steel embedded in his flesh. A groan rattled from his throat, ending in an awful gurgling. The strength fled his legs and he slumped to his knees. Pale-faced, he raised an arm as though to beg for mercy. Instead, blood burst from his lips and with one last, despairing cry he crumpled to the ground and lay still.

Behind the king, Kryssa gaped. The man's death inspired the same reaction amongst Janylle and her remaining followers, as they stumbled to a stop beside their fallen comrade. They had all heard of Braidon's feat at the temple, his power during the battle for the Castle, but to witness it first-hand…

Kryssa looked back at the king, as disbelieving as the others. Braidon had used the power he'd taken from the victims in the pantheon. She had not realised its potential until now, the deadly nature of the energies he'd stolen. Now having seen it, she was all the more terrified for what he had done.

Janylle's face could have been etched from stone. She stood staring at Braidon, lips drawn back in a snarl, teeth clenched, her eyes burning with such hatred Kryssa recoiled. It was the look of one who knew she was doomed but would fight on anyway. Taking a firmer hold of her sword, Janylle stepped over the body of her companion.

"I see what you are," she spat, waving the sword in front of her as though it might fend off Braidon's next attack. "You pretend to stand on the side of the Gods, but you are naught but a servant, a creature of your wife, your sister. You only claim to serve us so that we will open our doors to their evil."

Braidon said not a word as she approached, only stood watching, listening to her hateful words.

"But you have already betrayed yourself," Janylle cried. "You sent your soldiers to murder the faithful of the Three Gods, to butcher our people in the streets. Now they will rise against you, against your Order, against your *queen!*"

With the last words, Janylle lunged, driving her blade for Braidon's throat. At the last possible moment the king twisted, his hand flashing up to catch the woman by the wrist. He slammed his other arm into her elbow, and the blade clattered harmlessly to the ground.

Janylle screamed and kicked at him, but her blows could not seem to find their mark. Braidon waited in silence as she raged, trying her best to destroy him, but unable to even free her wrist. Lacking the courage to intervene, her followers stood in silence beyond.

Finally Janylle slumped in Braidon's grasp and stared up at him, defeat in her eyes. "Do it then!" she spat, her voice dripping with loathing. "Kill me, and stoke the flames of your doom! The faithful of the Gods will see who you truly are, King. They will not be blinded by your words."

Braidon shook his head, and when he spoke, his voice was cold as ice. "I am sorry for your husband," he said. "I can see now the mistake I made. I will not make it again."

Sensing what he was about to do, Kryssa opened her mouth to cry out, but Braidon was faster still. A sharp *crack* came from Janylle's spine as he twisted his hand and the energies went rushing from him. A second later, Janylle's lifeless body struck the ground with a *thud.*

Screams came from the other assassins as they turned to flee, but Braidon was already lifting his arms. The assassins stumbled to a stop and raised their swords. For a moment Kryssa thought they would make another attempt on the king—but then they launched themselves at one another, their blades hacking and slashing until all lay dead on the floor of the war chamber.

Silence fell as Braidon lowered his hands. Kryssa could only stare in shock at the carnage he had unleashed, unable to summon any words. Blood seeped slowly across the floor towards her, shimmering in the lanternlight. Not one of the assassins still breathed. With her own life no longer in danger, Kryssa saw now that they were young men and women, barely out of adolescence. Slowly her eyes were drawn back to the king.

Braidon stood in the middle of the carnage, his eyes dark and face pale, and for a second she thought it was not Braidon at all who stood there. Then he let out a long breath and his shoulders slumped, his eyes flickering closed for a half moment. Concern creased the king's forehead as his blue eyes found hers.

"Are you okay?" he asked.

She nodded, still struck dumb by his display of power, by the bloody nature of their assassins' ends. With a shudder, she broke from the trance. Finding the invisible barrier vanished, she moved forward to stand beside him.

"I'll…find someone," she croaked.

"No," Braidon whispered, his eyes on the body of Janylle.

"What?" Kryssa hissed.

The king's head came up. "You heard what she said, Kryssa," he murmured. "She *wanted* me to kill her, to become a martyr for her followers. If word of this reaches the people, there'll be open rebellion in the streets."

"But…" Kryssa trailed off. "What…what will we tell them?"

"The Order has made an attempt on my life," Braidon said. Kryssa shivered as his eyes bored into hers. Unable to hold his gaze, she looked away, and he went on matter-of-factly: "No one can know Janylle was ever involved in this."

"There will be people who knew her, Braidon, people who will ask questions."

"But they will not *know*," he hissed. He drew in a breath, as though summoning the will to do what was necessary, before facing her. "Leave me, Kryssa. I will deal with the bodies."

Kryssa's mouth fell open as she looked at the king. She might have argued, but his eyes were lit with a terrible rage, and the words died in her throat. Clenching her jaw closed, Kryssa spun on her heel. Retrieving her sword from the man she had killed, she fled for the door.

"Kryssa." Braidon's voice brought her up short as she reached the entranceway. She turned back, an icy fear sliding suddenly down her spine. Their eyes met from across the room. "Speak not a word of this, to anyone," he murmured.

Nodding, Kryssa practically fled into the corridor and swung the door closed behind her. She staggered several steps and slumped against the wall. Only then did she let the tears fall. She had only known Janylle for a brief time, but the woman had been kindly, welcoming. She deserved a better fate than this, and yet…what else could any of them have done? From the moment Dominic had lit the pantheon ablaze, had murdered all those innocent souls, their path had been set.

Gathering herself, Kryssa straightened. Whatever had happened, it was over now. All they could do was make the best of it. She may not entirely agree with Braidon's plan, but—

Her thoughts were interrupted as the softest of whispers carried down the corridor. Kryssa froze where she stood, the hairs on her neck lifting in sudden intuition. Holding her breath, she waited, and the sound came again. Her eyes settled on a nearby closet. Dropping a hand to her sword hilt, she crept to the door and threw it open.

A cry came from within the closet as a shadow leapt away from the light. Kryssa's sword leapt into her hand and she raised it to strike down the final assassin—but at the last moment she paused. Something made her hesitant, a wrongness to the shadow. Carefully, Kryssa pulled the door open wider, revealing a young woman crouched on the floor, barely Pela's age.

Terror shone from the girl's amber eyes and a short sword lay on the floor beside her, but she made no move to grasp it. Instead, her arms were wrapped around her knees.

Staring out from beneath long locks of brown hair, she looked ready to burst into tears.

Shocked to her core, Kryssa stared down at the girl. Time stretched out as she thought of her own daughter, lost in the currents of Malevolent Cove. Kryssa had failed Pela, failed to protect her, to prepare her for the darkness of this world. Now here was another young woman, led astray by Janylle's words, brought to her doom.

It was Kryssa's duty to show the girl to Braidon. She had been part of Janylle's group, of that there was no question. She must face the king's justice. And yet…Kryssa knew what Braidon would do with her. He could not afford to have his lie exposed, not with the fate of Plorsea resting on his shoulders. At best the girl would be thrown into a dungeon to live out the rest of her miserable days, at worst…

Kryssa shuddered, the image of the dead assassins lying not twenty feet away all too fresh in her mind.

The girl had not moved. She still crouched on the floor of the closet, staring at Kryssa as though she expected to be struck down at any moment. A shudder ran down Kryssa's spine, and suddenly she was stepping back, leaving the door unguarded.

"Go," she hissed, pointing with her sword, "and never come here again!"

11

The boat rocked wildly beneath Caledan as the captain pushed off into the swirling currents. He quickly sat himself on the narrow wooden bench. Marianne was already there, but she said nothing as he took his place. Her eyes were fixed on the opposite bank of the Jurrien, where the Lonian army awaited. They stood rank upon rank, their green cloaks and shining spears forming a forest of armoured men.

The rains had cleared during the night but the river remained swollen. Silt-laden waters rushed around their tiny vessel as the captain and another sailor set their backs to the oars. It would only take one mistake to hurl them all overboard, where the powerful currents would drag them straight to the bottom. Caledan had no fondness for boats, but he would rather be aboard the tiny vessel than facing the currents unprotected.

Across the river, a second boat was just pushing off from the banks. Caledan strained his eyes, counting four within the vessel, the same number as their own. Reassured that the Lonians were obeying the terms of truce, Caledan's eyes were drawn to their destination—a tiny island in the centre of the river.

Word had come from Servo in the night requesting a parlay before the battle began. Sensing a trap, Caledan had argued against such a meeting. There was no reason for the Elder to negotiate. He had the superior force, and it was only a matter of time before his power surpassed Marianne's—if it hadn't already. The parlay could only be a trap.

But perhaps Servo knew of Marianne's weakness, that she still cared for the Lonian people. She could not pass up an opportunity to spare their lives, though not even she believed the Elder would surrender so easily.

Caledan shook his head. This was a fool's errand, but at least she had allowed him to accompany her. After his folly during the night, he would not have been surprised if Marianne had ordered him to the front lines.

His hand drifted to his sword hilt as their boat approached the island. He was determined to do his duty. Turning his eyes to the other boat again, he watched as it bobbed and twisted on the currents, and sent up a prayer to the Storm God to drag it down into the river's murky depths.

But fate was not on their side, and both ships made it safely to the island. Standing on opposite shores, the two parties watched each other across the open ground. Though still high, the river had fallen during the night, leaving the earth damp beneath their feet. Twisted trees grew on the island further upriver, but where they stood was little more than slick mud and long grass pressed flat by the flood waters.

All this Caledan took in at a glance—but his attention never left Servo and his followers. They had not moved from where they had disembarked, their tiny boat tied to the trunk of one of the twisted trees, straining against its bindings. Two of Servo's companions appeared to be sailors, without swords or armour. They carried a third person between them, but as they stepped from the boat, they let their burden fall to the mud.

Caledan frowned, staring at the fallen figure. It took him a moment to realise it was a woman, for her hair had been hacked short and her face was so bruised as to be barely recognisable. A cry carried across the mudflat as she fell, her legs bent at a strange angle and obviously badly broken. Even so, she somehow found the strength to drag herself up and try to crawl away. One of the sailors put an end to her efforts by driving a boot into her side, flipping the woman on her back.

Only then did Caledan recognise Genevieve. His mouth fell open and unconsciously he took a step forward. A cackle answered his actions, and his gaze snapped back to Servo. Distracted, he had not seen the Elder advance to the centre of the island.

"I see you recognise my new friend," Servo said, wearing the slick grin Caledan remembered all too well from his time in the dungeons beneath Ardath. "I'm afraid she's a little worse for wear than the last time you saw her. Found herself a slave in one of your dear queen's mines, it seems."

"Set her free," Caledan snarled. His sword leapt into his hand and he started towards the man, but Marianne's arm snapped out, bringing him up short.

"Stop," she hissed, "before you get all of us killed."

Enraged, Caledan swung on the queen, but one glance at her face was enough to suck the rage from him. Teeth bared, her eyes did not flicker from Servo. Her jaw was clenched, and the muscles in her neck were bulging as though she held the weight of the world on her shoulders. Across the muddy ground, Servo stood seemingly relaxed, but as Caledan looked closer, he saw the Elder's eyes were aglow.

A silent war was taking place between the two, a battle of wills that Caledan could only imagine.

Then the Elder threw back his head and laughed. He made a gesture, and the glow faded from his eyes. A long, drawn-out hiss came from Marianne as she exhaled through her teeth. Her throat contracted as she swallowed; then flicking an angry glance at Caledan, she strode forward to confront her foe.

"My apologies, Marianne," Servo said lightly. "Though you cannot blame me for trying, can you?"

"What do you want, Servo?" Marianne growled. "I defeated you once, I would have thought you'd had enough."

The Elder spread his arms. "I did not seek this confrontation," he said, "but my people have placed this burden upon me, demanded I bring their message to the queen that claims to rule them."

"Oh really?" Marianne said dryly. "And what message would that be?"

"They demand Lonia be returned to the rule of the council, that the Order be free to practice its beliefs." A grin twisted his face. "And that you, Marianne, submit to their judgement for crimes committed against your homeland."

"The followers of the Order are free to follow the original message of the Saviour," she replied. "Of personal growth, of inner strength, and individuals standing together to protect the collective." Her face hardened and her eyes flashed as she looked at Servo. "But there will be no more of your vile cleansings. I am done with the bloodshed. As for your other…requests, I do not believe for a moment these few you have gathered represent the whole of my kingdom."

Servo chuckled. "You call my methods vile, but your hands are no cleaner than mine, gathering power from the deaths of slaves. We are the same, my dear—lions amongst the sheep. I do not judge you for it."

"My way did not require a single life to be taken before it was due," Marianne growled.

"Ay, such an inefficient use of your creation. Your slaves barely have a spark of power left when death comes for them." He nudged Genevieve with his boot as he spoke, a disgusted look crossing his face. "But enough of this. Surrender, woman, or I will destroy everything and everyone you ever held dear."

"My son is far from here, and out of your reach, Servo," the queen answered coldly. "And why would I surrender when we are so evenly matched?" A sly smile crossed her face. "But you are right; let this end now, between the two of us."

"Ha! You think I am such a fool to surrender my advantage?" Servo cried, throwing out his arms. Caledan tensed, readying himself for whatever trap the Elder was about to spring, but after a moment Servo lowered his arms again. "Besides, once battle is joined, your fate is sealed."

"Oh?" Marianne asked, edging forward.

Servo flicked an imaginary speck of dust from his cuffs.

"As I was saying, your collars were ingenious, but I have unlocked their true potential." He made a gesture at the two sailors standing behind him. "Do you not recognise your own creation, Marianne?" he asked, and Caledan saw now that each man wore an iron collar around his throat. "I took your invention, and gave it to my people. Now their every sacrifice will add to my own power. So even should you somehow defeat my army, even if you slay every one of my followers, still you will lose."

Beside Caledan, Marianne had gone pale at the Elder's words. She said nothing as he took another step towards them, eyes flashing in the dawn light.

"So bring your army, bring your swords and arrows and spears, Marianne. Kill them all, but in the end, I will come for you. I will burn your feeble champion to ash, enslave you to my will. Then, my dear Marianne, you will take me to your son, and you will watch as he dies by my hand."

Caledan gripped the hilt of his sword, his entire body trembling with rage. Servo towered over Marianne now, and she wilted before his threats. More than anything Caledan wanted to draw his blade and drive it through the Elder's heart, but instead he stood frozen, listening to the awful words.

"In the end, Marianne, you will sit beside me as queen, obedient to my every whim. Just as you once were for Braidon. But this time, there will be no scheming, no secret plots. You will be mine, body and soul, a slave to my power."

"You would sacrifice a thousand lives for the sake of a crown?" Marianne croaked, her voice barely a whisper.

"I would sacrifice ten thousand to destroy the witch who shamed me," Servo snarled.

"Please," the queen rasped. "This fight is between us. Let us settle it, the two of us. There is no need for anyone else to die."

Caledan's heart thundered in his ears at the queen's words. Her whole body was shaking; she was practically begging the Elder now. He recalled their conversation so many nights ago, about how she had suffered, trapped in her unwanted marriage, been forced to bear Braidon's child. Servo threatened to do far worse: to enslave her entirely to his will. There could be no fate more awful for Marianne, no greater fear.

Servo laughed in her face. "You think to negotiate? Who do you think you are, witch? You were nothing more than the daughter of a pig farmer before we raised you up. And yet you thought to destroy me, to rule in my stead. Such arrogance! No, I will not negotiate with the likes of you. There is only one way to save yourself. Kneel in the mud like your precious pigs, or I will send my army. A thousand might die before I have power enough, but the end will be the same. You will kneel."

Silence fell across the island at the Elder's words, punctuated only by the roar of the river as it raced around the little patch of mud. It rolled over them like the distant rumble of thunder, like the howling of wind through tree branches, or a thousand voices raised in anger…

Caledan frowned, his gaze drifting past Servo, across to the opposite bank of the river where the Lonian forces waited. Except they were no longer standing still, but rioting up and down the riverbanks, their weapons raised to the sky. Even as Caledan watched, the roar of their rage grew louder, rolling out across the turbulent waters to where their leader stood.

"Trait…basta…kill him."

The individual words could not be heard, but their meaning was clear, the subject of their anger indisputable: Servo.

Caledan stared at the queen in disbelief. "What did you do?"

A smile touched the queen's lips as the fear fell from her face. "Nothing at all," she said, straightening. "I only shared the Elder's words with his own people. It seems they are none too happy with his plans to sacrifice them for his own power."

A desperate snarl crossed Servo's face as he looked from his rioting army to the queen. "You little witch!" he screamed, lifting a fist. "I'll tear you limb from li—"

"Ah, ah, ah," Marianne interrupted, wagging a finger at the Elder. Her smile spread, and Caledan realised everything had played out exactly as she had planned. "We are evenly matched, remember. But don't worry, I'll wait for you to send a few of your men to their deaths. Off you go, it looks like they're excited to receive you!"

Servo looked ready to explode. His jaw was clenched so hard Caledan could almost hear his teeth grinding. Eyes wild, he dragged his sword from its sheath. Genevieve still lay at his feet. He pointed the blade at her throat.

"I'll kill her!" Servo screamed.

The huntress did not move—did not even seem aware of anything that was happening around her, in fact.

"Now, now, there's no need for that," Marianne replied, showing little concern for Genevieve's life. Indeed, the woman had been Marianne's enemy when last they'd met—there was no reason for her to care. But Caledan's heart beat faster at the thought of the huntress's peril.

"My offer still stands, Servo," Marianne continued. "A fight to the death, sword against sword, without powers. Let the Saviour's hand guide the victor."

The Elder stared at Marianne, looking half-mad with rage. His hands shook and the tip of his blade was mere inches from Genevieve's throat. Caledan held his breath, though he wasn't sure what he was hoping for. What was Marianne thinking, offering a duel now? She was decent with a bow, and she had shown some proficiency with a rapier in Malevolent Cove, but she was far from a master. Servo was almost twice her size—that alone gave him a terrible advantage in a sword fight.

The same realisation seemed to have occurred to Servo. A wild grin spread across his face. "I accept!" he screamed, stepping away from Genevieve. "A final gambit then, to decide the fate of our nations." He pointed his blade at Marianne. "Are you ready, witch?"

Marianne's eyes widened in feigned surprise. "Me?" she gasped. "Why, Servo, I am a queen! It would be unseemly for me to participate in such a competition. As you said earlier, Caledan is my champion. He will stand on my behalf." She inclined her head and Caledan's eyebrows lifted in surprise at her announcement. "You may, of course, select a champion of your own, should you fear the skills of a mere sellsword."

Servo bared his teeth as fresh rage twisted his face, but he had little choice now. With his army in open rebellion, he had only one chance to snatch back the initiative. His eyes narrowed as they focused on Caledan. Caledan stared back, his heart suddenly racing.

"Very well, Marianne," Servo snapped. "You had best bid farewell to your favourite sellsword."

Letting out a long breath, Caledan looked from Servo to his queen. What game was she playing? Had she planned this as well, as punishment for his insolence? Without any power of his own, Caledan could not counter Servo's magic if the Elder tried to cheat. And with such high stakes, there would be no room for mistakes.

Marianne only smiled, her sapphire eyes glinting as they met Caledan's gaze. "Fight well, my Champion."

12

Standing on the ramparts of his Castle, Braidon looked out over the rooftops of Chole and wondered where he had gone wrong. Just a short few weeks ago, Janylle had been serving them breakfast in her house with Dominic. Now they were both dead—and by his hand.

Regret touched him as he thought again of Dominic's fate. Why had he acted so rashly, sentencing his own men to death for slaying some followers of the Order? It had forced a wedge between himself and the people of Chole, when they should have stood united against the Knights of Alana. And it had created an enemy in Janylle.

At least she'd made her assassination attempt in private. Had she attacked him publicly, forced him to take her life in front of others, how many more of Braidon's followers might have abandoned the cause? As it was, he had managed to spin things in his favour, to make a lie of Janylle's final words.

If only unrest in Chole had been his sole problem. With Loyla's rejection, his last hope of matching Marianne in the field lay in ruins. His five hundred recruits could not even hope to defend the city walls, let alone meet the queen in open battle. As things stood, Marianne would take the city within a day, and power or no, there was little Braidon could do to stop her.

Rage bubbled up within him, burning in his veins. Marianne's betrayal still cut deep, and every rejection and failure since had only added to the wound, feeding his pain, his hatred. His mind was a mess of self-loathing, that despite all his efforts, all his planning, he was still no closer to reclaiming his crown than he had been while lying half-dead on the shores of Malevolent Cove.

Well, maybe a little closer.

Braidon shivered as he turned his mind inwards and felt the power respond. It was his only comfort, the only reminder he was not entirely helpless against the forces that opposed him. He had spent precious energy defeating Janylle, but it had almost been worth it to feel the rush of his power.

It was *soldiers* he needed, though, men and women who could stand against the Knights of Alana, and whatever other allies Marianne had found. His spies claimed her army numbered some two thousand, the Lonians more than five. Even if he could match Marianne's magical abilities, Braidon could not create several thousand warriors from nothing.

Silently he cursed Loyla a fool, for refusing him, for shaming him with her outrageous challenge. Could she not see what was coming for them, that if they did not stand together, Plorsea would fall? What then for her people?

Grinding his teeth, Braidon looked again at the city and wondered how many of Janylle's followers survived. The crowd that had gathered while he'd been outside the city had numbered in the hundreds. How many were still plotting against him? Janylle had said the followers of the Three Gods stood with her, but Braidon was not so gullible as to believe her words. He had *saved* the Temple of the Earth, its priests would never think to betray him…

But then, he had once thought his wife beyond suspicion. So he had taken precautions, placing the temple under watch. If only he could trust the watchers. His sergeants had proven themselves worse than useless, ordering the attack on the crowd. How he missed his King's Guard now, their utter loyalty, their dependability. His chest ached as he recalled the familiar faces that had once stood alongside him. All dead now, the first casualties of his wife's so-called vengeance.

Balling his fists, Braidon ground his knuckles against the stone crenulations. He was again thinking of events he could not change. The past was fixed, his friends dead, his family stolen away. He had to find a new way, new powers to counter the forces Marianne would bring against him.

They didn't have long now. The queen's army could be at their gates in a week and his recruits remained untrained, unprepared for a major battle. At least they had weapons enough, with the stockade they had taken from the Castle— armour and swords and dozens of the deadly crossbows the Knights had brought from Lonia. He had blacksmiths around the city trying to replicate them, but so far they were having little success creating steel that could bend and flex as the Lonian weapons did.

Braidon needed something more, something to restore the confidence of his people, something to silence his doubters and restore the city's morale. Something to convince them all of his power.

A smile touched Braidon's lips as an idea came to him. But was it possible? Dragon Country was a long way off, far beyond normal calling distance. Perhaps with his new power…who knew what his limits were?

Closing his eyes, Braidon focused on his breathing, sinking slowly into the meditative trance. Light flickered in the darkness, blue and red and green and a hundred other colours, leaping and dancing in place, the life forces of the souls lost in the pantheon.

He drew the light to him, feeling the surging power as it touched his consciousness, feeding confidence to his wasting soul. For a moment he lost sight of his plan, felt only the rush of energy, but with a wrench he refocused. Opening his inner eyes, he sent his soul soaring.

Out across the plains of Chole he flew, as he once had as a true Magicker, across the scrublands and pastures, up the steep slopes of the volcanic range, between the twisted snow-capped peaks, until far below him were the wild forests of Dragon Country.

Nidryt!

He called the dragon's name in his mind, sending his voice rumbling out across the bowl-shaped land, to ring from the peaks, to whisper through the twisting branches below, to seek out its owner.

King?

Nidryt's voice sounded surprised, and back on the ramparts of the Castle, Braidon smiled.

Did you think I was dead, dragon?

Laughter sounded in his mind. *You humans are sickly crea-*

tures, the dragon's voice rumbled. *Your fate must have changed, to have power enough to reach so far.*

Ay, Chole is mine, Braidon replied. *Though enemies still assail me on all sides.*

Such is the fate of kings, the dragon growled.

I would have your help to destroy them.

You ask much of us, came Nidryt's reply, *for a man yet to fulfil a single promise.*

Braidon's stomach twisted as he recalled the oath he'd made with the dragons—that he would grant them fresh territory, gift them broad swaths of Plorsea in exchange for their aid.

I can offer you nothing until Plorsea is won, he replied, hoping the beast would accept his excuse.

Laughter was the answer. *Ay, we would have that promise too,* Nidryt reverberated, *but I speak of your pledge to drive the Knights from our land.*

They left, did they not? Braidon asked, surprised.

They have returned, the dragon replied.

Images flashed into Braidon's mind's eye, almost too quick to follow. They revealed a great encampment rising from the cliffs of Malevolent Cove. The amphitheatre that had once stood on the sands had vanished, but now great walls of sandstone rose from the blackened clifftops. They were only a few feet tall, but out in the cove, a dozen ships bobbed at anchor. They must have been ferrying supplies from Lon—Braidon knew it was only a matter of time before the walls would be finished.

They build anew, some foul structure from your stinking cities. We will stand for their desecration no longer. My people have pledged to drive them from our lands forever, though it may cost every one of our lives.

No! Braidon cried out, his voice ringing with power as he reached for the beast's mind.

A wrenching sensation followed, and suddenly he *felt* the dragon, the rippling of its muscles, the bulk of its wings, the power in its terrible jaws. Fear touched his mind as he sensed the beast's uncertainty—then a terrible rage as it realised what the king had done. Walls of fire encircled Braidon and he cried out, hurling his power at the flames. An opening appeared and he darted through, returning instantly to his disembodied state.

Now though, he found his spirit drifting before the dragon itself. Nidryt's scarlet head swung around, its one good eye swivelling in search of its attacker.

Where are you, King? the dragon growled, its voice now so loud Braidon felt his soul shiver. *Why do you seek to control me?*

My apologies, Nidryt, Braidon said, adopting a consoling tone. *I am still…new to this power.*

The growl increased in pitch, but after a moment the dragon gave up its search. Lowering its head, it spoke once more into Braidon's mind:

You once bade my people fight. Why do you now demand our cowardice?

Because I need you, Braidon replied. *If you throw your lives away against the Order, my last ally will be lost.*

What do we care for your fate, King, the dragon snarled, *when iron men trespass in our lands?*

Back in Chole, Braidon ground his teeth. He needed the Red Dragons desperately, but how could he convince Nidryt the true fight was with him? If Marianne could be defeated, the Knights that had set up camp in Malevolent Cove would be quick to follow, cut off from their supporters back in Lonia. But he sensed the dragon did not care for logic or strategy, that it was determined to end their strife now, whatever the consequences might be.

There was only one option left. Braidon could not convince the dragons to join him, so he must give them reason. He turned again to the power curling around his soul, the burning heat of a hundred lives. Would it be enough? Whatever Knights the Order had sent to build their new Castle, they would not be alone. They were bound to have at least one Elder with them, someone with power to protect the fledgling fortress. Would Braidon have the strength to match them?

It was a risk he would have to take.

Because I will help you, Nidryt, Braidon said at last. *Allow me to fulfil my part of our bargain. If we are to be allies, the Knights must learn to fear us. Where better to start than their most sacred of places?*

The golden eye of the dragon swivelled, seeming to stare straight at Braidon's spirit form. *Your power can stretch so far?*

Braidon frowned. It was doubtful—he was already beginning to feel the strain of reaching this far, and he was only using his energy to communicate, not to fight. If he was to go up against an Elder, he could not afford such waste. Finally he shook his head, though the beast could not see him.

No, he murmured into the dragon's mind. *I will need your aid, Nidryt. Come to Chole, my friend. Carry me back to Dragon Country, and together we will watch our enemies burn.*

13

"**A**re you ready to meet the Saviour, sellsword?"

Caledan did not rise to his foe's bait. Servo was younger than most of the Elders he had seen, closer to Caledan's thirty-three years. His shoulders were muscular and he moved with confidence on the slick ground—though the way Servo held his blade suggested he had not spent much time practicing with the weapon. His guard was too low, leaving his throat open to a sudden attack.

But Caledan could not forget the other energies Servo had at his command. Marianne had said this was a battle of blades, but Caledan was not about to trust his life to the word of the treacherous Elder.

"Very well," Servo said when it became obvious that Caledan would not reply. "Send my regards when you see her. I hope she condemns you to the darkest pits of hell for your blasphemy."

Caledan smiled at that. "Are you afraid, Servo?"

A scowl twisted the man's face and he leapt forward with a roar. Aware of the slick mud beneath his feet, Caledan moved carefully, his sword flashing up to deflect an over-hand blow. Spinning sideways, he tracked Servo's movement as the Elder followed him, holding back his attack. Caledan knew from years of practice that a reckless attack would open him to a riposte. A master swordsman must bide his time, studying his opponent for weaknesses, before launching his assault.

Servo had no such patience. A growl rumbled from his throat as he came at Caledan again, moving faster than the sellsword would have thought possible. Slowed by the mud, Caledan would have struggled to deflect the blows if not for Servo's habit of dropping his shoulder before each attack, warning Caledan just in time.

Turning aside a third blow, Caledan twisted on his heel and lashed out with his free hand. The blow crashed into the side of Servo's face, sending him reeling back. With his opponent bent in two, Caledan saw his opportunity and moved in for the kill—but at the last moment he pulled back, sensing a wrongness to Servo's stance.

Quick as lightning, Servo leapt, his blade slashing through the space where Caledan would have stood if he'd continued the attack. A snarl crossed the Elder's face as he realised his deception had failed. Caledan laughed in his face.

"Enjoy your last breaths, sellsword," the Elder snapped. "Soon you will drown in your own blood!"

With the words, Servo made a gesture. Caledan gasped as he suddenly found himself unable to breathe. A metallic taste filled his mouth as a desperate gurgling came from his throat. For a second, he was back in Marianne's apartment, dying on the tile floor with the Knight's blade embedded in his chest.

A fiery warmth ignited in his palm, and the sensation vanished, returning him to the muddy island. He blinked, glancing at his sword, before a scream returned his attention to Servo. The man's blade arced for Caledan's face and he leapt back—but not fast enough. The razor-sharp edge slashed through his shirt, opening a shallow cut across his chest.

Cursing, Caledan slipped in the mud and went down on one knee. Instinctively he thrust his sword above his head and the shriek of clashing steel followed as Servo's blade connected, almost jarring the weapon from Caledan's hands. Clinging to the hilt, Caledan threw himself to the side, rolling smoothly and coming back to his feet.

"Afraid, sellsword?" Servo laughed, blood now dripping from his sword tip. "You should be. The Saviour will torment your soul for a thousand years. Your agony will be the fuel in her eternal battle against the False Gods."

"You talk too much," Caledan snapped.

It was time to end the subterfuge, to finish the Elder before he had a chance to use his power again. Taking a two-handed grip of his sword, Caledan edged forward, eyes on the man's feet, waiting.

The second Servo lifted a boot, Caledan leapt. His sword drawn back for a strike, the Elder's eyes widened in shock. Caledan aimed high, taking advantage of the gap in the Elder's guard. But to his surprise, Servo's blade moved faster than thought, flashing upwards to catch Caledan's blade on its razor edge. Steel shrieked as the impact left chinks in both blades, but Caledan was already twisting, his boot coming up to catch his foe in the chest.

Servo staggered back from the blow, the breath hissing between his teeth as he struggled to inhale. Caledan followed, his blade arcing for the Elder's exposed neck. Servo threw himself sideways, crashing face-first into the mud, and Caledan's attack missed by inches.

Unwilling to surrender his advantage, Caledan pressed the attack. Servo was still struggling to regain his feet and made a clumsy swing at Caledan's legs as he approached. Caledan deflected the Elder's blade into the ground. A scream tore from Servo as his fist collided with a stray rock, knocking the sword from his hand. Caledan quickly kicked out, catching the hilt with his boot and sending the weapon hurtling away.

"No!" Servo screamed.

Suddenly the Elder was back on his feet, eyes wild, face red. Realising what Servo was about to do, Caledan leapt, bringing up his sword to stab for the man's heart. The blade arced out, its aim true, but with a cry Servo threw out his arms.

A brilliant red leapt from the Elder's outstretched hands, a terrible, burning glow that seemed to light the very air aflame. It rushed at Caledan, coalescing into an inferno that could not be avoided. A cry came from Marianne, but she was too far away, too slow to save him. Grim-faced, Caledan lifted his blade and screamed into the firestorm.

Heat seared at his face, searing, burning. He smelt the faint stench of burning hair—then the fire was upon him, so hot he no longer felt anything, no longer knew anything but the brilliant, burning white. Eyes clenched shut, Caledan thrust out with his blade, determined to kill the Elder before he took his last breath, to do this one last thing for his queen.

The blade shook in his hand, vibrating as though the very metal had come alive, as though the flames were about to hurl it back in his face. Teeth clenched, flesh searing, Caledan screamed into the inferno.

Then as quickly as it had appeared, the light was gone, leaving Caledan standing unexpectedly on a patch of scorched earth, blade still outstretched. A second later the pain struck him, a wave of agony that drove him to his knees. The sword slipped from his fingers as he toppled to the earth.

Lying there, he waited for death to find him, for the cold release of the afterlife. Instead, the sounds of the world came rushing back, and he became aware of someone groaning, the gurgling of liquid in lungs, the gasps of a dying man. He thought they must be his own desperate, dying cries, but as he drew in a breath, he tasted only fresh air in his throat.

Caledan's eyes snapped open. Light blinded him, then the world resolved, and he found himself looking across seared earth to where Servo lay nearby. The Elder's hands were clutched at his chest, where Caledan's sword was now lodged. The wound should have killed him instantly, but Servo was still trying to tear it loose, even as blood bubbled from his purpling lips.

Beyond the Elder, his sailors stood transfixed, either unwilling or unable to help their master. Groaning, Caledan turned his gaze on himself, and was surprised to find his clothes only singed, his flesh untouched by the fire.

The crunch of footsteps on burnt ground sounded as Marianne strode past, her sapphire eyes on the dying Elder.

"Oh my dear Servo," she murmured. "Do not waste your precious life force trying to remove it. I invested enough of my power into the blade that your magic cannot affect it." She knelt beside the man, drawing his head into her lap. His hands were bloody from trying to grip the blade, and now he turned them on the queen. He fumbled weakly at Marianne's arms, leaving red streaks on her pale skin. She laughed. "Relax, my dear Elder," she whispered. "It will all soon be over. The Saviour awaits, remember? I trust you will send my blessings?"

With her words, Marianne drew a dagger from her waistband. A desperate, drowning cry came from Servo as he tried to fend her off, but the queen swatted his hands aside and drove the blade through his eye. She held the blade there as Servo's legs drummed against the earth for a few seconds more, then yanked it clear when he finally grew still.

"Yesss," moaned Marianne as her eyes flickered closed.

Sitting up on his elbow, Caledan struggled to comprehend the sudden turn of events. The queen's hands were on the Elder's chest. Multicoloured sparks leapt from Servo's corpse into Marianne, lighting her skin aglow, until with a final flash, all sign of power vanished from sight.

"Ah, but that is better," Marianne murmured, opening her eyes again. They settled on her foe, and she reached down to remove a bracelet from his arm. "And this ensures my victory," she added, removing her own bangle and replacing it with Servo's.

"What did you do?" Caledan asked, staggering to his feet.

"Reclaimed my power," Marianne replied.

Before Caledan could enquire further, a moan came from nearby. His eyes lit on Genevieve, still collapsed in the mud on the other side of the island. Servo's sailors stood nearby, but at a look from him, they raised their hands and backed away. Ignoring them, Caledan staggered to his friend's side and knelt beside her. She flinched away at his touch, another moan rasping from her throat.

"Genevieve, it's okay," he whispered. "It's me, Caledan."

Her eyelids flickered, but her eyes were so swollen he doubted she could see him. She didn't react the next time he touched her, though. Her skin was burning and her lips were cracked and dry, sure signs of dehydration. This close to her, he realised Genevieve was far worse off that he'd first thought. Every part of her was bruised and there were gashes on her arms and legs, many still seeping blood and worse. Both legs were twisted at a terrible angle, no doubt broken in a dozen places.

"Gods, what has he done to you?" Caledan whispered.

"Caledan," came Marianne's voice from nearby. "Come, we must move quickly, before Servo's army breaks up."

Caledan looked around, surprised at the coldness of the queen's tone. "What are you saying?" he hissed, gesturing at Genevieve. "She needs my help!"

Her brow creased and she did not reply, but after a moment she flashed a glare at Servo's soldiers. They seemed to freeze in place, and with a nod, she joined Caledan. Crouching beside him, she stretched out a hand to Genevieve. The huntress must have been unconscious after all, for she did not pull away from the woman who had tried to kill her the last time they'd met.

Marianne's eyes narrowed, but after only a few seconds she withdrew her hand.

"Her fever is well advanced. Her body cannot last much longer." She offered Caledan an apologetic look. "I am sorry, my Champion. She is not long for this world."

"Can't you heal her?" he asked. "Like you did for me?"

"I…" She hesitated. "This is…different. Her wounds are physical, but the infection now stretches all throughout her body. It would take a tremendous amount of energy…"

Caledan caught the hesitation in her words. "But you *can* do it?" he insisted.

Her lips tightened. "She is my enemy, Caledan."

"She is my *friend*," Caledan snapped.

He bowed his head until it touched Genevieve's brow, remembering how the huntress had stood strong in Malevolent Cove, how she had rescued Kryssa and Pela when all others had failed. The whisper of Genevieve's breath touched his cheek, and he heard the crackling from her throat, as though the very act of breathing was becoming difficult.

"Please, Marianne," he said, looking again at the queen. "You told me once how you regretted your actions in Malevolent Cove. This is the partner of Kryssa, the woman you tried to sacrifice. You owe her this!"

Marianne's eyes shimmered and for a moment Caledan thought she would refuse. Then the light faded and her eyes slid closed, her face falling. She gave the slightest of nods, then pushing Caledan aside, she placed her hands on Genevieve's chest. A groan came from the huntress as rainbow light seeped from the queen's palms. Her hands came up, fumbling at Marianne's wrists.

"Hold her down," the queen ground through clenched teeth. Her eyes did not so much as flicker from her patient. "This is hard enough as it is."

Obeying, Caledan took the huntress's wrists in his hands and pulled them away from Marianne. Genevieve was so weak that it took little effort, though she still managed to dig her nails into his flesh before he got a good grip.

Grimacing, he glanced at the queen, then back to the huntress.

Genevieve's face contorted as the light spilling from Marianne intensified, her mouth opening in a silent scream. Her back arched as she strained against his grip. He held her tight, but it was a full minute before she collapsed back to the earth. Marianne kept on, her face tight as she concentrated, the multicoloured light flickering from her hands. A trickle of sweat ran down her face and dripped onto Genevieve's cheek.

Caledan wondered if he was doing the right thing, asking this of the queen. An army still waited on the other side of the river. What if one of Servo's fellow Elders managed to take command and attack while they sat here unawares? What if healing Genevieve drained too much of her strength? What if the huntress died anyway?

He swallowed, his throat suddenly parched, but he pushed his fear back down. Whatever trials Genevieve had suffered these past few weeks, she deserved a chance at life, whatever the cost. Besides, after Servo's little speech, Caledan doubted if a single Lonian soldier remained loyal to the Elders.

Time stretched out, and Caledan began to wonder whether Marianne would fail after all. Genevieve lay unmoving, her breath faint, her skin so pale she might have already passed to the other side. Then Caledan began to notice changes coming over the huntress—a touch of colour returning to her cheeks, the slight easing of her breathing, the agony slipping from her face. Half an hour passed before Caledan finally believed Marianne might truly save her.

Finally the queen sat back with a gasp, though her

hands remained on Genevieve's chest. She swayed where she sat and her eyes flickered open, though it was a long time before they focused on Caledan.

"Water!" she croaked.

Caledan rushed back to their boat, where the sailors still stood waiting. They handed him a waterskin and he returned to the queen, holding it out for her.

"You...do it," she said. "I cannot stop until every trace of infection is burnt from her body."

With that, she bent her head back and opened her mouth. Caledan hesitated, then removed the steel cap and awkwardly shifted the bulging skin into place. He did his best to pour just a splash, but the thing was large and unwieldy, and he managed to spill a small torrent over the queen's face.

By the time Marianne had finished coughing and spluttering up the extra water, Caledan had regained control of the skin. He opened his mouth to apologise, but to his surprise, the queen only laughed.

"I guess that will have to do," she said, returning to her patient.

Now she moved her hands to and fro along Genevieve's body. Wherever the rainbow light fell, bruises faded and gashes knitted themselves back together, leaving hardly a mark.

Caledan swallowed, finally seeing the true power in the queen's fingertips, her control over life and death. If she could do this to save his friend, what else might she be capable of? The inferno Servo had summoned had been awful, but this...this was something else, a power at once miraculous and terrifying.

Finally Marianne moved onto Genevieve's legs, where

the worst of Servo's cruelty had been inflicted. Here she paused, glancing at Caledan with worry in her eyes.

"Her legs are broken in a dozen places," the queen whispered. "I must move them back into alignment. You will need to hold her tight now."

Caledan grimaced and got a better hold on the huntress. The queen gripped Genevieve's leg tightly enough that her nails left marks, then slowly straightened the limb.

A hair-raising shriek clawed its way up from Genevieve's throat as she began to thrash. If Caledan had not been warned, she would have torn herself free. As it was, he hung on grimly, using his weight to pin her down, his hands fixed like shackles around her wrists. But he could not block out the screaming. The sound seemed to come from her very soul, as though her flesh were being peeled back from her bones.

Marianne moved as quickly as she could, struggling against Genevieve's thrashing to straighten each leg, and all the while light poured from her fingertips. The queen's face was pale now, her brow soaked with sweat, but still she kept on.

By the time she reached the second leg, Genevieve had ceased her thrashing. Her screams had died away too, but a dull keening still came from the back of her throat. Her face was screwed up tight, her eyelids flickering as though she were trapped in a nightmare from which she could not wake. Caledan held her close, whispering to her beneath his breath, doing whatever he could to reassure her.

Finally Marianne let out a gasp and sat back. The light died in her hands as she released the huntress, and swaying on her haunches, her eyes flickered closed. Caledan released

Genevieve and placed a hand on the queen's shoulder, supporting her in case she fell.

Marianne's eyes snapped open at his touch. She looked from him to Genevieve, exhaustion writ across her face. Then leaning across Genevieve's body, the queen tapped her on the forehead. A long breath whispered from his friend as she relaxed, as though passing from nightmare into a dreamless sleep.

"There," Marianne said, drawing back. "It is done. Your little friend is healed."

"Thank you, Marianne," Caledan whispered, giving her shoulder a squeeze. "I don't know how I can ever repay you."

Marianne smiled at that. "It was but a small thing," she murmured, though the exhaustion etched into her face said otherwise. "More than earned. Now," she continued, standing and offering him her hand, "it is time I spoke with my new army. I would have my Champion beside me, should he still want the role."

"I do." Caledan smiled, and taking her hand, he stood. Then he frowned as he realised the significance of her words. "But why do you think they will follow you?"

"Revenge," Marianne replied, her eyes drifting out across the waters. "They might love me because I freed them, but they will follow me because their hearts still scream for justice. Lonia has but one enemy left—the son of the Tsar." She grinned, and light spilled from her eyes. "Let Braidon try and stop me now."

❧ 14 ☙

Pela paced up and down the room, fists clenched, her entire body shaking. After Ruebyn had collapsed at dinner, Rayan had helped her carry him back to their room. The place was sparsely furnished, containing only a pair of beds and a washroom where they had cleaned themselves earlier. The stone walls were unadorned and even the blankets on the beds were an unattractive grey.

Another tremor ran down her spine and she looked at the unlit brazier, wishing they'd at least been left fuel for a fire. Night had fallen an hour ago and the temperature in the windowless room was falling quickly.

Ruebyn himself lay in one of the beds, the covers tucked up to his chin, eyes fixed on the ceiling. His face had lost all colour and every so often another bout of coughing would overcome him. Each time Pela would race to his side, though there was nothing she could do but watch as he doubled up beneath the sheets in agony. Every spell seemed to last a little longer, to take more from him.

She returned to his side as another bout started. Specks

of blood stained the sheets as he gasped into the pillow. She stretched out a hand and stroked his hair. Her eyes stung, but she refused to cry. To cry was to accept his fate, to accept that there was nothing she could do to save him. And Pela would rather die than surrender.

Finally Ruebyn's coughing faded and he relaxed back into the pillow. His eyes fluttered closed and his breathing eased.

Silently, Pela resumed her pacing. Rayan and the king had said there was nothing they could do for Ruebyn now. The *morbus* was almost always fatal, and while water and warmth might help ease his suffering, there was little that could be done to save someone once infected. Ruebyn was doomed: she had seen it in the eyes of the king, in the grim-faced look Rayan had offered.

Doomed, unless she did something, unless she found a way to save him.

"Pela."

She jumped as Ruebyn's voice carried across the room. Bracing herself, she turned to face him.

"What?" she whispered.

She could hardly bear to look at him. His eyes were like sunken pits, his face so pale he might have already been a ghost. How had the life left him so quickly?

"Come here," he breathed, so softly she barely heard.

Pela went without thinking, dropping down beside the bed and hugging him tight. Whatever her own doubts, she could not deny him that small comfort now. Sitting back, she ran a hand across his forehead and shivered. He was burning up.

A sigh slipped from his lips as his face twisted in pain.

"I'm sorry," he whispered just as she thought he'd fallen asleep. "It's not your fault, you know."

Steel jaws closed around Pela's chest and she had to force the words out. "Of course it is. You wouldn't be here if not for me. I should have listened when you said to go back."

"No." He shook his head weakly. "I made my own choices. Truth is, I wanted to follow you. You're…nothing about you makes sense, you know." A smile touched his lips. "I still can't figure out how you made the soldiers obey you."

Pela laughed. "Magic, silly," she croaked, and now the tears did spill across her cheeks.

Ruebyn chuckled, but the action quickly turned into more coughing. By the time they left him, Ruebyn's strength had gone, and he lay back in the bed with his eyes closed. Pela sat beside him, gently stroking his brow. She longed to do something, but in the face of the *morbus*, her newfound confidence had evaporated. She'd been a fool to think her victory over the Knight had ever meant anything, that she would ever be good enough to make a difference.

"I'm so sorry," she gasped, burying her head in Ruebyn's chest.

Why was this happening? Was this her fate, to watch everyone she'd ever loved die? First it had been Devon, then Genevieve. Now Ruebyn seemed destined to follow them.

His breathing had deepened now, its rhythm steadier, and he did not respond to her words. She watched him sleep, fighting the urge to flee. She could do nothing here, nothing but wait for her friend to die—then whatever she felt for him would be meaningless. There would be only pain.

Shivering, she ran her fingers across the curve of

Ruebyn's face. Their night in the cave flickered into her mind and she flushed. In the danger and creeping cold, there had been no time to think, to pollute her mind with doubts and reservations. Perhaps that had been a good thing. The Gods only knew, she had been overwhelmed by those doubts ever since.

Meditation helps to regulate our emotions.

Pela shivered as her mother's voice whispered from the past. Letting out a long breath, she focused her mind on the action of breathing. In the rush of the last week, in the excitement of her discovery, she'd forgotten why she had first learnt the mindfulness technique. Meditation was more than power or magic; it was a pathway to peace, to tranquillity of spirit.

In, out. Think of nothing else.

Simple in theory, something altogether more difficult in practice. Ruebyn's forehead was still hot beneath her fingers, and she could not block out his breathing, could not help but hear his every agonised inhalation. Pain radiated from him in waves, so powerful she could almost *feel* it, could sense it calling to her, twisting the fabric of her mind.

Pela started, her eyes snapping open as she returned to the room. What had *that* been? For a moment, she had felt separated from her body—at once herself, but also something else, able to view the world around her in an entirely different way.

Looking at Ruebyn, she remembered the agony she had sensed, a violent, almost tangible thing that seeped from him like an outgoing tide. There was nothing now. It had only been her imagination, surely?

The hackles on her neck stood on end. What if it

wasn't? What if she had unwittingly tapped into her own power, if she had reached out for him subconsciously?

A lump lodged in her throat as an idea came to her. Swallowing, she wondered if it was possible, if she might actually have a chance of helping him.

A candle flickered into life in her mind's eye—her life force, burning bright in the darkness. But was it enough for what she planned? Or would she fail, as she had in the village, in Malevolent Cove, on the Queen's ship?

Pela shivered, but she could not submit to her fear. If she did nothing, Ruebyn's fate was sealed. She had to try.

Closing her eyes, Pela focused on the trance, following her breathing inwards, on the light in her mind, before reaching out for her friend.

This time the transition was jarring, a sudden tearing sensation that left her suddenly hanging in the air, staring down at her own body. Fear touched her, a sudden terror that she was actually dead. Then she saw the slight movement of her chest. Opening the fingers of her spirit hand, she saw the tiny flame burning in her palm, felt its warmth.

Steeling herself, she turned her attention on Ruebyn. An angry red glow radiated from his body, an inaudible agony only she could see. It seemed to come from every part of him, and Pela trembled as she realised the scale of the task before her.

But she could not waver now. Drifting closer, she reached out a spirit hand and touched it to Ruebyn's chest. Her vision spun, and then it was as though his whole body was all around her. She saw at once every intricate part of him, every bone and muscle and organ, felt his life force, diminished but still burning, still fighting. She felt his pain as well, an agony that she grasped in her hands, and followed deeper into his core.

Pela shuddered as she found herself in his lungs and finally saw the damage there. The pink flesh was bleeding, seared by the angry red flames burning in his core. Her courage was shaken by the sight, but she held on, gathering herself in preparation for what must be done.

Ruebyn was burning up, his entire chest aflame. Focusing her mind, Pela imagined the cooling touch of water, then drew on her own energies to bring the thought to life. A swirling wave of blue swept from her, an icy breath that immediately lessened the angry glow filling Ruebyn's lungs. She kept on, willing the flames of his agony away. With a touch of surprise, she watched the flickering red crumble to embers.

Elated, Pela retreated from Ruebyn and looked at him again. He still slept, but his breathing seemed lighter now. The angry glow still burned elsewhere though, and returning to his body, she followed the light to his heart.

Its rhythmic pounding filled her ears as she surveyed the damage. Here the glow was green rather than red, forming sickly vines that weaved their way around the pounding muscle, forming a strangling cage about his heart. Wherever they touched, his tissue sickened, turning to black.

Her stomach swirling, Pela summoned flames and hurled them at the vile things. To her delight, they fled from her spirit, burning in the face of the inferno.

Her confidence growing, Pela continued through Ruebyn, destroying the *morbus* in all its forms, using her power to chase the illness from his frail body. It surprised her, how little energy it consumed, as though his healing took no effort at all. The sickness might have overwhelmed Ruebyn's life force, but it could not stand against hers.

Finally she turned her attention to Ruebyn's mind. Here the sickness was worse, clinging to his brain, creating a fever that would destroy him if she did not stop it. Pela poured herself into the effort now, turning back the heat, cooling it, taking the pain from her friend.

When that was finally done, she retreated from Ruebyn, hopeful she'd defeated the awful virus. Drifting in her bodiless state, she gave an inner smile at the sight of Ruebyn sleeping peacefully in his bed. The angry colours had vanished, revealing the soothing blue of his true aura…

Pela frowned as a spot of red appeared amidst the blue. Fear touched her as it began to spread, growing from the tiny seed, spreading rapidly to encompass his chest. A racking cough struck Ruebyn as his breathing became strained again.

No, no, no!

Desperate, Pela returned to Ruebyn's body. She poured all her energies into the effort now, determined to burn every last trace of the *morbus*. Swirling through him like a hurricane, she tore the illness from its roots everywhere she found it.

Outside their bodies, time ticked slowly past. Exhaustion crept over Pela as her life force flickered, lessened by her exertions, but she kept on, determined to succeed.

But as she destroyed the sickness in Ruebyn's lungs, more appeared in his heart, then brain. She attacked each of these in turn, only to find new vines had taken root elsewhere. However fast her efforts, the *morbus* sprang up again each time she turned away, its spread unstoppable.

A moan rasped from Pela's throat as she retreated to her

body and felt the weight of her exhaustion. She slumped against the bed, gasping for breath as though she'd just run ten miles. An ache had begun in the back of her skull and she sensed her entire body would be hurting by morning.

Ruebyn still lay asleep in the bed. His breathing was better, but a touch to his forehead confirmed his fever burned on. Despite her efforts, the *morbus* was winning.

In despair she turned her eyes inwards and watched the red slowly spreading through Ruebyn's body. She felt drained, as though she had poured her life force down a bottomless hole rather than into Ruebyn. He was coughing again, and there was blood on his lips. She wiped it away, but a second later it was back, gurgling up from the depths of his chest.

How much longer could he last like this?

Pela shivered and forced the thought from her mind. She drew in a breath, battling with despair, and sent her spirit soaring again. The process came easily now, almost instinctively.

The last of Ruebyn's blue was already succumbing to the red. She drifted closer to her friend, still searching desperately for something she could do, some way to help him. Perhaps a single, overwhelming wave of energy was needed, to burn the illness from him all at once?

Did she even have enough energy left for such an attempt? A shiver passed through her as she looked at the dwindling flame of her life force, then back at Ruebyn. It was their only hope. Drawing on her power, she readied herself…

…then frowned, suddenly aware of a strangeness to Ruebyn's aura. The red aura swirled about his body, but not in a random manner as she had first thought. There was a pattern, a spiral that led inwards to his chest. She watched in curiosity as the aura continued to flicker. The blue was almost gone now, draining away through that strange spiral.

Then she noticed something else, something utterly out of place. The finest of threads twisted from Ruebyn's chest, so thin she had not noticed it until now. The silver string hung in the air before her, and without thinking, she followed it across the room. It disappeared through the wall, but that was no obstacle to her spirit, and she drifted after the silver glow. Something was terribly wrong here, and Pela intended to find out what.

Unseen, her spirit traversed the citadel, passing down corridors and kitchens and dining rooms, through closed doors, until Pela no longer knew where she was, how long she had been gone from her body.

Then Pela realised the thread she followed was not alone, that she had entered a room where a thousand trails of light converged on one another. They crisscrossed the room like the web of a spider, all directed to the centre, where a ball of multi-coloured light shone so brightly Pela could hardly see.

Though she was only present in spirit, Pela couldn't help but tremble at the energies burning in the room. Fist clenched tight about the flame of her own life force, she drifted closer. Her whole being vibrated as she passed through the webs, straining to discover what lay at their centre.

Confusion touched Pela as she found herself floating over a canopy bed, looking down upon the aged face of the king. She looked again at the shining threads and finally realised what they were—slivers of life force, gathered from across the city, maybe even the nation. Every one of them must be connected to a soul like Ruebyn, but why…

No, no, no.

A scream built in Pela's throat as her gaze was drawn back to the king. Each of the threads had been drawn to this place, to this man, igniting a brilliant light in his chest. Betran was connected to all of his subjects, was somehow drawing on all their energies at once.

The king was stealing the lives of his people. Surely it could not be true, not after the man had been so generous with them, after his people had suffered so much, not unless…

Pela groaned as she realised the terrible, horrible truth. There had never been a *morbus*—only a terrible deception. Ruebyn did not have the plague. He had not gotten sick until he'd worn the opal necklace. The illness had only ever been an excuse to force the Trolan people to wear the black opals. The king only need draw slowly on their life forces to make him stronger than any living soul, and ensure his deception was never discovered. But Ruebyn though…with his apparent exposure, there'd been no reason to use constraint.

Staring at the monster lying in his bed, Pela thought of all the empty pastures stretching across Trola, of the despair in the eyes of his people, the lifeless looks of even the nobles. She thought of all the innocent lives this man had destroyed, the pain and misery he had unleashed upon his own people.

Rage wrapped its fiery fingers around Pela's heart. She drifted closer, her whole spirit trembling. King Betran lay unawares. Despite the power that burned in his core, there was no barrier to keep her away, nothing to stop her. All she had to do was use her own life force against him, to channel all her rage, all her grief into a single killing blow.

Pela's life force burnt hot in her fist. Slowly she reached out, then afraid he might suddenly wake, went forward in a rush. Thrusting her fist at the king's skull, she readied herself…

A gasp tore from Pela as her spirit was spun around, surrounded suddenly by a cacophony of light. Images jarred her vision, memories that were not hers. She found herself looking out across a great expanse, a land of giant forests and lush pastures. People moved across the land with joy on their faces, and at the centre of it all stood their king.

Then a darkness crept into the land, and soon the people were fleeing, falling to their knees before a shadow they could not resist. Blood flowed freely in the streets as the scenes progressed. Pela saw a father clutching a child to his chest, watched a mother trying desperately to wake her baby, heard the screams, smelt the decay.

A scream tore from Pela's throat as the creature appeared amongst the dying, a monster clothed in shadow. Its outstretched arms reached into the souls of all it encountered, tearing the life from them. Their energies disappeared into a void at the creature's centre, consumed by an insatiable hunger. Some tried to stand against it, but with a flick of a finger the strength was drained from them.

Before long there was no one left to fight. The only option left for the Trolans was to run, and Pela watched as they fled into the wilderness, into the mountains and forests, but even there they could not escape. Drawn to its power, men with black hearts and blue armour joined with the monster. They rode after their former comrades, rounding up the innocent and driving them back to Kalgan, back to the creature's embrace.

The king had not lied when he spoke of a plague that had swept across the land. It had not come from any illness, but from a creature of darkness. A word sprang into Pela's mind, one that had not been spoken since the time of the Gods.

Demon!

$\maltese$ 15 $\maltese$

The days passed quickly after Caledon's defeat of Servo. The confrontation with the Lonian army had played out just as Marianne had predicted. She'd won their hearts by revealing Servo's true nature, but it had been revenge that finally motivated them to join her. For decades, Lonia had suffered beneath the yoke of Braidon's father— then at Braidon's own hand, during the ten-year-long war between the north and south. Now Marianne offered them retribution, a chance to unleash their fury against the man who represented every hurt, every injustice they had ever suffered.

They had shouted her name to the skies.

And so Marianne's newly enlarged army had taken to the Gods' Road. Now two days later, they were already nearing Chole. Caledan expected to come within sight of the city walls by the morning. Reinforced by the Lonian army, he did not doubt their victory would quickly follow.

Even so, his mind remained heavy. Marianne had thrown herself into organising the army's march, becoming more withdrawn with each passing day. Caledan was saddened to see her retreat into herself, and as the final battle approached, he noticed her smiles becoming less frequent. Her eyes would often take on a distant look, as though she were already imagining her confrontation with Braidon.

Then there was Genevieve. The huntress still had not woken from her sleep, and while Caledan had ensured she was well cared for, he was beginning to fear Marianne's healing had not taken. He longed to ask the queen what was wrong, but she already had too many worries on her shoulders.

Instead, as the sun set on the makeshift camp that Marianne's forces had erected for the night, Caledan found himself carrying a bowl of broth to the tent that had been set aside for the injured. Other than Genevieve, there were only a couple of occupants, those who had sprained ankles on the march or injured themselves while training.

He ignored them as he entered, crossing directly to the corner where the huntress lay sleeping. As Caledan approached, he saw her eyes flicker. His heart began to race as he quickly knelt beside her.

"Gen—"

Before he could finish, Genevieve surged up and her fist careened into his chin. The broth went flying as Caledan tumbled backwards, the huntress crashing down atop him. He cried out as she raised her fist again, and now he saw a glint of steel there.

"Genevieve, wait!" he cried. "It's me, Caledan!"

For a second it seemed she had not heard him—then her eyes widened and the dagger tumbled from her fingers.

"Caledan!" she gasped, sitting back suddenly. "What are you doing here?"

"That's…a long story," Caledan replied with a grimace, still smarting from the hot stew that had spilled on his lap. "But…you're safe."

Genevieve swallowed visibly. "Servo?"

"Dead," Caledan said. "Marianne made sure of that."

"Marianne?" Genevieve croaked, the panic returning to her voice. "The queen is here?"

"She is."

"You're working for that witch?" Genevieve whispered, her eyes flicking around the tent as though expecting the queen to appear at any moment.

"I am," Caledan replied.

Despite himself, he felt hurt as Genevieve pulled away from him. But then, the huntress would not have forgotten Devon's death at Marianne's hand. A part of Caledan still felt shame, that he now served the hammerman's killer.

"I don't understand," the huntress whispered. "She tried to kill us all. How could you betray your friends like this?"

"If not for her, you would be dead," Caledan shot back, anger touching him now. "She healed you, though it cost her dearly."

"That doesn't make any sense."

Caledan sighed. "There is much for you to catch up on. Where have you been? How did you survive Malevolent Cove, after we capsized?"

Genevieve scowled and sat back on her haunches. "Well, while you were making friends with the enemy, Pela and I were taken by Baronians."

"Pela?" Caledan asked, his heart quickening. The girl hadn't been amongst Servo's people.

"She's alive," Genevieve replied. "Last I saw her, she was fleeing into Trola."

"*What?*" Caledan gasped.

"She didn't have much choice," Genevieve growled. "It was that, or be sent back to your queen's precious mines."

"You were *slaves?*"

Genevieve nodded, and for the merest of seconds, Caledan glimpsed the terror in her eyes. She swallowed visibly before adding, "Pela…she had it the worst. I didn't know what had happened to her, the first few weeks. When I found her…she was in poor shape. But she is Kryssa's daughter. In the end, it was Pela who found a way to escape." She hesitated, drawing in a deep breath. "And… what of Kryssa?"

Caledan looked away. "She lives," he said softly.

"What is it, Caledan?" Genevieve asked.

"She's with Braidon in Chole," Caledan replied, forcing himself to look at the huntress. "A day's march from us. Marianne intends to put an end to the king's little rebellion. She's going to storm the city."

"*What?*" Genevieve gasped, staggering to her feet.

Caledan rose with her, gripping Genevieve's hands to keep her from doing anything rash. "*Calm down,*" he hissed. Glancing around, he looked for listeners, but the other injured didn't seem to be paying them any attention. "Do not forget where you are," he added with a glare.

"In the camp of my enemy," Genevieve said coldly. "The prisoner of a traitor."

"You are not a prisoner," Caledan snapped. "And I'm no traitor—Braidon was never my king."

"Yes, I remember," Genevieve growled. "You would have killed him and let Kryssa die, had I not intervened."

"I wouldn't…" Caledan couldn't finish the sentence. He looked away again. "We saved her in the end, didn't we?"

"From your queen, Gods damnit!" Genevieve snarled. "And now you seem determined to correct the error. Did Devon die for nothing, that you spit in the face of his sacrifice?"

"I saved the bastard King!" Caledan hissed, raising a fist. Genevieve did not so much as flinch. "I half-drowned myself, dragging Braidon from the waters of Malevolent Cove. My obligation ended there," he finished, though now his words lacked conviction.

"And now you're actively trying to kill him." Genevieve shook her head. "She must be a fantastic lover."

"She is my queen!" Caledan lashed out, then sucked in a breath, seeking calm. "Don't you see, Braidon cares only for himself, for his own power. Otherwise, he would have marched against Servo, instead of sitting in his fortress while the Elder led a Lonian army into our lands. He did *nothing*, while Marianne did what he never could—brought peace between our two nations, with hardly a drop of blood spilt."

"Ay," Genevieve murmured, "and in doing so, she earned the loyalty of the Lonians, and tripled the size of her army."

Caledan's stomach twisted as he stared at Genevieve. He could see the fervour in her eyes, knew she would never listen, not while her lover stood with the other side.

"She is a better ruler than Braidon could ever hope to be," he breathed finally. "*That* is why I support her."

"Very well," Genevieve said. "In that case, I would like to see her for myself."

The huntress darted suddenly forward. Ducking past Caledan, she was across the tent in two strides. He cried out and leapt after her, but she had already disappeared through the flaps. By the time he found her, she was already a dozen yards away, darting through the men and women still trying to set their tents for the night. In the distance, the gold-tinged pavilion of the queen's tent rose above the surrounding camp.

Cursing, Caledan set off after her, keeping pace as she weaved through the workers, but slowed by the press of bodies, he was unable to catch her. Only at the entrance to the queen's tent did Genevieve stop, her path barred by two of the Queen's Guard.

"Genevieve," he gasped, taking her by the shoulder before she got herself killed. "You can't just go running up to the queen's quarters."

"Be damned," Genevieve snapped, shrugging him off. She spun on him, eyes aflame. "Your *queen* tried to murder the woman I love. She killed Devon, and…" Genevieve's voice trailed off, and she took a deep breath before continuing. "And her people put a collar around my neck and made me a slave. *You* may have forgotten what kind of woman this queen of yours is, Caledan, but *I* have not."

"I—"

"Caledan," came the queen's voice, interrupting whatever argument he'd been about to make. The two of them spun, surprised to find Marianne standing between her guards. A smile touched her lips at the sight of the huntress. "Enough, my Champion. I will see her. Why don't the two of you join me for a drink?" She disappeared into her tent without a backwards glance.

Steel rattled as the guards stepped aside, granting them passage. Caledan exchanged a glance with Genevieve, but whatever doubt the queen's words might have given the huntress, it quickly vanished as she spun and stepped through the canvas flaps. Letting out a long breath, Caledan followed her inside.

Within, he found Marianne standing at her war table, already pouring wine into three glasses. She might have had any number of retainers do such a menial task, but she generally preferred to serve herself when it was practical.

Genevieve still stood in the entrance, her courage lost now that she had crossed the threshold into Marianne's lair. Caledan hesitated beside the huntress, but after a moment's hesitation, moved to join his queen.

"Welcome back, my Champion," Marianne said with a smile, offering him a glass of wine.

Caledan took it reluctantly, still mindful of his duty to defend her. Taking a sip, he stepped aside and placed it on the table. Chuckling, Marianne turned her eyes on the huntress and held out a glass. Genevieve had her hands clenched at her side, but drawing in a breath, she accepted the offered wine.

"So, you're awake," Marianne murmured as she picked up the final glass and took a seat at the table. "I am glad all my hard work did not go to waste."

"What do you mean?" Genevieve asked. She did not sit, and held her glass out in front of her as though it were a snake about to strike her.

"Caledan begged me to save you," the queen explained, reclining in her chair. "So I used my power to mend your broken bones and cleanse your body of fever."

"Why?"

"Because Caledan did me a great favour, not too long ago," Marianne said simply. "I owed him a debt."

"Even if it meant healing your enemy?" Genevieve questioned.

Marianne shrugged. "Caledan was also once my enemy. Now he stands as my Champion. Perhaps it will be the same with you."

Genevieve slammed her glass down on the table so hard that the wine sloshed over the sides. "You tried to kill the woman I love," she hissed. "I will *never* be your ally."

"So be it." The queen did not flinch from the woman's anger. "You have every reason to hate me. But I will say this: I regret what took place in the cove. Braidon was my enemy, not Kryssa or her daughter. I let thoughts of power corrupt me." She hesitated, and Caledan thought he glimpsed doubt on her face. Her eyes flickered to the bracelet on her wrist, then back to Genevieve. "I will not let it happen again."

Caledan held his breath, waiting for the huntress's response, but Genevieve seemed at a loss for words. She swallowed visibly, glancing at Caledan, before finally managing to croak, "So you have changed?"

Marianne spread her hands. "I am doing my best."

A sneer twisted Genevieve's face. "Pretty words, but your actions prove them a lie."

"Oh?"

"You say you regret the blood that was spilt in Malevolent Cove, but here you are again, expecting others to bleed to settle your grievance with Braidon."

Marianne's sapphire eyes stared up at Genevieve. "I did not seek this fight," she said. "It was Braidon who attacked Chole. I cannot stand by while he still claims to be king."

"Yet he speaks the truth. He is the rightful king of Plorsea."

"By what right?" Marianne asked mildly. "By the right

of his father, who enslaved the Three Nations for decades? Or do you claim that his years as king were prosperous, that he is a fit ruler for Plorsea?"

"Braidon was never perfect," Genevieve shot back, "but at least he didn't condon coldblooded murder."

"No?" Marianne asked mildly. "Then you have not heard the news. Under his command, the Castle in Chole was stormed by his followers. Innocent believers had gathered there, seeking protection from the riots he had stirred up in the city. Braidon's people murdered them all—locked them in the pantheon and burned them alive."

"No," Genevieve whispered. Her face had lost all its colour. "Braidon would not…"

"It's true," Caledan said quietly. "I read the reports myself."

All the fight seemed to go from Genevieve as she slumped into a chair. Her glass still sat before her, and almost unconsciously she reached for it and downed the wine in a single gulp. Marianne picked up the bottle and refilled her glass before continuing the story.

"If it helps, I do not believe murder was Braidon's intent," she said. "Just more of his general incompetence."

A shudder passed through Genevieve as she looked at the queen. "What is wrong with you people?" she whispered. "You play with our lives, hold our fate in your hands, but do any of you even care?"

"I care," Marianne replied softly, her eyes taking on a distant look. "With Caledan's help, I have put an end to the faction within the Order who were intent on murder. The cleansings ended with Servo's death. And the Great Sacrifice will return to what it once was—a celebration of strength, of devotion to the Saviour, to mankind's future. I would have peace."

"Peace?" Genevieve gave a hollow laugh. "You just have to fight one little war first, right? Why is it always so? All of you powerful men and women, you all claim to want peace. But somehow it's always one war away." She shook her head. "No, don't tell me you want peace, woman. Blood, revenge, power, any of that I would believe, but peace?" Genevieve laughed again and finished her second glass.

A strained silence followed her words. The queen said nothing, only sat swirling the wine in her glass. Every so often she took a sip, her face pensive. Still standing at her side, Caledan held his breath, wondering how Marianne would react to Genevieve's challenge. What game was the huntress playing at here? Surely she must see there was no other way, that Marianne must take the fight to Braidon now, or risk the fallen king drawing the nation into a bloody civil war.

Finally the queen sighed and placed her glass aside. Steepling her fingers, she fixed her eyes on the huntress. "And what would you have me do, Genevieve?" she murmured. "Braidon took my childhood, my innocence. I cannot turn my back on our past—nor the threat he poses to myself and my son. I do not want a war, but neither will I give up my crown to a man who again and again has proven himself unworthy of the title."

Genevieve stared back at the queen, eyes angry, defiant. "I would have you find another way."

❧ 16 ❧

Wind tugged at Braidon's hair as Nidryt circled the cove. Each stroke of the beast's massive wings sent them soaring upwards, only to drift slowly down again, the constant beat holding them aloft as he studied the terrain.

The dragon had caused a panic in Chole as it swooped down to his Castle. By then, Braidon had gathered his sword and warmer clothing from his quarters and was waiting on the battlements. The beast had dropped in low, settling only long enough for Braidon to leap upon its back. Shouts had chased after them and a solitary figure with silver hair had come running into the courtyard, but Nidryt was gone before Kryssa had a chance to call them back.

Braidon had not told her of his plan. This was something he had to do alone, to prove he was still worthy of being king, that he was not destined to fail in this as he had in everything else. That, and a part of him knew he was alone now, had been alone since the day he'd gathered the energies of the dying in the pantheon.

Now high above Malevolent Cove, Braidon looked

down on his enemy. They were little more than ants from the height at which Nidryt soared. Braidon wanted to be sure they went unnoticed until he was ready for the attack.

The scene below was exactly as the dragon had shown him back in Chole. Scorched timbers lay scattered across the cove, where the Red Dragons had destroyed the amphitheatre abandoned by the Knights. Now though, a new structure stood atop the cliffs, the makings of a Castle, its sandstone walls cast red in the setting sun.

Braidon smiled, determined to make the scarlet display a foul omen for the Order. At least a hundred were camped around the structure, nestled within a wooden stockade they had been raised to protect them from the dark creatures lurking in the jungles of Dragon Country.

Of course, wooden walls could not stop the Red Dragons, but that was not their only protection. Hidden behind each wall and atop the cliffs were dozens of sleek steel catapults, their arms already loaded with the familiar barrels. Braidon knew from experience that within each was an explosive black powder that could tear through stone and steel alike. The catapults had been a match for the dragons the last time they'd attacked the Knights, though they'd still managed to wreak havoc before their defeat.

Braidon had not been awake to see that though, having been half-dead and drowning in the cove himself. Now though, an army of Red Dragons swirled around him, the five that Nidryt had chosen to take part in their attack. But if all went as Braidon planned, they would not even need five to defeat the Knights.

Letting out a long breath, Braidon closed his eyes and sent his spirit soaring. The process came easily to him even now, thirty years after his grandmother had first taught him the ability. Drifting free of his body, he gathered the power of the dead around him like a cloak. He shivered as the energies formed a protective shield, his spirit tingling at their touch, then shot down towards the fortress.

Braidon slowed his flight as he neared, reaching out with his senses for the enemy. Still new to his powers, he had no idea what tricks the Elders might be capable of, what traps they might have set for wandering souls.

While the weapons of the Order were formidable, the Elders themselves were Braidon's greatest fear. Only they could sense his flight through the camp, and had the power to threaten his spirit. It was the Elders of the Order who performed the ritual cleansings, drawing power from the innocents they murdered. Braidon knew at least one must be in the camp, but there was no way of knowing yet how powerful his foe would be.

But their sacrilege would at least reveal them to Braidon's spirit gaze. Every man and woman within the camp glowed with a unique aura, the essence of their life force. But the Elders would be different, their aura warped, marked by the multicoloured hue of those lives they had taken.

The camp was massive, occupied by more than a hundred men and women now, each there with the sole purpose of raising a new Castle on behalf of the Order. It took long minutes for Braidon to sense his target, as the Elder's tent was much like the others—its only difference were the two Knights stationed outside. That, and the brilliant glow of the man's aura within.

Slipping unseen past the guards, Braidon hesitated on the threshold. The interior of the tent shone with the Elder's aura, so bright it sent a shiver through Braidon's soul. How many lives had this man stolen to become so powerful?

Doubt touched him then. Did he have enough power to go up against such a man? And even if he did, the energies he'd taken from the lost were finite—if he used his power here, what would be left to him when Marianne finally came with her army?

Reaching for his own power, Braidon felt reassured as it surged through his spirit, reinforcing his courage. What was the point of having such strength if he was too afraid to use it? Power or no, he could not defeat Marianne without allies, and there were none more powerful than the Red Dragons. Even should he use all the energy he had collected from the pantheon, it would be worth the sacrifice to have the beasts at his side.

Then an idea came to him. Perhaps there was a way to have both—to destroy the Elder and the camp, and to still preserve his own power.

Gathering his nerve, Braidon drifted closer, studying the Elder's aura. The man was asleep, his consciousness trapped in the depths of his dreams. What was to stop him from attacking now, while the man lay unaware? Braidon could kill the Elder before he ever realised his danger.

Energy crackled through Braidon's spirit as his excitement rose. He scanned the room one last time for traps the Elder might have set, but there was nothing. Why would there be? The man was far from any threats, in the centre of his own encampment. The dragons might pose a risk, but they were not magical creatures; they could not harm him here.

Braidon smiled at his enemy's arrogance. Nowhere was safe now, and Braidon made a mental note to find some way of protecting himself while he slept. He would learn from the Elder's mistake—even as he took full advantage.

Hovering over the Elder, Braidon wondered how best to dispose of the man. With the energy held at his disposal, the Elder would be a fearsome enemy should he wake. Fire or suffocation might be effective, but they could also alert the man to Braidon's presence. In those few seconds before death took him, the Elder might have time to lash out, to save himself.

But what of his own body? The man was old, and despite the power he wielded, frail. Braidon drifted down, allowing himself to merge with the Elder's body—though he took care not use too much power, lest he wake his foe.

A dull, unsteady pounding carried to Braidon's ears, the rattling whistle of breath, the hiss of blood through veins. It was a strange sensation, being cocooned inside another man's body, listening to the sounds of his life—a life Braidon was about to snuff out. For a moment he considered what he was about to do—to kill a man as he lay unawares—but this was the only way. Allowing him the chance to fight back would risk everything. Braidon could not afford to take that risk.

Thump, thump, thump.

Inevitably, Braidon's attention was drawn to a distant thumping. The pounding muscle of the Elder's heart rushed into focus, covered by a chrysalis of brown and yellow, sickly strips of fat clinging to flesh. Such a simple thing, little different from the great pumps used to ventilate a black-smith's forge. Yet it meant the difference between life and death.

Looking at the twisted organ, it was clear the man was already in poor health, his heart practically decaying in his chest. With his power, Braidon might have healed him, burned away the fat and restored the dying tissues. He had not realised such a feat was possible until that very instant. With his own life force, it would have been exhausting, but with the power Braidon had collected…

But he had not come here to heal his enemies.

Reaching out with his mind, Braidon wrapped the Elder's heart in his power. He steadied himself, drawing on more energy to shield his soul in case he failed. Then with a gesture of his spirit, he sent fire rushing into the man's heart.

At its touch, a single cry tore from the Elder, a scream of horror quickly cut off. The man lurched upright, mouth open wide, and for a second Braidon thought he had miscalculated. He threw up his arms, summoning all his strength in preparation for battle—but there was no need.

A long, drawn-out sigh whispered from the Elder, his life's breath leaving his body, and he slumped back onto the bed. Shouts came from outside, and behind Braidon the tent flaps were yanked aside, admitting the Knights as they came racing to their Elder's aid.

But it was already too late.

Braidon watched in fascination as the energy left his foe's body, his life force and all those others the man had stolen cut loose from the ties of the flesh. Here was an opportunity Braidon had not expected, but he did not hesitate now. Quickly, he drew those fresh energies to himself, gathering the swirling colours like a cloak around his spirit.

He gasped as power surged into him, almost overwhelmed by this new force. Bending in two, Braidon was momentarily unaware of the Knights crouched over the Elder's body, of the sobs that rattled from their helmets as they tried to wake the man. All he felt was the power, the surging energies of so many fresh lives.

When Braidon's senses finally returned, he found the tent empty again, the Knights departed for he knew not where. Now the Elder lay covered by a sheet. Braidon stole a moment to look at the body, wondering if the man had known in his last moments what had killed him. Then a smile touched Braidon's lips.

"Thank you for your sacrifice," he whispered to the night. "It might not have reached your precious Saviour, but her brother appreciates it."

King?

Braidon jerked as the voice of Nidryt shook his spirit. His gaze was drawn upwards, though the dragon could not have been seen from the ground, even had he stood outside. Elation swept through Braidon as he rejoiced in his victory.

I live, dragon! he replied. *You have only to wait a few minutes more, then revenge will be yours.*

The dragon did not reply, but Braidon sensed a rush of emotion from the beast, its lust for blood, to tear and rend and burn those who had dared to invade its homeland. Laughing in the darkness, Braidon returned to the night, ready to complete his part of the plan.

With the Elder dead, there was no one to stop him now, no supernatural force to oppose him, and he walked freely through the camp. He started with the catapults, quietly burning away the hinges that drew the firing arm back. Now if the Knights tried to operate them, the catapults would tear themselves apart rather than fire.

Next, he searched out the deadly crossbows. There were many more of these, but he did not need to destroy them all, only enough that they could not drive off the dragons.

One by one, he made his way through the camp, slicing wire strings and bending firing arms, whatever he could do to sabotage the Knight's last defence against the scarlet beasts.

A wave of exhaustion touched Braidon as he returned to his body. He swayed on the dragon's back, eyes closed, trying to readjust to the sudden weight of his flesh, the hardness of the scales beneath him, the wind in his hair.

Then the full force of the power he had gathered struck him, burning through his veins. His eyes snapped open and he gasped, heart suddenly racing. In an instant his gaze fixed on the camp far below, on the unsuspecting souls he was about to sweep away.

"It's time," he said.

What of their weapons? the dragon asked.

Braidon laughed, the sound carrying across the sky so that every one of the beasts heard his next words.

"Their weapons are destroyed. The camp lies unguarded."

Nidryt rumbled beneath him, and throwing back its head, the dragon unleashed a blood-curdling roar. Answering cries rose from the other dragons and their flames lit the sky. Braidon crouched low on Nidryt's back as the beast folded its wings and dove towards the enemy.

The bellowing of horns greeted their approach as watchmen sounded the alarm. Braidon grinned as the ground came rushing up towards him, bemused at the desperation of his enemies. They had been so confident, so assured of their own power. Now they would pay for their arrogance.

The night had passed unnoticed while he had haunted the camp, and now the rising sun marked the horizon. Its brilliant light shimmered on the armour of the Knights as they rushed for their weapons. In moments, a dozen crossbows were aimed at the sky, while others leapt to the catapults, swinging them to face the new threat.

Braidon had to admit, the camp was better prepared than he had expected. Within seconds, the full might of the Knights was trained on the dragons, ready to tear them from the skies. The *clack-clacking* of catapult arms being drawn back whispered up from below, and Braidon sensed the sudden hesitation in Nidryt, the faltering of the dragon's wings.

"Fly!" Braidon bellowed, pointing to their enemies. "Let the Order feel the wrath of the Red Dragons!"

The beasts roared around him and he sensed their fear evaporating, replaced with a terrible resolve to burn their enemies from the earth. They flew on, the camp rushing up at frightening rate now, until it seemed they must surely crash into the unforgiving ground.

At the last second, Nidryt spread its wings. A sharp *crack* followed as they caught the air, bringing them to a halt so suddenly Braidon was almost torn from the beast's back. He clung to its scales with all his strength, even as his eyes fell on the camp below.

With the dragons in range, the Knights were desperately seeking to ready the catapults. The *clack-clacking* was like thunder in Braidon's ears, but as the arm of the first device neared its apex, there came a *crack*—then men were falling back as the catapult disintegrated, the great arm tearing from the base and hurling shards of wood in all directions. Screams filled the dawn as the other catapults followed suit.

Now silence fell across the camp, as a terrible realisation came over the Knights, that their most deadly weapons had been rendered useless. Without them, they had no defence against the Red Dragons. With that realisation came terror, and suddenly the followers of the Order were fleeing, tripping over one another in their desperation to escape.

But penned in by their own fortifications, there was nowhere left to run, and with a roar, the Red Dragons set upon them. An inferno fell from the sky, the rage of the beasts unleashed. The wooden stockade burst into life, becoming a boiling wall of flame that none could pass. Trapped within the camp, one by one the Knights of Alana burned.

And atop the back of Nidryt, Braidon reached out as each Knight perished, and plucked the life force from their burning bodies.

❧ 17 ❧

"R*uebyn!*" Pela screamed as she found herself back in her body.

Gasping, she flailed about in the darkness, trying to find Ruebyn's bed. The lantern must have burnt out while she was trying to heal him. She swore as her hand struck a wall, but she followed it until she finally found Ruebyn's hand. Dragging herself up, she threw herself across him and fumbled at his shirt.

"Wha…Pela…" Ruebyn's voice was faint.

Ignoring him, Pela cried out as she found the necklace Rayan had given him. She yanked it with all her strength and felt a satisfying *clink* as the chain tore. The thing burned hot in her hand, and crying out, she tossed it to the floor then brought her boot down on it. There was a satisfying *crack* as the opal shattered.

"What…have you…done?" Ruebyn gasped.

Movement came from the bed as he tried to sit up, and she imagined him reaching for the necklace. She threw her arms around him and hugged him tight, ignoring his cries of protest. Finally she released him and sat back, switching to her spirit eye to see him in the darkness. Already his aura was returning to a steady blue. Shivering, she sent up her thanks to the Gods.

"It was killing you," she said shortly when Ruebyn tried to sit up again.

She rose and stumbled her way to the lantern. They had been left a spare, and after several minutes struggling in the darkness, she had it lit. Holding it up, she returned to Ruebyn's side. There was no time to waste now. She did not think the demon had sensed her questing about the king's memories, but they could take no chances.

"That's…insane."

Moving faster than she'd thought him capable of in his current state, Ruebyn tumbled from the bed and scrambled for the necklace. She quickly kicked the remains out of reach and moved to bar his path. Growling, he clutched at the bed and tried to haul himself to his feet.

"It's the truth!" Pela snapped, her irritation returning now that she could see he was no longer in mortal danger.

Grinding her teeth, she took him by the shoulder and pushed him back onto the bed. Though he had already regained some of his colour, his strength had not returned so quickly, and he succumbed with hardly any effort on Pela's part. Tears streaked his cheeks as he collapsed on his back and lay there panting.

"Please, Pela," he whispered. "You have to give it back. I don't want to die."

"You're not going to die," she grated. Seating herself beside him, she took his hand in hers. "I promise."

Pela wished she could make him see, that he would understand. Almost unconsciously she reached for the flicker of her life force. Ruebyn gasped as heat rushed down her arm and into him, and his eyes lost their focus. A tremor shook his body, followed by a desperate moan. Terrified of what she'd done, Pela snatched back her arm.

A scream hissed from Ruebyn's throat until she lurched forward and slapped a hand over his mouth.

"Don't!" she gasped. "You'll wake it!"

His eyes widened and she saw the terror there. She knew then what her power had done, that it had revealed to Ruebyn the vision she'd had at the king's bedside. After a moment, he nodded, and warily, Pela released him.

"We have to get out of here," he whispered.

"Finally you're talking some sense," Pela muttered, struggling not to roll her eyes.

Her mind was already far ahead, thinking of the dawn. They would need to be a long way from the city when the sun rose, or they would never escape the demon's grasp. She swallowed, feeling again the collar's iron embrace. The Gods must have been looking over her after all, that the hateful thing already had a black opal in place. She didn't understand why, but the demon must only have a connection with its own devices, or she would have been in the same state as Ruebyn by now.

Then realisation struck her like a blow. It could not be a coincidence that the slave collars were inset with the same black opals the demon used to drain the energy from its subjects. She shivered as memories rushed before her eyes, and she found herself back on the deck of the queen's ship.

The Elders discovered long ago there was a power in death. They just lacked the creativity to use it efficiently.

"*No,*" she whispered as another piece fell into place.

"What?" Ruebyn croaked, his head whipping around to stare at her.

Queen Marianne had said that long ago in Malevolent Cove, as she'd slipped the necklaces over her and Kryssa's heads. Those had had black gems set into them as well. And on the shore of Malevolent Cove, the queen had crouched beside the body of Ikar and had spoken of death and power again. Only then had she revealed the strange magic that had held them in her thrall.

Rayan had called her collar a primitive design. Indeed, it had never made her sick as Ruebyn's necklace had. But Pela recalled now how it had warmed when she'd been close to death, as though preparing to steal the life from Pela the second her soul departed.

Shuddering, Pela stood. "Do you remember the way out?"

"Wait," Ruebyn murmured, shaking his head as though to clear a fog from his eyes. "How…how did you show me that?"

Pela stared down at Ruebyn, one eyebrow raised. "Magic."

He stared back at her for a long moment, then a grin broke across his face, and suddenly he was laughing. Climbing ponderously to his feet, he wrapped her in a bear hug.

"I'm sorry I ever doubted you," he croaked, still pale but looking a thousand times better than a few hours earlier. "You're…incredible, Pela."

Pela found herself smiling back. "Thanks, Ruebyn," she replied, her cheeks growing warm. "But I'll be even more thankful if you remember how we got here?"

The citadel was huge and she had hardly seen a fraction

of it. What she had seen, she could barely remember for all the winding back and forth they had done to get to this room. Coming from tiny Skystead, she was unused to large buildings, and she would never find her way out alone, not by dawn.

"I think so," Ruebyn replied, his face turning serious.

He made to step towards the door and his legs almost gave way. She was at his side in an instant, lending him a shoulder, though she was by no means at her best either. Her earlier efforts had left her drained and she wasn't sure how much strength she had left, how long she would last.

"We'll need food, supplies," Ruebyn rasped, "and water, or we'll never reach Plorsea. Come on, there was a kitchen attached to the dining hall."

"How will we get past the guards?" Pela hissed as they staggered for the door. They had no possessions but the clothes on their backs. At least she was free of the rags she'd worn in the mines.

"I don't know," Ruebyn whispered. "We'll think of something, somehow."

Pela wasn't convinced. "We should kill the king," she croaked, though just the words sent ice shooting through her veins.

The idea was suicide. They had seen the king's memories, the ease with which the demon had destroyed its opposition. Not a man or woman could stand against it. And yet…

"If we don't, one day it will come for us," she added.

"If it could be done, someone would have already done it," Ruebyn replied. They were staggering through the corridors now. With the late hour the halls were thankfully empty, though Pela kept glancing back, expecting someone to discover their absence at any moment. "Come on," Ruebyn continued, tugging at her arm. "We're close."

Pela fell into step beside him, though his words had not convinced her. She was thinking again of her uncle. The legends told how Devon had stood alone against the Tsar— a mortal against the all-powerful Magicker. People had said the same then, that the Tsar was immortal, that he could not be defeated. Yet still Devon had defied him, and with Alana and Braidon's help, they had cast him down.

In the kitchens they found cured sausages and cheeses, fruits and a wine skin that could be emptied and used to carry water when they were on the road. Ruebyn managed to fashion a canvas sack into a bindle that he could loop over his shoulder. He was recovering well from his sickness, though he could still move no faster than a hobble.

"Come on," he murmured when they had collected all they needed. "The gate to the city is this way."

Pela did not respond. Her eyes had fallen upon a carving knife that had been left on the steel bench. Gingerly she picked it up, watching as the razor edge glinted in the lanternlight. Clutching it to her side, she followed Ruebyn to the door and found him in the corridor outside, his eyes flicking back and forth as he searched for enemies. Watching him, she felt her heart swell, and she allowed a smile to touch her face.

"You go," she whispered. "I can't leave, not yet."

"What?" Ruebyn hissed. "You can't kill him, it's suicide!"

"I know," she replied, trying to keep the terror from her voice, "but I still have to try. It's what my uncle would have done if he were here."

"Devon had the Saviour on his side," Ruebyn croaked,

stepping forward and taking her hand in his. "Here, now, there is only the two of us against that demon."

Holding back tears, Pela nodded. "All the more reason for me to try. At least I have my power."

"Pela," Ruebyn gasped, his eyes shining, "I…I believe in you, but…whatever power you have discovered…it's no match for that thing. It has harvested thousands of lives."

"Even so."

Releasing her, Ruebyn scrunched his eyes closed. Knuckling his forehead, he turned away, and for a moment Pela thought he would do as she bid and leave. The breath caught in her throat and her heart pounded at the thought of facing the demon alone.

"Okay, Pela," he whispered, turning again to face her. "Lead the way."

She stood staring at him for a long moment, hardly daring to believe she'd heard him right. Then she spun on her heel and set off down the corridor. Silence clung to the citadel as they made their way through the night, following as best they could the path Pela had taken in her spirit state. Thankfully, the king's apartments had not been far, and whenever Pela was unsure of the way, she had only to open her inner eye to see the threads hanging in the air.

Finally they stood before a door, the way barred to them. There had been no guards as they walked the citadel, and Pela now knew why. Nothing could threaten the demon, with an entire nation in its thrall. Nothing, until now.

The door swung open with a push—it had not even been locked—and they advanced into the king's chambers. Pela held the carving knife clenched tightly at her side. Ruebyn had claimed a knife of his own, though he still had the bag of supplies looped over his shoulder. A lantern had been left partly shuttered in the corner, casting a sliver of light that illuminated a sofa and meeting table. They slipped through the shadows, searching for danger, but there was no sign of the demon.

Breathing a sigh of relief, Pela crossed the room to where a second door led to the king's private chambers. Her mind was fixed on what waited beyond, on what must be done. Reaching out, she placed a hand on the panelled wood, readying herself.

"I would not do that, were I you."

Pela's heart almost leapt from her skin as a voice spoke from behind them. Stifling a cry, she spun and raised the carving knife. But no attack came, and staring into the darkness, she found a man standing in the doorway to the corridor. It was Rayan.

There was sadness in his eyes as he looked at them. "You cannot kill it."

A lump lodged in Pela's throat as she struggled to reply. Ruebyn found his voice first. "You know what it is?"

"How could I not?" Rayan whispered. "The day my father changed…but I could not let him go, could not believe what he had become. I looked for a way to save him, but I waited too long, and then…" He made a gesture, as though the creature beyond the door needed no explanation. "The creature was starving. It took to the land, and wherever it walked, death followed. There were some who believed the story, that it was a plague, but I knew the truth. With every life the demon stole, its power grew, until all of us were faced with a choice. Submit, or perish."

"Then why are you here?" Pela gasped finally, unable to believe Rayan would willingly help such a monster.

The king's son bowed his head. "I will not let you suffer

the same fate as my people," he whispered. "I came to your room to remove the necklace and help you escape, but you were not there." He looked up then, his emerald eyes glinting in the darkness. "My father spoke of Devon often. I knew there was only one thing his niece could do, should she discover the truth."

Pela swallowed, her heart swelling at his praise. Shuddering, she took a firmer hold of the knife. "We have to stop it."

"You cannot," Rayan repeated. "The second you open that door, the demon will wake and destroy you."

Pela froze. Her hand was already halfway to the knob. A tremor shook her as she stared at the copper handle, and somewhere within a voice screamed for her to grasp it, to try anyway, though it would surely cost her life. Then she saw again the eyes of the demon, the dark depths that would tear her soul from her body and cast it into the void, and with a shudder she turned away.

"What can we do?" she croaked to Rayan.

The muscles in his jaw tightened. "Live," he whispered. "Bring word to your nations of what happened here. Maybe this King Braidon or Queen Marianne of yours can find a way to defeat him."

"They are already paving the way for his victory," Pela replied, gesturing to her collar. "The queen created these to channel the life forces of her slaves from all across Lonia."

A frown passed across Rayan's face. "Truly?" But shaking his head, he pressed on. "All the more reason for you to return, to warn them of their folly."

"Will you help us?" Ruebyn whispered.

Rayan's eyes drifted to the king's door, as though he feared even now the demon would burst forth and destroy them all. But lips tight, he nodded. "I will," he said grimly, turning and gesturing towards the corridor. "Come, I know a secret passage through the walls. I will show you."

He disappeared into the corridor. Ruebyn followed, Pela just a step behind. Only in the doorway did she hesitate. Glancing back at the darkened room, she wondered whether they were making the right decision. But there was no more time for second guesses, and swallowing her doubt, she followed the others out into the corridors of the citadel.

"Guard up!" Kryssa shouted a second before she leapt, and watched with displeasure as the recruit clumsily raised the wooden practice sword above his head.

For a second she was tempted to take her frustrations out on the young man, to deliver a beating he would not soon forget and hope it hammered in the lesson. But the morale of Braidon's makeshift army was already low enough. Kryssa had told the populace that the king was enlisting the Red Dragons to their cause, but that had been two days ago now. With their scouts placing Marianne's army at little more than a day's march from the city, many were openly suggesting surrender.

So as she faced the recruit, Kryssa forced her practice blade to slow, and only tapped him lightly on the wrist.

"There goes your arm," she said, then stepped back and turned to the other recruits who had gathered in a circle around them.

Irritation touched her as she saw the doubt in their eyes,

the fear that they had been abandoned. What had Braidon been thinking, leaving on the back of a Red Dragon? And why had he not told her of his plans? Yet again she had been left behind, blindsided, forced into a corner by the king's reckless actions.

"Drop your guard on the battlefield, and you're dead," Kryssa announced. "Since none of you seem able to remember that, we will return to the shield drills. Partner up with one shield and sword between you. Take turns with each, drills three and six."

Eager to avoid being partnered with her, the recruits rushed to obey, grabbing practice blades and shields from the piles of equipment. Kryssa claimed a shield of her own as she watched the men and women retreating into two lines. Taking her place in the centre, she gestured to the young man she had beaten earlier. He held only a shield now, and his eyes were on the ground. His defeat had left him shamed, and now he needed to regain his confidence.

Lifting her sword, Kryssa saluted him. "Defend yourself!"

His eyes widened as she leapt. The time for patience was over and she attacked quickly this time, her wooden stave flashing for his face. Instinctively, he raised the shield, catching her blow on the steel rim.

"Better," Kryssa said, stepping back.

The man's mouth hung open, as though he could hardly believe he'd blocked the attack. Polite clapping came from the other recruits and Kryssa suppressed a sigh. He might have deflected her blow, but he had overcompensated with the shield, lifting it so high his stomach had been left exposed. Had it been a real battle...

"What are you all standing there for?" she bellowed. "I said drills three and six!"

Flinching at the volume of her voice, the recruits leapt to obey and the rattle of swords on shields followed. Leaving her partner to pair up with another recruit, Kryssa marched up and down the line.

'Drills' were perhaps too strong of a word to describe the exercises she had assigned. With only a few weeks to prepare, the sergeants had only taught the recruits the most basic of blocks and strikes. The first she had assigned was a simple stab to the chest by the attacker, countered by a thrust of the defender's shield, the second a high strike and block combination.

Striding through the ranks of men and women, she corrected several pairs on their stances and technique, then gestured for her sergeants. Marching forward, they snapped her a quick salute and then looked to the recruits.

"Take them through the drills for another hour," Kryssa commanded. "Then break for lunch. If a battle is coming, I want them fresh."

"Yes, sir!" the sergeants bellowed and then spread out amongst the lines of recruits.

Kryssa watched them for a while longer, a weight settling in her stomach. Marianne had joined with the Lonians, as expected, and now marched with a force of almost seven thousand. She outnumbered Braidon's fledgling army seven to one. Even with the walls of Chole, those were impossible odds. And if the king did not return soon to lead them...

With an effort of will, Kryssa forced the worry from her mind. Braidon would return—he had to. It was his duty, his destiny. Yet even as she thought it, Kryssa recalled their conversation on the plains of Chole, how he had talked of leaving it all behind.

No, he wouldn't…

Kryssa was lost. It seemed there would be no choice but to surrender when Marianne came…but what would that mean for Plorsea's future? The queen had already shown her true colours in Malevolent Cove, when she'd coldly attempted to sacrifice Kryssa and Pela to her precious Saviour. Kryssa couldn't just step aside and let the woman enforce her twisted religion on the rest of the nation.

Yet if Kryssa stood against the woman, she would be dooming herself and everyone in Chole. Maybe if there was some slim possibility of victory…but Kryssa had been a soldier most of her adult life. She knew a lost cause when she saw one. Not even her father and all his heroics could have turned the odds in their favour.

Turning her eyes upward, Kryssa wondered again at Braidon's fate. Had the Red Dragon come in peace, or to seek revenge for the king's broken promises? The sky was clear overhead, the blue heavens stretching all the way to the distant volcanic peaks.

A frown touched Kryssa's brow as she glimpsed movement above the mountains. Squinting, she made out several specks on the horizon. Unsure of what she was seeing, Kryssa watched as they flickered in the light of the sun, waiting. Her heart started to race as they grew larger, swelling as they approached, becoming scarlet blobs drifting between the snow-capped peaks.

Dragons.

A cold sweat dripped down Kryssa's back as the sounds

of clashing weapons fell away, others now noticing the coming creatures. Whispers spread through the recruits, of fear, of excitement. They knew the king had gone with the beasts, but in a thousand years of history, the Red Dragons had always been the enemy of man.

They might still be, for all Kryssa knew. After all, the beasts had promised to wage war on humanity should Braidon fail them. Had that time finally come? Had the beasts grown tired of the king's excuses and murdered him? Did they now come to burn his cities to the ground?

Kryssa knew what needed to be done. She needed to take command, to order her soldiers to the walls, to arm the catapults, to protect the city. Yet all she could do was watch as the dragons approached, frozen by her memories from Dragon Country. This was an enemy she could not fight, no matter how skilled she might be with a blade. The tiny flame of her life force might offer some resistance, but against a Red Dragon…what was she but an insect to such a beast?

Minutes raced by as the dragons swept on towards the helpless city. As they neared, the blobs resolved themselves into individual creatures. There were five in all, a terrifying, unstoppable force of nature. Mount Chole might as well have erupted again, for all Kryssa could do to save the city and its people.

Finally the beasts were directly overhead, over the Castle. Their broad wings cast the courtyard in shade, sending fear rippling through the gathered recruits. A hundred eyes turned to Kryssa, looking for guidance, but she could do nothing as a single creature spiralled down.

A mighty *thump* came from the ramparts as the dragon landed atop the walls. Shuddering, Kryssa forced herself to face the creature. A wave of exhaustion swept through her as she found the beast's eyes on her. She had worked so hard these past days to prepare Braidon's recruits, but now none of it would matter. In an instant, she would be gone, and all her aspirations with her. Kryssa almost felt relieved, that she might finally rest.

"My people!"

Kryssa started as a voice called down from the ramparts. A figure leapt from the dragon's back, one arm raised high in greeting. Braidon's sapphire eyes swept over the courtyard as he spoke: "I have returned with new allies!"

There was a moment's silence—then a ragged cheer rose from the recruits as they thrust their blades skywards. Their cries rang from the walls, becoming a roar of triumph, of renewed hope for the cause they had sworn their lives to. Wearing a satisfied grin, Braidon moved to the edge of the crenulations and raised his arms, basking in the love of his people.

Yet looking up at the king, Kryssa could not find the same joy, the same cause for celebration. All she could think of was how Braidon had abandoned her. He had expected her to be here, to make up for his absence, yet he had not even warned her of his mad quest.

"The dark queen comes to take our freedom!" Braidon was saying, but Kryssa was no longer listening.

Feeling sick, she turned away, even as the dragon threw back its head and unleashed a roar. Heat washed over the courtyard and Kryssa saw the flames flickering in the corner of her eye. The recruits screamed their enthusiasm, but Kryssa felt nothing but a dull emptiness as she moved through their ranks.

The king might have returned with fresh hope for their

cause, but once again he had betrayed her. While she had suffered here alone, worrying and wondering, Braidon had been off on his own quest, plotting his own victory.

The cries of the crowd faded as Kryssa left the courtyard. The darkness of the Castle engulfed her and she smelt again the acrid tang of smoke, the constant reminder of her failure. She went quickly through the corridors, finally emerging before the gates to the city. The guards saluted as she strode past, well used to her comings and goings—though this time she had no plan, no destination, only the sense she must get away.

Mindlessly, she wandered through the twisting alleyways of Chole, her thoughts drifting to other times, other places. She thought she'd left this all behind long ago, when she'd first quit the King's Guard and retired to Skystead. Tired of war and death, she and Derryn had been ready to begin life anew.

Yet now Kryssa had somehow found herself in the centre of a new war. Once she had railed against her father for returning again and again to battle, but now Kryssa realised she was little better. She had been all too quick to encourage Braidon to take up the fight against Marianne, to retake his crown. And all the while, Kryssa's own daughter had been missing, lost in the darkness of Malevolent Cove. She should have left in search of Pela long ago, rather than staying to fight for the ungrateful king.

And now it was too late.

Kryssa didn't known where she was heading until she turned a corner and found the triple spires rising from the street ahead. Realising her feet had unwittingly led her to the Temple of the Earth, she crossed the road and strode up the long marble staircase to the entrance. There she was met by several men and women in the long emerald robes of priests.

"Daughter of the Earth," they greeted her. "How might we help you?"

"My mind is clouded," Kryssa said truthfully. "I've come to meditate."

"Then welcome," came the reply.

A sense of peace fell over Kryssa as she entered and breathed in the earthen incense they burned to honour Antonia, Goddess of the Earth. Candles flickered in the entrance hall, guiding her through marble columns to the inner sanctum. Here, she carefully removed her boots and put them aside, before following the priests across the velvet carpets to the altar.

She had spent a day here while Braidon lay unconscious after his battle on the steps outside, but had not been back since. There had been too much to do, too many fears and threats, to take the time for herself.

The temple was almost empty, and Kryssa knelt in silence, thinking how wrong it felt to be practicing her worship so openly. Even in Skystead, her belief had been a hidden thing, not forbidden, but something people preferred not to think about. But then, that was the people of Skystead with most things—kind, but hard, welcoming, but closed off.

In Chole though, all forms of worship had been celebrated openly—at least until the Knights of Alana had ridden into the city two weeks ago, threatening to burn down the temple. If Braidon had not intervened, they would have succeeded.

Shivering at the reminder, Kryssa closed her eyes and began the gentle *in-out* of breath that she had learned from her mother, Selina. Meditation had been an escape for Kryssa as a child, a way to rise above the nightmares when they'd come, to free herself of the fear that sometimes still plagued her even now. She had begun her life on the streets, and if not for Selina, she might have lost it there as well. She still thanked the Three Gods every night for the old woman's kindness.

She missed them both more than ever now, Selina and Devon, her adopted parents. At least with her mother she'd had more time. They'd known the end was coming for a long time. With Devon though…Kryssa had hardly spoken to him in years, not since he'd left for war with her husband, and returned only with his body.

But Devon had never stopped being her father, not even from afar. She had not been surprised when he'd come to rescue her—but his death had shocked Kryssa to her core. As a child, she'd been terrified of the giant hammerman. From the start, he'd made it clear she was not part of his plans, that she was not his daughter. But as she'd grown and had shown her affinity with the blade, Devon had finally warmed to her, had even taken her under his wing as a warrior.

The day she'd been named amongst the ranks of the King's Guard, she'd seen the pride in his eyes, felt the love in his hug, even if he had never spoken the words.

Tears stung Kryssa's eyes. They flickered open and she looked to the panelled ceiling.

"You are distracted, my daughter," a priest murmured from nearby.

Kryssa shuddered as a sob tore from her throat. "I don't

know what I'm doing anymore," she said, sitting up and angrily rubbing away the tears. "I thought helping Braidon was the only way to get my family back, but I'm no closer to finding my daughter than I was when we started."

"And now we stand on the brink of a new war," the priest added sadly. He seated himself across from her and crossed his legs. "You were with the king, when he came and stood against the Knights who would have destroyed our temple."

Nodding, Kryssa swallowed the lump that had lodged in her throat. A sad smile crossed the man's face.

"A dark day for my Order," he said. "To see so many led astray from the path of the Goddess."

"What?" Kryssa asked with a frown.

"The death of the Knight was regretful, but he came here with hate in his heart. It was a noble act, for the king to stand against him." The priest drew in a breath. "Less so, when he led a mob against the Castle."

"They were sheltering the Knights who attacked you."

"Ay, and many more innocents." His eyes bored into Kryssa's, as though daring her to refute his words. "Now they are dead, their power given over to your king."

Kryssa shivered. "That was an accident."

"It was inevitable from the moment the king broke down the gates of the Castle."

Frowning, Kryssa was about to respond when she realised the significance of his earlier words. "Wait," she gasped, her head jerking up. "How did you know what the king did in the pantheon?"

The priest's eyes fell to the floor. "We have always known of the potential within each of us—and the risk for its abuse."

"He did not kill them," Kryssa insisted. "I was with him. It was his followers…"

"And it was Braidon who led them there, who fed the anger in their hearts, when we would have preached forgiveness. Why do you think *we* did not strike against the Knights when they came for us?"

"What do you mean?"

"We were not helpless." As the priest spoke, he lifted a hand and turned it palm up. A flame leapt to life, dancing across his flesh until he closed his fist, snuffing it out once more. "We could have done as Braidon did, could have struck down those men in their steel armour. But their deaths would only have stoked the Order's hatred—then more would have come seeking blood. Peace would be impossible."

"You would have died rather than defend yourselves?"

A smile touched the priest's lips. "Evil must be opposed wherever it is found, my daughter. But it does not always take a sharp blade or magic to stand against the darkness. Sometimes mercy is all it takes to change a man's heart."

As he finished, footsteps came from behind Kryssa. Suddenly fearing deception, she spun and reached for her sword, but there was only a young woman standing nearby. Kryssa's heart lurched as she recognised the assassin she had spared. Her amber eyes were wide with terror, but she made no move to flee as Kryssa drew her blade.

"So Janylle spoke the truth," Kryssa croaked, her legs trembling as she faced the priest. "The temple *was* behind the assassination attempt of Braidon."

"No," the priest whispered as he came slowly to his feet. "We only offered the girl shelter and forgiveness, after her anger led her astray."

"Why should I believe you?" Kryssa snapped.

"Have we not kept Braidon's secret?" the priest murmured. "Are the streets buzzing with word of Janylle's death by the king's hand? Or of the mercy you showed his would-be-assassin?"

The anger drained from Kryssa in a rush. She swallowed. "I betrayed him, letting her go," she said, her eyes fixed to the ground.

"She is naught but a child," the priest replied. "Surely it is no crime for the king's lieutenant to spare such an innocent."

The sword shook in Kryssa's hand. Maybe the king did know of her betrayal. Was *that* why he had not told her about the dragons? Why else would he have left so precipitously, without a single word of warning?

"I trust this secret will not leave these walls," Kryssa said finally.

The priest nodded. "The girl will remain in our protection until the war has ended."

"Very well," Kryssa said, turning away.

Looking around the temple, she thought about returning to her meditation, but it was an impossible task now. She was too distracted, too fractured, to centre herself. A sigh slipped from her lips and she was about to sheathe her sword when the doors at the back of the hall banged open.

She swung around as two men raced into the temple, both armed with short swords and shields. She recognised them as two of the recruits she'd been training that morning. Sliding her sword back into its sheath, she strode across the hall to greet them before their boots tramped dirt into the fine carpets.

"Lieutenant Kryssa!" one gasped as she strode up. "The king sent us to find you."

"And so you have," Kryssa said, inclining her head. "What does Braidon require of me?"

"It's the queen!" the second recruit burst out before the other could answer. "Her army is at the gates!"

❧ 19 ☙

Braidon stared across the packed earth at Marianne. He could barely believe she was actually there, standing boldly outside the gates of his city as though she were there under invitation. So many months had passed now since Malevolent Cove, since her betrayal, that she had almost become a caricature in his mind, a dark and demonic woman who sought only to destroy everything he had ever built.

Now though, he was forced to face the reality his hatred had allowed him to forget—that she was still the woman he had loved for the better part of a decade, who had lain beside him for nights uncounted, who had listened to his private fears, who had born him a son. For half a moment, Braidon found himself wondering whether they might turn back the clock, if he could restore their lives, if they could be together once more.

Then an image flickered into his mind—of Marianne towering over him in Malevolent Cove, of the hatred that had twisted her face, and all his hope withered away. Marianne had never loved him. All that time the woman had claimed to be his queen, she had been scheming behind his back. It had been *her* plan to invite the Knights of Alana into his nation, her reign that had seen the streets of his capital run thick with the blood of innocents.

No, there could be no turning back for either of them now, no redemption. The past as he remembered it, the love and shared companionship, it had never been anything more than a construct, an act to manipulate him.

Grinding his teeth, Braidon flicked his gaze to the man standing alongside his wife, and now he could not keep the rage from his face. Caledan stood there, one hand resting on the hilt of his sword. The sellsword wore a casual smile, as though he were exactly where he belonged.

They had come together in neutral territory midway between the city gates and the grounds upon which Marianne's army was setting camp. Both had a dozen soldiers at their back and a champion at their side. With Caledan standing beside Marianne, Braidon had been relieved when Kryssa joined him in time for the meeting.

Although Braidon was still surprised he'd received the call for a truce at all. Marianne's forces greatly outnumbered his own. Word of the Red Dragons must have reached her, or…perhaps she now sensed the power reverberating in Braidon's core, and feared it.

The thought put a smile on his face, though it faded when a quick check of the queen's aura revealed that she too had been busy collecting lives.

"So, here we all are," Marianne said finally, opening her hands in a gesture of peace. "I am glad you agreed to see me, Braidon. It is my hope that we can settle our…disagreement without bloodshed."

Braidon gaped at his wife, stunned by her words. She had tried to kill him twice already, had stolen his son, slaughtered his King's Guard. Now she spoke of avoiding bloodshed, of peace. If he hadn't already suspected some trap before, he was certain of it now.

Rage touched Braidon as he realised she thought him a fool, that he would fall for her sweet words. She still wore that smug grin, as though she alone ruled the world, and everyone else on the field were beneath her. He fought an overwhelming desire to reach out and throttle her, to wipe the grin from her face. Let the sham continue; eventually Marianne would show her true colours, would betray herself. Then the whole world would see her for the monster she truly was.

"So, this is how you repay Devon's loyalty, sellsword?" Braidon spoke finally, ignoring his wife. "I thought you were his friend, yet now you stand beside his murderer."

"Devon *was* my friend."

Braidon laughed. "Then I am glad you do not count me amongst your friends."

Caledan stared back, his brown eyes cold as ice. "I stand with the side I believe in," he growled. "You have failed Plorsea one time too many, Braidon. It is time for you to step aside."

"I am the rightful king," Braidon snapped, "and when your queen lies dead at my feet, I will—"

"*Enough!*" Marianne snarled, speaking over him.

She took a step forward, and from behind Braidon came the rattling of steel as his soldiers reached for their blades. Braidon raised a hand, bidding them to wait.

"You should be thanking Caledan," Marianne continued, her voice returning to a calm tone. "His council is the only reason I am not already knocking down your gates."

Braidon sneered. "You think you could take Chole so easily?" he asked. "Not even Archon could breach its walls."

"You have less than a thousand soldiers, husband," Marianne said. "Not even enough to man the walls of which you boast so loudly." She took another step forward. "But let us not quarrel over the trivial. I have come to talk of peace."

"Peace?" The word slipped from Braidon before he could stop himself. "You want to talk about peace?"

When Marianne only nodded, Braidon started to laugh. "Very well then, my beloved!" he gasped. "What are the terms of your surrender?"

Marianne clasped her hands behind her back, her smile unchanged. "I see your failures these last few months have not dented your arrogance, husband," she murmured. "The only surrender which interests me is yours."

"Ha!" Braidon cried. "And what would your terms be? Last I knew, you wanted to watch me bleed to death on the shores of Malevolent Cove." He shook his head. "No, I will not be surrendering to the likes of you, Marianne. You say you care about peace? Well it was you who broke it in the first place. If you wish to repair the damage you have wrought, kneel before me and I might consider sparing your life."

"I did what I had to for my freedom!" Marianne snarled. The smile finally slipped from her lips as rage twisted her face. "I wouldn't expect you to understand. I'm sure you would have been happy to have me in your bed until I withered away to nothing."

"I wouldn't touch your corruption with a ten-foot pole," Braidon shot back.

"Ah, so finally you know how I felt all those years, forced to lie in the arms of a vile old man," Marianne spat. Then she took a breath, and when she looked at Braidon again, the mask of calm had been restored. "You know, everyone else who had a hand in our marriage is dead now. My father, the Lonian senators, the Elders. Only *you* have not suffered, my dear husband."

"You think I have not suffered?" Braidon asked, his voice dropping to a whisper. "After being betrayed by the woman I loved? After you stabbed me in the heart, murdered my friends, and turned my people against me? No, it is *you* who have not suffered for your evil. But then, I would not expect you to see that, Marianne. You care only for yourself."

Silence fell across the plains as Marianne stared at him. She said nothing, but there was a distant look to her eyes, as though she were weighing the truth of his words. Finally though, she shook her head.

"That is not true," she replied, then gestured with a hand.

The soldiers behind her parted and Braidon tensed, preparing for treachery. Instead, he stood frozen in place as a woman appeared through the ranks of Marianne's followers. A gasp came from beside him, then in a blur of movement, Kryssa threw herself forward.

"Gen!" she cried.

Braidon watched in disbelief as Kryssa and Genevieve came together. Clasping desperately at one another, they kissed. He hadn't seen Genevieve since the disaster in Malevolent Cove, though he'd sent out messages asking after her and Pela when he'd won Chole. In truth, he'd thought them both long dead. It beggared belief to see the huntress here now.

Finally the two broke off their kiss, but they did not separate, only pressed their foreheads together, eyes closed as their tears flowed freely.

"You see?" Marianne said quietly, drawing Braidon's attention back to the queen.

His heart raced as he realised he'd been distracted. With Kryssa's attention elsewhere, Marianne might have struck at him, overwhelming his defences and destroying him before he knew what was happening. But she had not moved from where she stood, only looked at him with sadness in her eyes.

"The Elder Servo had her," Marianne continued, "when we met on the River Jurrien. He had been using power to manipulate the Lonian army, but Caledan destroyed him. Genevieve was amongst his prisoners. She was on the verge of death, but I saved her, at great cost to my own power."

"Why should we believe you?" Braidon hissed.

"It's true," Genevieve interrupted. Breaking away from Kryssa, she stepped between the two monarchs. "It was Servo who was intent on eradicating the followers of the Three Gods."

"Ay, the entire Order is corrupt," Braidon snapped. "Whether they are led by Servo or Marianne, there is no changing that. If she killed the Elder, I have no doubt it was only because he stood in her way."

"Perhaps that is true," Genevieve frowned, glancing at the queen. "I only know that she freed and healed me. But...I want to believe she is telling the truth when she claims to want peace."

"It's true, Braidon," Marianne said. "I do not want war. I only want what's best for my people, to finally bring peace and prosperity to this land." Then her face hardened. "And for you to pay for what you did to me."

"Me?" Braidon growled.

He clenched his fists and the energies within him went crackling to his fingertips. For a second he was tempted to launch an attack, to destroy Marianne before she could defend herself. But he swallowed back the urge and lashed out with his tongue instead.

"What of your crimes, dear wife? It was not by my command that Knights were allowed free rein in our lands, not my rule that saw innocents stolen from their families and sacrificed in the name of the Saviour." He shook his head. "No, if that if your idea of peace, I want no part of it. So bring your foreign army and your Knights; they will break on the walls of Chole, as every invader since the Great Wars has done."

A ragged cheer came from the recruits behind him, but Braidon did not glance back. His eyes were fixed on Marianne, sensing the anger radiating from her, a mirror of his own. Any second now she would lash out, would try to strike him down, but this time he would be ready for her. When the attack came…

"Very well, dear husband," Marianne said, a sigh whispering from her lips. He was surprised to hear sadness in her voice. "You will have your war. But when the prairies are stained with the blood of our people, do not forget: it was you who asked for this."

"I will fight until my dying breath to protect my people," Braidon hissed.

"Ay, and they will bleed for it," Marianne said sadly. She

turned to go, then hesitated, her sapphire eyes lingering on Genevieve. "You may stay, Genevieve," she said at last. "As I told you, you are not a prisoner. Enjoy your lover's embrace while you can. Tomorrow, we will be at the gates."

❧ 20 ☙

Pela let out a long breath as they emerged from a side door into the gardens of the citadel. Moonlight bathed the world, casting everything in black and white, and she paused to stare at the scene, remembering the vibrant colours of the flowers, hidden now by darkness.

Shuddering, she shook off her dread and followed Ruebyn down the steps. Rayan was just ahead, moving down a narrow path between the rosebushes. Their scent touched Pela's nostrils as she stepped onto the path, but now they seemed overly sweet, setting her stomach to roiling.

Pela moved quickly between the rows of bushes. The beauty of the garden had been nothing more than a thin veneer, an act to conceal the true corruption at Trola's core. The demon's greed, its hatred, had infected everything.

How could they stop such a monster? An awful sorrow gripped Pela as she hurried after the others, a sickly sense of despair. The Gods had truly abandoned them if such evil could take root in the land. They were all alone now, each and every one of them, their lives but candles before the vastness of the world. And the demon was the storm that would snuff them all out.

Ahead, Rayan left the path and cut across the lawns towards the outer walls of the citadel. Following him across the uneven grounds, Pela stumbled against something. She paused to check what had tripped her in the otherwise perfectly manicured lawn. A block of slate the size of a small table lay in the grass, smooth and unadorned, though amidst the grey, tiny specks of crystal shone in the moonlight.

She remembered then what Ruebyn had said, about how the Sword of Light had once been kept in these gardens, before Alastair and King Thomas had passed through The Way and claimed its power. Tears sprang to her eyes as she thought of those ancient heroes. How easy it must have been in those days, knowing the Three Gods were on their side.

Now Pela stood in the very spot those ancient powers had once gathered, alone and defeated, fleeing the dark creature that had taken residence at the heart of Trola. But what else could she do? What was her fleeting power against such darkness?

Her shoulders heavy, Pela crossed the lawn to where Ruebyn and Rayan waited in the shadow of the wall. The king's son gave her a quick glance before pressing a small stone in the wall with his thumb. Then he put his shoulder to a larger block and heaved.

To Pela's surprise, the stone swung easily inwards, revealing a hollow. Rayan continued pushing until the entire opening was unearthed before stepping back. The block had been the size of a small person, though the space revealed was low to the ground. They would have to crawl to enter.

Then Rayan cursed. "Did either of you bring a lantern?"

"We left it behind," Ruebyn whispered.

Pela swallowed, looking from the tunnel to the sky. The eastern horizon was just beginning to brighten. There was no time left.

"What is inside?" she whispered. "Maybe we can manage in the dark."

Rayan looked uncertainly at the tunnel. "After a few feet, you can stand," he said. "From there, you follow the wall to the right. Eventually you will come to a turn that leads down a series of steps, into a tunnel ends in an abandoned building."

"We'll be blind," Ruebyn croaked. His strength was fading fast. He looked almost as bad as he had at dinner.

"We'll manage," Pela replied.

"I must leave you here," Rayan said, looking gaunt now. "I will try to delay your discovery as long as possible, but…"

He trailed off. Pela knew what he meant, though. Their newfound friend could do little against the demon. Silently she nodded her thanks, and without anything else to say, she dropped to her hands and knees and started into the darkness. The knife she had taken from the kitchen she tucked into her waistband, though it would do little good against those that would come after them. Shuffling came from behind her as Ruebyn followed, and then a grinding noise echoed in the dark as Rayan sealed the door behind them.

Pela suppressed a scream as the faint light from outside vanished and the darkness swallowed them up. For a moment, all she could do was kneel there in terror. The black was so absolute it was like a physical thing, so thick Pela felt she could hardly breathe. Suddenly she was back in the mines, the collar cold around her throat, the weight of a mountain pressing down from above. A moan built in her chest as she sucked in a lungful of air.

"Pela?" Ruebyn's voice came from behind her. A second later his hand touched her leg. "Are you okay?"

No!

Pela wanted to scream, to thrash and scramble back to the light, but they were trapped now in the dark, just as she had been in the mines. She had escaped her servitude, had vowed she would never go back, but now…

"Just breathe," Ruebyn whispered. "What was that exercise your mother taught you? Meditation?"

"Yes," she managed to croak.

"In, out, right?" he said, and she could almost see him smiling.

Despite herself, Pela laughed. "Well, when you put it like that."

She closed her eyes all the same, focusing on her breathing, allowing everything else to fade away. She sank into the darkness of her mind, but this was a familiar darkness, a part of her, and slowly she began to relax. Her life force flickered into her mind's eye, and she let out a sigh, reassured by its presence.

Edging forward, Pela felt above her head and found she could stand. Carefully, she pulled herself to her feet and then reached down to help Ruebyn to do the same.

"By the Saviour, I wish we could see *something*," he muttered. She heard his boots scuffing on stone as he shifted on his feet.

"Reminds me far too much of where we first met," Pela agreed.

Working by instinct, she closed her eyes and reached within for her life force. Then she held her hand out before her, imagining the energies gathering in her palm, and a tiny flame flickered into life. She grinned as a glow appeared against her eyelids, but before she could open her eyes, Ruebyn's scream thundered in the tunnel.

Panicking, Pela stumbled backwards and reached for her knife. Before she could draw it, a hand jabbed at her back. She spun, expecting to see Ruebyn, but he was standing across from her, his face a mask of horror. His hand lifted to point across her shoulder.

Pela cried out as she saw their assailant. He stared back at her, eyes wide, his face a mask that mirrored her own terror. Leaping back, she placed the knife between them, expecting him to give chase.

But he did nothing, only stood fixed in place, almost statue-like for his stillness. The blood pounded in Pela's ears as more figures took shape beyond the man. Dozens—no, hundreds—of men and women hid in the hollow beneath the wall, their faces showing looks of rage and terror.

Pela retreated another step, gesturing for Ruebyn to follow her, but he did not move. His eyes were on the watchers, his face so pale he could have been a ghost.

A shiver ran down Pela's spine as she faced the man who had attacked her. He had not moved an inch, had not even changed expression. It was as though…

Breath held, Pela took a trembling step forward, then another. The light grew in her hand, illuminating the glassy sheen in the man's eyes, the wax-like tone of his skin. Pela's scalp crawled as her eyes darted from face to face, but not one of them moved.

A scream built in Pela's throat as she realised what she was seeing—mummified corpses, frozen in their final moments by some spell and hidden here. This could only be the demon's work. Pela slapped a hand over her mouth to silence her scream and looked at Ruebyn. Why had Rayan brought them here?

Laughter echoed through the cavern as movement came from amongst the corpses. For a moment she thought they had returned to life, but then footsteps echoed loudly in the narrow passage, and a figure emerged from the shadows.

"Welcome to the hall of the damned," Rayan said quietly.

"What?" Pela whispered. She stared at the man, though as he approached she found herself retreating, until Ruebyn brought her up short. "What are you doing here?"

"*My* hall of the damned, should I say," Rayan said with a laugh.

"No," Pela hissed as realisation struck her. She shook her head. "No, that's not possible. It was the king, I saw!"

Rayan only smiled. "Anything is possible, with power." He waved a hand, and a single golden thread appeared, winding its way into the amulet that hung about his chest. "A simple deception, though only necessary in my early days, when I was still weak and feared discovery. Long since redundant—or so I had thought."

Pela stood frozen in place as Rayan approached, clinging to Ruebyn as though her life depended on it. She could feel him shaking, could see the terror in his eyes as he watched the creature come for them. Fear gripped Pela's mind, robbing her of reason, even as she tried to find a way out.

"What did you do to Betran?" Ruebyn's voice rang suddenly from the walls, thin and trembling, but it cut through Pela's fear like a dagger, bringing her back to the present.

Rayan waved a hand. "My father, like most of my vassals, has come to believe his own lies. To them, the *morbus* is real, a dark shadow hanging over our lands." His smile grew and Pela watched as the colour seeped from his eyes, turning them to the deepest black. "But then, my power does not allow them to think otherwise."

"Why did you bring us here?" Pela rasped. Drawing on every ounce of her courage, she stood hand in hand with Ruebyn against the monster.

"Your collar, of course," Rayan replied. "When I saw it through my soldier's eyes, I feared the rise of a rival in the east." He laughed. "But it seems your queen is still far beneath me. When I come, she will bow to my power, or perish like all the rest."

Pela's entire body was trembling now. Ruebyn must have felt it, for he hugged her tight. She shivered at his embrace, and for a second almost felt better.

"Everything's going to be alright, Pela," he whispered before pulling away.

"How?" she gasped, staring up at him.

"Because I believe in you." He smiled. "You'll find a way."

"I'm afraid your friend is overly optimistic," Rayan interrupted. He spread his arms, as though to encompass the rows of mummified corpses. "Or do you not yet understand the reason for my collection?"

A shudder passed through Pela as she looked at the host standing behind Rayan. "They're still alive…" The words left her mouth before she knew what she was saying.

The creature's laughter rose to a fever pitch. "They are my crowning achievement," Rayan whispered. "The strongest of those who opposed me, frozen forever by my magic, for me to feast upon whenever the hunger takes me."

As Rayan walked, he drove his boot down on the foot of one of his collection. Pela's stomach tied itself into knots as a distant scream rasped from the desiccated body, a dry, far away thing that spoke of untold horror. Her every hair stood on end as they stumbled back.

"No, no, no," Pela whispered, her tone rising to a scream. She gripped Ruebyn's hand tight enough to break bones.

The demon continued towards them, a dull light seeping from its fingers. "The people of this sweet nation no longer prosper." The voice was Rayan's, but it was darker now, cold like steel. "The light in their souls is a dull, dwindling thing. I have not tasted lives as sweet as yours in decades. Such a delight cannot be wasted." A smile morphed his face into something awful. "It must be savoured."

Rayan made a gesture, and a sharp *shriek* came from Pela's collar. She cried out, thinking it would snap closed around her throat, but instead it cracked apart and crashed to the ground with a heavy *thunk*.

"Now you are *mine*," the creature cackled, throwing out its arms.

"Pela!" Ruebyn cried as a wave of darkness swirled towards them. "Use your power!"

"How?" she screamed back, clutching at him.

There was nothing she could do, not against Rayan, but

at Ruebyn's cry she reached for her life force all the same. She could have sobbed as the light appeared, little more than a drop before the ocean of darkness that rushed for them. She had wasted so much this night, and now she stood on the brink of exhaustion. One push was all it would take to drain the last of her strength, to hurl her into the void.

"Find The Way!" Ruebyn was screaming nonsense in her ears now, his voice barely audible above the pounding in her ears, the cries of the demon. "You can open it, I believe in you!"

But there was no way out of this. There was no escape for them, not unless some miracle of the Gods blessed them…

The Way!

Her heart lurched as she realised the meaning in Ruebyn's words, that they stood at the entrance to the fabled gateway from Kalgan to Plorsea. But that was just a story, a figment of her people's collective imagination—Ruebyn had said so himself. Even if it existed, only magic could open such a gateway, only the Gods themselves, surely.

Instead, there was just her. She turned to look at Rayan, at the darkness pouring from the demon's hands. His eyes glowed with all the lives he had collected, and Pela's confidence wilted. She was weak and small, untrained, a useless girl who thought to stand against an eternal beast. She could not do it, could not see the way, could not even grasp the light of her own feeble life force.

"Pela!" Ruebyn cried again. Then his hands were on her face, turning her from the beast, so that all she could see was him, all she knew were the depths of his hazel eyes. "Pela," he repeated. "You can do it. You can do anything."

Pela swallowed. She could feel the darkness pressing down, the weight of the demon's power. For a second, all she could think about were those terrible mummies, about being trapped in this place for eternity, unable to move, only wait for the awful creature to come and feed…

Ruebyn's fingers tightened on Pela's arm and finally she heard him. Blinking, she found herself back in the cavern beneath the wall, but now she looked out not with her own eyes, but those of the spirit. A thousand golden threads filled the cavern, spiralling inwards, with the beast at the centre of it all. A shiver shook her soul as she saw finally the corroded black of Rayan's aura. She could sense his elation, his arrogance that victory was assured, that they could not escape.

But perhaps he was wrong, perhaps there *was* a way.

Grasping the candle of her life force, Pela used its power to send tendrils of herself out into the night, questing, seeking something different, something unlike anything else in the ancient citadel…

…and to her shock, she found something respond. Deep beneath their feet, a power stirred at her presence, a rumbling giant that had lain dormant for a hundred years, now waking. She gasped as the ground itself rocked beneath them, as the air suddenly shimmered, changed. An unworldly light filled the cavern around them.

"What are you doing?" the demon roared, its eyes burning with sudden rage.

Pela did not respond. Her mind was still turned inwards, fixed on the dwindling flame of her life force. Whatever she had done, it was consuming her. Weakness spread through her body and she slumped into Ruebyn, still clinging to the flame, even as it crumbled to embers. She groaned as her spirit slammed back into her body, the weight returning to her soul.

"Hold on!" Ruebyn cried out and she clung to him, too weak to even open her eyes.

An explosion of colour burst through her eyelids, and then they were falling, spinning, hurtling through some unseen vortex, and Pela felt the last traces of her consciousness slipping away, the darkness rising up to embrace her.

21

"I still can't believe it," Kryssa murmured, cupping Genevieve's cheek in her hands. Her vision blurred as tears stung her eyes. "I can't."

They were back in Chole, back in her room in the Castle. Now though, the place no longer seemed so dark. It was as though someone had just lit a candle, and she'd discovered the monsters she'd feared had all been in her imagination. Even with Marianne's threats, even with the battle to come on the morrow, Kryssa was not afraid.

Because Genevieve was here. Because Pela lived.

Genevieve had just finished telling her about their ordeal in the Lonian mines, and of their escape. Kryssa could hardly believe the things Pela had done, the challenges her daughter had risen above. She knew now that whatever came to pass tomorrow, Pela would be okay.

And after hearing the truth about Lonia, of the awful cruelty of their overseers, the horror in their mines, Kryssa also knew that Braidon had been right. They could never surrender to Marianne, could not give up their sovereignty to such callous masters.

"I'm here," Genevieve whispered, leaning in and pressing her lips to Kryssa's. Their tongues met, and Kryssa savoured the familiar cinnamon taste of her lover. She moaned as Genevieve pulled away with a whisper: "Believe it."

Smiling, Kryssa ran a hand through the huntress's hair. "Thank you," she whispered. "For everything you did for Pela."

They were sitting together on the sofa in Kryssa's room. She had one arm around Genevieve's shoulders, while her other traced slow circle's over the huntress's leggings.

"She is her mother's daughter," Genevieve chuckled. "She hardly needed my help to send those Lonians fleeing."

"And yet you were willing to sacrifice your life to protect her."

Genevieve looked away at that, and Kryssa felt the tremor in her lover's body. She pulled the huntress closer, holding her tight. Genevieve had spoken only briefly of her capture. She had fought the Knight that had pursued them, almost defeating him before the man managed to disarm her. He had gone on alone, yet with a storm bearing down and an arrow through his shoulder, he could not have gotten far.

But Genevieve had been left in the tender care of the Knight's attendants. They had carried her back to Lonian lands, where they had met the Elder Servo. There was no mistaking the fear in Genevieve's voice when she had spoken of the man, how he had tormented her, taking sick pleasure from her screams.

Kryssa could only imagine how long the torture might

have lasted if not for Marianne, and despite her misgivings, she found herself thankful for the queen's mercy.

A shiver ran down Kryssa's spine and she quickly shook off the thought.

Remember, Marianne is a masterful manipulator. She killed your father!

Recalling that night in Malevolent Cove, anger touched Kryssa. How could Caledan have given his oath to such a woman. The sellsword had travelled with Devon for weeks, had fought alongside him against the Order's evil. Yet now he stood beside the hammerman's killer. She could not understand such a betrayal.

"What of Pela and this boy?" she murmured after a time. "Do you truly think they will be safe in Trola?" Her greatest fear was that Pela might have escaped from one danger, only to step straight into the path of another.

"As safe as anywhere right now," Genevieve said wryly. She rubbed her hand across Kryssa's back. "Your daughter is smart. So is the boy, for that matter. They've probably already made it south and crossed back into Plorsea. They could be safer than either of us right now, for all we know."

"I pray you're right."

"I am," Genevieve replied with a smile.

Kryssa shivered as her partner's fingers moved to her neck and gently began to massage the stress from her muscles. A long sigh whispered from her lips and she relaxed into the huntress, her eyes flickering closed.

"I missed you so much," Kryssa whispered, thinking of the endless days and nights since they'd last been together, of all despair and grief and guilt she'd felt since that fateful day in Skystead. "I can't believe you're really here."

"You already said that," Genevieve chuckled, her lips nuzzling Kryssa's ear.

Opening her eyes, Kryssa looked up at the huntress. "I mean it."

Still smiling, Genevieve leaned down and kissed her. This time it was no soft thing, but hard and urgent, and Kryssa gasped as the huntress's fingers tightened in her hair. They fell sideways together onto the cushioned sofa. Heat lit Kryssa's stomach, and growling, she ran her hands over Genevieve's chest, fingers plucking free the buttons of her lover's shirt.

"Kryssa," Genevieve whispered.

A tremor shook the huntress as Kryssa's fingers slid inside her shirt. Wearing a wicked grin, Kryssa moved her lips to Genevieve's neck, enjoying the soft moans as her lover responded. Then Genevieve was tugging at her own tunic. Kryssa gasped as the buttons gave way and Genevieve's lips traced fiery paths across her breasts and stomach.

She slid her fingers through Genevieve's hair, savouring her lover's touch, pulling her down. An answering moan came from Genevieve and the huntress's head lifted an inch, their eyes meeting across her naked body.

"I missed you too," Genevieve whispered, her emerald eyes alight with desire.

Afterwards, Kryssa lay dozing in Genevieve's arms, her mind adrift. Memories of the past weeks and months and years danced across her thoughts, of her father and daughter, her husband and the king, and a million other things both important and insignificant. They had moved from the couch to her bed, and now lay curled together beneath the blankets, insulated from the frigid air that hung about the Castle.

"You truly think Pela will return?" Kryssa murmured when Genevieve stirred.

The huntress's eyes flickered open, shining emerald in the faint light. "I do," she said, propping herself up on one elbow. "Like I said, she is her mother's daughter. Whether you wanted her to be or not."

Her words made Kryssa shudder as she recalled the day Devon had returned with her husband Derryn's body. She had been so angry at her father then, so determined to prevent her newborn daughter from following the warrior's path. And so Kryssa had locked away her sword, turned her back on that life.

Somehow, it had found her daughter anyway, and now Kryssa found herself regretting her decision. If only she'd been more open, Pela might have been prepared for what the world had thrown at her these last months. Maybe then they would not have lost each other in the cove, maybe they would have all been together…

Grinding her teeth, Kryssa forced her mind back to the present. There was no changing the past and whatever her feelings, there was nothing she could do for Pela now. She had to have faith, had to believe the girl could fight her way back to Plorsea.

"Then we'd better make sure there's something for her to return to," Kryssa said finally, smiling at Genevieve from her pillow. "Marianne will come tomorrow. You've seen her army up close—did you notice anything that might help us?"

Genevieve sighed, her eyes turning distant. "I don't know, Krys," she said. Then her eyes flickered back into focus and she looked down at Kryssa. "Are you sure we're fighting on the right side? Caledan…he told me what happened here, about the civilians in the pantheon. Is it…is it true?"

Kryssa swallowed as her guilt came rushing back, and she lowered her eyes, suddenly unable to meet her lover's gaze. "It's true," she whispered. "Though it was not by any order. Braidon wanted them protected, but he was betrayed by his followers. Those responsible were hung for their crime…but it was I who failed. I promised to protect them."

"Promised who?"

"The Elder who served this Castle," Kryssa croaked. "He had power, admitted to performing their vile cleansings. He claimed to want only peace, but I didn't care, not after everything I had lost. I drove him from the pantheon—from the people he was protecting. We hunted him down, saw him killed. And while we were occupied…" She broke off as her grief spilled over, choking her throat.

Warm arms wrapped Kryssa in their embrace. She folded into the huntress and sobbed onto her shoulder until the tears finally dried. Then Kryssa sat back, wiping the tears from her cheeks.

"It's not your fault, Krys," Genevieve said, lifting her chin so their eyes met. "You could not have known."

"I should have."

"It's done, Krys," Genevieve insisted. "You can't change it, so you must find a way to live with it. To make things better."

Kryssa swallowed and said nothing, but when Genevieve refused to look away, finally she nodded. A long breath whispered from her throat. "Okay, Gen."

Genevieve kissed her brow. "Good," she said. "Now, it's

your turn to tell a story. I've only heard up to where Caledan left you. Tell me the rest, my love."

So Kryssa did, starting from Braidon's fight with Caledan, how it had woken the king from his stupor and put him on the path of vengeance. How they had bartered with the Red Dragon, then ridden the beast to Chole. How Dominic had recognised them, had sheltered them in his home, and led them to the Temple of the Earth. How Braidon had stood alone against the Knights of Alana and used the power of his own life force to defeat them. How Kryssa herself had used the same power against the Elder, when the mob stormed the Castle.

And how Dominic had murdered all those innocent souls who had taken refuge in the pantheon.

She finished the last parts in a croaky whisper—about the execution and the assassination attempt, the tribal leader's rejection of Braidon's kingship, and of the Red Dragons' arrival in the city.

"You've had quite the adventure yourself," Genevieve said when Kryssa finished, gently running a hand across her cheek. "I wish I could have seen you in action," she added, kissing her on the cheek.

Kryssa smiled and kissed Genevieve back. "I should never have stayed," she replied. "I should have followed my instincts and left, gone looking for the two of you."

"As single-minded as you can be, my love, I don't think even you could have plucked us from the depths of that mine," Genevieve replied gently. "It was better you were here, protecting the king." Her eyes darted sideways for a half a second, before returning to Kryssa. "You are sure about him?"

A lump lodged in Kryssa's throat as all her doubts came

rushing to the fore. Braidon had never stopped fighting for the side of good, had sacrificed so much for Plorsea, and yet…

No, she insisted to herself. *My father believed in Braidon.*

How she missed Devon now. He had always been so calm, so reassured. Even in the face of battle the hammerman had been undaunted, giving courage to those who stood around him. If only she could hear his voice, to know they were on the right path.

But there was only her own voice, her own conscience now, and drawing in a great breath, she nodded.

"I'm sure," she whispered, then: "He's all we have."

A smile touched Genevieve's lips. "Then I will stand."

22

P ela woke to the warmth of light against her face. Blinking, she pushed herself up, then suppressed a groan as her entire body screamed out in protest. Sinking back to the cold earth, she placed a hand across her face to shield herself from the sun. Her heart was racing as though she'd just run a great distance, but she could not recall why.

Cracking open her eyes, she took a moment to look around, trying to remember what she'd done the night before. She'd had such strange dreams…but they must still be on the road to Kalgan, for now she found herself in a narrow canyon with tall cliffs stretching up towards a red sky. The earth was hard beneath her and after a moment she tried sitting up again. This time it was slightly more bearable.

Her eyes alighted on Ruebyn, lying nearby, but there was no sign of the Trolan soldiers. She frowned—they had never been left unattended before, nor did she recognise the land around them. She looked upwards again. The sun must have still be rising for the sky to be so red…and yet she could not find its orange glow anywhere.

She crawled across to Ruebyn on screaming arms and shook him. He gave a groan, and then his eyes flickered. He frowned, then suddenly snapped bold upright.

"Where is it?" he gasped, struggling to his feet.

Pela groaned as he tried to drag her up, her muscles protesting. "Where is what?"

"Rayan!" Ruebyn cried. "The demon!"

The demon!

His words set off an explosion in her mind. A scream built in her throat as memory of Kalgan and Rayan came rushing back. She saw again the smiling king, the armies marching across the land, the desiccated bodies and Rayan stalking towards them, his eyes changing to the pitch-black of a demon…

Coming to her feet, she clasped desperately at Ruebyn. They swung around, searching for their foe, but there was only the narrow canyon, only the warmth from above.

Pela frowned, her sense of wrongness growing. She stared at the scarlet sky, realising it had not changed since her waking, that there was not a cloud or sun or moon in sight. A shiver went through her as a desperate, terrifying thought came to her…

"The Way," Ruebyn whispered. "It's actually real."

A lump lodged in Pela's throat, but she swallowed it back down. They stood there for a long moment, struggling to comprehend what had happened, where they were. The land around them was barren, without any sign of life—not even a blade of grass grew between the cracks in the cliffs.

"Can it follow us?" Pela whispered at last.

"I…" Ruebyn frowned. "Like I said before…The Way

was a meeting place during the Great Wars. Only one party could enter from either end, so there could be no treachery. If that's true, no, it cannot come after us so long as we're inside."

Relief struck Pela like a blow. She slumped against Ruebyn, sobbing great gasps of joy. They had escaped, they were safe! Somehow, inexplicably, they had eluded Rayan and all his power. Clutching at Ruebyn, she remembered those last, desperate moments, how his words had steadied her, how he had found his courage in the face of the demon's darkness.

Pulling away slightly, she found him staring at her, just as he had back in the tomb. His eyes shone with unspoken emotion and she swallowed.

"How?" she whispered, feeling safe in his arms. "How did you know it could be done?"

"I didn't," he replied, "but I knew *you* could do it." With the words, he leaned in close and pressed his forehead to hers.

"Why?" she croaked.

"Why not?" he chuckled. "After everything I've seen you do, what was one more miracle? If anyone was going to open an imaginary doorway to another world, it would be you." He smiled as he said it, taking any sting from his words.

Pela cupped his cheek, seeing again the man she had found in the mountains, his kindness, his courage. "I've been so terrible to you," she croaked, scrunching her eyes closed to keep the tears from falling. One escaped anyway, the hot liquid streaking her cheek. "I should have trusted you, should have gone back when you said something was wrong with Trola."

Chuckling, Ruebyn wiped away the tear. "No," he replied. "I was the fool, for not believing you about your magic."

Laughter bubbled up from Pela's throat. "You are a fool," she said with a smile. Then standing on her tiptoes, she kissed him on the lips. "But you're my fool."

Ruebyn chuckled as he kissed her back and then they were falling to the ground. Pela's heart raced as their kisses slowed, their tongues dancing against one another to a music of their own making. The smoky taste of him filled her mouth, and she shivered as his hands traced patterns across her back.

Desire burned in her chest, a need for them to be together, to celebrate their very existence. They were alive, had escaped, were safe! She plucked at the buttons of Ruebyn's shirt, suddenly regretting all the cold nights they had spent separate.

They broke apart and Ruebyn's lips moved to her neck, raising goosebumps wherever they touched. By then she had his shirt undone. He shivered as she slid her hands over his chest, enjoying the warmth of his skin, the fire in his body. Suddenly she could hardly feel her own aches, could barely remember the fear that had so filled her just a short while ago. Beneath that strange, sunless sky, there was nothing but herself and Ruebyn, only his body and hers.

A moan built in her chest as Ruebyn's kisses moved to the small of her throat. Impatient, she sat up, and taking the hint, Ruebyn helped to pull the shirt over her head. Before it was even completely gone, he was back at work. Flames lit in Pela's stomach as his tongue traced circles around the mounds of her breasts.

Growling, she slid her fingers through his hair, directing

his mouth where she wanted it to go. A gasp escaped her as he obeyed, the heat in her centre swelling to a roar. Blood pounded in her ears as she tugged the shirt from his shoulders, as her fingers trailed down his stomach, plucked at his belt…

Afterwards, Pela lay nestled against Ruebyn's chest as he snored softly, the flames at her core finally sated. She could hardly believe it had happened, but she knew now there would be no more doubts, no more hesitation. Whatever happened, wherever this strange land took them, she wanted Ruebyn at her side.

Ruebyn twitched in his sleep and his eyes flickered open. He smiled when he saw her awake, and reaching, he stroked a hand through her silver hair. She smiled, moving her body closer to his.

"What are you thinking about?" he whispered in her ear.

"Oh, everything," she replied, "and nothing."

He grunted. "They're not our worries anymore."

"Aren't they?" She tried to give him a stern look, but the innocent glint in his eyes made her smile. "And why is that?" she whispered, kissing him on the cheek.

To her disappointment, Ruebyn sat up. She felt so at peace entwined around him, she never wanted to let go. She remained on the ground as he stood, her naked body inviting him to return to her arms. Flashing her a grin, he nudged her with his foot, and with a dramatic sigh, she joined him. Looping a hand around her waist, he pulled her close.

"We're in a whole other world," he said, "a whole other place. Even time is said to move differently here. The demon can no longer touch us, nor the Knights or the queen or anyone else. Why don't we just stay?"

"Stay?" Pela's eyes widened at the thought. "We can't stay!"

"Why not?"

"I…" She trailed off, then managed: "It's a wasteland, we would starve."

Her stomach rumbled at the words and casting her eyes around, she found their bag of food nearby. Rummaging inside, she pulled out the sausage and sat on a rock. Ruebyn raised an eyebrow as she tore a chunk off the salami with her teeth, and grinning, she held it out to him.

Taking it with a nod, he joined her on the rock. "It doesn't look like a wasteland anymore," he said as he ate.

Pela frowned, but as she turned to the rocky canyon, she saw what he meant. All around them, The Way had changed as they slept—was still changing. Where before there had been barren rock and broken gravels, bare cliffs and a blood-red sky, now life sprang unbidden amongst the stones. Grass grew from the earth and here and there around them, daisies blossomed, bright yellow beneath a now violet sky. Vines twisted their way up the cliffs, swirling and changing, red and yellow and blue roses appearing amidst the thorny tendrils.

"What is happening?" Pela whispered.

"A better question would be why?" Ruebyn replied.

She sighed as he ran his hand through her hair again, her eyes fluttering closed. "Why?" she whispered absently.

"Because of us? Because of you?"

Pela shook her head, her eyes still closed. Now she could smell the scent of the flowers, taste the freshness on the air, as though it had just been raining. Shivering, she opened her eyes to look at Ruebyn, wondering at his words.

"This was a tormented place once," he explained. "Cursed by the Gods or by Archon, the tales differ. But all say it had become the domain of a demon."

Fear shot up Pela's spine at his words and she tried to pull away, to grab for her clothes, but Ruebyn held her tight.

"Relax, that demon was destroyed long ago!" he gasped, a grin on his face. "Now, where was I? Oh, yes. Some of the earliest tales have it that The Way was a beautiful place before its corruption, a place of peace. But even though that demon is gone, the balance was never restored. *Life* was never restored."

"I still don't understand," she said.

Ruebyn slid his fingers under her chin and lifted her head to kiss her. She shivered as he held her close, enjoying the feel of his body against hers.

"Maybe I'm just a romantic," Ruebyn said finally as they broke apart, "but I wonder at this place. It is strange, different to anything in the Three Nations. If we follow your legends, it was Archon's hatred that corrupted this place." He swallowed, locking eyes with her. "Perhaps…perhaps our love is restoring that balance."

Pela stared at him for a long moment, then burst into laughter. Bending in two, she let her mirth ring from the canyon walls. It was a long time before she recovered, and all the while Ruebyn sat alongside her, a sheepish look on his face. Finally she straightened, and catching her breath, offered an apologetic grin.

"Sorry," she murmured, leaning forward to kiss his cheek, before adding: "I love you too, Ruebyn." Her laughter burst out again. "But you really are too much sometimes!" She danced away as he tried to grab her.

Leaping to his feet, Ruebyn snatched her back and kissed her. A soft *oh* slipped from her lips as she sank into his embrace.

"So what do you think?" he asked finally, resting his temple against hers.

"About staying?" she whispered, eyes closed, breathing in the scent of him.

The thought sent a tremor down to her very soul, and for a moment she truly considered it. Perhaps they *could* stay here, away from the darkness, away from the war and strife that had gripped the Three Nations for a thousand years. The demon could not reach them, and no one else in Plorsea even knew The Way still existed. They would be safe…

…But her mother would not be. She and Ruebyn might have escaped the demon, but eventually Rayan would come for the east. How long before he marched with his armies? In the vision she had seen, the blue-armoured soldiers had been legion—ten thousand men just as cruel as the patrol that had taken them. Divided, the east would not stand a chance.

Not in two hundred years had the Three Nations seen such a threat, not since the days of Archon.

And no one even knew it was coming.

What would Devon think if Pela did nothing? What would her uncle say, if he knew Pela had turned her back on those she loved?

Letting out a long breath, she pulled away. Her vision blurred as she looked up at Ruebyn. "I'm sorry," she croaked. "I can't. I have to go back. I have to warn them, Ruebyn."

He stared at her for so long Pela began to think he had not heard her, that she had only imagined speaking the words, that this had all been some hallucination in her mind, and she was truly back in the cavern beneath the wall, trapped in the webs of the demon's spell.

With a smile, Ruebyn suddenly hugged her tight. "I expected no less," he said softly. Looking around, his eyes settled on their clothes. "Come on then," he added, "we'd best get going. If time really does move differently here, who knows what's happened back in the real world."

Watching him move way, it was Pela's turn to smile. Quickly, she stepped up behind him and slid her arms around his waist.

"Not just yet," she murmured in his ear. "I think we still have a few minutes to spare."

❧ 23 ❧

Standing outside the gates of Chole, Caledan looked up at the ancient walls. They stretched high above, the giant blocks of granite shining in the rising sun. No army had ever taken them, and without scaling ladders they would be impossible to climb. But that mattered little against what Marianne and her forces would hurl against them. The explosive powder had already been loaded into the catapults. The gates would fall within the hour.

If the information Marianne's spies had provided was correct, the battle would not last much longer. Braidon had less than a thousand fighters inside the walls, plus a handful of Red Dragons. The beasts concerned Caledan, but Marianne was confident she had power enough to handle the creatures should they try to intervene.

Caledan had stationed their army well back from the walls, well outside the range of the defender's longbows. The seven thousand-odd men and women of Marianne's army waited behind him, their eyes fixed on the distant ramparts. A squadron of veterans and Knights who had joined Marianne's side waited around him, the backbone of the army. They would be the first through when the gates fell, to face whatever threat waited on the other side.

Marianne did not have the numbers to completely encircle the city—not without thinning her army enough to be vulnerable—so they had chosen to launch a frontal assault, relying on their superior numbers and weaponry to sweep away the defenders.

The king must have guessed their strategy though, for a glance at the walls revealed only a few dozen defenders on the ramparts. Braidon had seen first-hand in Malevolent Cove the power of Lonia's black powder. He knew the walls could not be defended against such a weapon. The bulk of his forces had no doubt been stationed beyond the gates, ready to defend the inevitable breach.

A horn sounded behind Caledan, back amongst the ranks where Marianne waited. It was the order to begin the attack, and Caledan swallowed, casting one glance back. He had argued his place was at the queen's side, but she had insisted he lead the assault, that no one else could be trusted. She was protected by her Queen's Guard, yet even so…

No, it was too late to second-guess their plan now. Casting one last glance at the sky, Caledan pointed his sword at the gates.

"Set distance!" he bellowed.

At his command, two catapults lurched against the hard earth, their arms springing forward to hurl rocks at the distant walls. Each had been carefully measured to weigh the same as the barrels of black powder. The engineers watched the projectiles closely as they arched high and then plunged back down towards the enemy. There was a dull *thud* as they struck empty earth a dozen yards short of the gates.

"Adjust!" Caledan shouted. The engineers leapt to obey, resetting their machines with the new distance. When they were done and Caledan received the confirmation, he pointed again. "Fire!"

Another set of rocks arced upwards, and this time they fell true, slamming into the gates with a double *crack*. The heavy timbers shook on their hinges but held tight.

Caledan stared at the walls of Chole, waiting, praying that Braidon would signal the surrender. The king had to know what would come next. The gates could not withstand the black powder, and once they were gone…no force within the city would stop the invaders. Anything could happen then, and while Marianne had given strict orders for the citizens to remain unharmed…Caledan did not trust the Lonian forces to obey. Bitterness ran deep amongst the Lonian soldiers, an anger embedded by the decades their nation had been enslaved beneath the rule of the Plorsean Tsar.

Beneath Braidon's father.

Now their time for revenge had finally come, it was difficult to see them holding back. Caledan could not blame them for their anger, but he would do everything in his power to see his queen's orders obeyed. If only he could spare Kryssa and Genevieve…but his friends were warriors. They would go wherever the fighting was thickest. There was nothing Caledan could do for them.

"*Fire!*" he bellowed finally when it became obvious the surrender would not come.

Two barrels arched into the sky, a thin cloud of smoke trailing out behind them from the fuses. If the engineers had been successful, the powder would ignite at just the right moment—

Boom.

Caledan staggered as a tower of flame erupted from the gates. A cry went up from the Plorsean veterans gathered around him—they had never seen this new weapon in action—while the Knights of Alana only stood in silence, watching as the black powder devoured their enemies.

The column of flame engulfed the gates and rushed upwards, the power of the explosion slamming into the stone ramparts above. For a moment it seemed the ancient walls would resist the terrible inferno—they had survived beasts and dragons and Archon himself, after all. But then the stones itself seemed to lift. Time seemed to slow as Caledan watched the enormous granite blocks surrounding the gate begin to crumble.

The inferno surged on, swallowing wood and stone and human flesh in an instant, then dying back to embers as its fuel was spent. Then there was only a thick column of smoke left where Chole's gate had been, only rubble where once an impenetrable wall had barred their path.

It was time.

"Ready?" Caledan bellowed, raising his sword and pointing the way. "Charge!"

The Knights and veterans gave an answering roar, and then they were racing across the two hundred yards to the rubble-strewn breach. Chole's walls still stood to either side, but the remaining defenders were scattered and broken, their morale shattered. A few recovered their bows and began to fire down at the oncoming army, but Caledan had Lonian crossbow men stationed on either flank, and they began to fire back, their steel bolts peppering the ramparts.

With their superior range, the steel weapons took a terrible toll, and the defenders soon ducked back behind the crenulations.

Reassured Braidon's archers were occupied, Caledan risked another glance at the sky, but there was still no sign of the Red Dragons. He had held back several catapults, loaded with barrels of the black powder and steel shrapnel. Detonated mid-air, they would tear the dragons from the sky should they decide to attack. But perhaps the beasts had already seen the futility of the king's cause, and abandoned the fight?

Several of the veterans had drawn ahead of Caledan, their eagerness to reach the fight overcoming their training. He bellowed an order and all but one slowed, reforming into their ranks as they approached the smoking ruin that had been the gates. The wall might already have fallen, but Braidon's forces still waited within. A man alone would quickly be cut down.

They slowed again as the wind sent smoke swirling around them. On either side of Caledan he glimpsed the ruin of the walls, the battlements warped and broken by the explosion, even where they still stood. Giant blocks of stone lay scattered all around, impeding their advance.

Caledan tried to organise his men into tighter ranks, but shouts came from behind them as the less disciplined of Marianne's followers caught up with the vanguard. Cursing, Caledan found himself wishing he'd ordered the rest of the army to hold back.

But the way ahead was clear. All they needed to do was pass through the rubble and the city belonged to Marianne. Bellowing above the voices coming from behind, Caledan urged his force onward. The smoke swallowed them up, acrid and tasting faintly of sulphur, thick enough that Caledan's eyes were soon watering.

Forcing himself through the press of bodies, Caledan strained to reach the front ranks and take command. Braidon was no strategist, but neither was the king a coward. He would not be hiding in his Castle, and it was only a matter of time before he launched a counterattack. Caledan intended to be ready when it came.

The ruined walls lingered like shadows amidst the smoke to either side of Caledan as he neared the front ranks. Just a few more yards and the battle would begin in earnest—unless Braidon attacked before Marianne's forces escaped the rubble. The thought gave Caledan pause and he strained to see through the smoke. It was finally beginning to thin. He watched as buildings took shape, the red slate roofs of the city, rippling and shining in the sun.

Caledan frowned. Something wasn't right…

Then an awful roar thundered in the breach, and all hell broke loose. Suddenly men were screaming and throwing down their weapons, fighting against one another in their desperation to retreat. For a moment Caledan could only stare in disbelief and confusion—and then the last of the smoke blew away, and finally he saw the truth.

A dragon sat crouched behind the breach, its scarlet scales shining in the morning sun. Staring into the maw of the beast, Caledan had only a moment to appreciate the brilliance of Braidon's plan. The king had known Marianne could thwart any outright attack the Red Dragons might launch.

But he had also known the gates would fall, and that Marianne's forces would quickly storm the breach. He'd left just enough soldiers atop the walls to assuage their suspicions, so that they would not realise the dragon waited beyond the gates.

A brilliant glow appeared in the throat of the dragon as its jaws stretched wide. Men were streaming past Caledan now, shrieking and scrambling over one another, becoming a stampede. But Caledan had seen a dragon's flames first-hand in Malevolent Cove. There would be no escape, not for any of them.

With another roar, scarlet flames belched from the beast and rushed across the killing ground into which they had been lured. The first ranks of soldiers vanished into the inferno, Knights and veterans incinerated in an instant.

Caledan closed his eyes, and lifting his blade, he waited for the end to come. A wall of heat swept over him, and the screams of his comrades fell abruptly silent. His arms shook as his flesh began to sear, but an answering vibration began in his sword, and the heat lessoned.

His eyes snapped open. They immediately began to water, as the flames bore down on him—but somehow, he wasn't burning. The inferno was all around him now, but it came no closer, held back by the rainbow glow of the sword in his hands.

Then a sharp screech came from the blade, and the multi-coloured light flickered. Caledan watched in horror as a crack spread through the steel. Whatever spell Marianne had cast was fading beneath the dragon's onslaught. Shuddering, Caledan started to back away, even as he felt the heat returning.

But the firestorm was dissipating as well, the roar of the dragon fading away. Caledan choked as the flames suddenly flickered out, to be replaced by the stench of burning flesh. Now he saw the bodies lying around him, the blackened remnants of his Plorsean comrades, the twisted scraps of metal that had been the Knights.

The roar of human voices carried over the crackling of flames still burning amidst the ruins. Caledan's head jerked up as a great gust swept away the smoke, revealing the soldiers charging from the city. They rushed across the blackened ground, swords and shields held high, screaming their triumph.

And at their head was a man in shining armour, his sword lit from within by a brilliant white, a golden crown upon his brow.

Braidon.

Caledan watched as his lifelong enemy rushed towards him. For a moment he was filled with a desire to meet the man with sword in hand, to finally take his revenge. But Marianne's army was in disarray, her vanguard destroyed. If someone did not take control, the battle would be lost.

Gritting his teeth, Caledan turned and fled. Not one other soul who had entered the breach had survived the dragon fire, and as he leapt from the rubble, Caledan found the ranks that had come after them in disarray. Men and woman stumbled across the parched earth, many sporting burns, while others had lost their weapons in the chaos. With the best of Marianne's fighters already dead, the army was on the brink of collapse.

"Soldiers, on me!" Caledan bellowed.

Several faces turned in his direction, but their eyes showed only shock and few seemed to understand what he was saying. Cursing, Caledan grabbed the nearest man and spun him to face the enemy.

"Swords up!" he screamed, and finally the man seemed to understand.

Caledan continued the process, until more than two dozen men and women stood with him, weapons held at the ready. The sight seemed to bring order to the rest of Marianne's forces, and for a moment calm returned to their ranks.

Then the king emerged from the smoke, walking slowly now. Two women appeared behind him, and Caledan's heart fell as he recognised Kryssa and Genevieve, both decked now in the scarlet and golden uniform of the King's Guard. More soldiers followed, hundreds of them marching in line.

At their front, Braidon lifted his sword, and the white light flashed out across the battlefield.

"This is your last chance, traitors!" His words crashed across the plains like thunder. "Surrender, and I will spare your lives!"

A tremor swept through the ranks around Caledan and he cursed, sensing their fear. The king was still badly outnumbered, but Marianne's soldiers had already seen the best of their comrades obliterated before their eyes. Now the King of Plorsea stood before them with a magic sword offering survival…

"Enough!"

Caledan swung around as Marianne's voice carried over the battlefield, an equal to Braidon's command. Stillness fell as every soul held his breath. Ripples spread through the ranks of soldiers behind him, and then the queen herself appeared. She strode through her followers, her scarlet dress swirling with each step and lightning crackling at her fingertips.

"Enough of the bloodshed, Braidon," she cried. "It's time this ended."

The king and his soldiers had frozen at Marianne's appearance, and now they waited as she emerged into the open. Caledan shivered as she glanced back at her army, seeing the silent resolve, her determination to end this battle once and for all. Her gaze seemed to focus on him, and for a second her mask cracked, and he saw the joy in her face, the relief he had survived. A smile touched her lips, then her attention returned to the enemy.

"Marianne," Braidon said softly. He stepped from the ranks of his soldiers, arms spread. In his silver armour and with shining sword in hand, he looked for all the world like the battle king of his early days. "Your army is sundered," he continued, "your power proven naught but illusion. Now you stand here begging for leniency?"

"I would face you myself."

Braidon laughed in her face. "You, or your champion?" He grinned. "Did you think I would not hear the tale?" His eyes flickered to Caledan, then back to Marianne. "No, Marianne, I will not fight you. But I offer the same bargain you extended to me. Surrender now, and your people will go free. Only you need suffer for your crimes."

"I spent eight long years suffering you, sweet husband," Marianne spat. "I have no intention of returning to my bonds." Then she smiled. "And I wasn't asking your permission."

At that the queen threw out her arms. An awful *boom* rang from the walls as lightning leapt from her hands. Braidon recoiled and raised his sword as though to defend himself, but the blade became a lightning rod, and with a *crack*, the blue fire exploded through the steel.

Blazing light lit the plain and Caledan was forced to cover his eyes, even as the shriek of rending metal tore at his ears. He clenched his teeth and waited for the brilliance to dim, then spun to face the enemy again.

Smoke clung to where Braidon had been, but now a breeze blew across the battlefield. The air cleared, revealing the king standing untouched—though his apparently magic sword now lay in the dirt, a mess of molten steel. Rage twisted Braidon's face as he looked at Marianne.

"Oh my dear wife," he whispered, "how I have waited for this moment."

His hands flashed up, though no lighting or fire emerged from the king. For a moment it seemed his magic had failed —then a dozen yards away, Marianne gasped. Her hands clasped desperately at her throat, though not a mark showed on her flesh.

Sneering, Braidon stalked closer, one hand outstretched as though to throttle her. Behind him, Kryssa and Genevieve watched on from the ranks of soldiers, their faces pale.

"I am not powerless anymore," the king hissed. "Your disciples gave me power when they died in my Castle, and on the shore of Malevolent Cove. Enough to match your hateful curses."

He was closing in now, barely ten yards from the queen. Caledan's heart throbbed in his chest as he watched the silent battle, sword still clutched tightly in one hand. It was ruined, the steel cracked and broken, the spell probably destroyed. But he was still the Queen's Champion. He could not stand by while Braidon murdered her.

Silently he slipped closer. The two armies had drawn close together now, almost forming a ring around the two monarchs, but the soldiers were watching the silent battle and did not notice the sellswords movements. Dull gasping noises came from Marianne as she clutched at her neck, as though she were trying to breathe through a reed pipe.

Caledan's hands shook and his heart beat faster. He was as close as he could get, at the very edge of the crowd. Another step and Braidon was sure to see him. There was no other choice. Gradually, he drew back his arm, then with sudden speed, he hurled his sword.

The blade hissed as it slashed the air, flashing for Braidon's chest. Caledan saw the surprise flash across Kryssa's face, but Braidon had left his King's Guard behind and now they were too far away to intervene. Caledan's aim was true—but at the last second a flicker crossed Braidon's face, and suddenly he was spinning, his arm coming up…

Boom.

Caledan staggered as an explosion rang out over the plains. The earth rippled beneath him like a wave, as though Braidon's magic had turned it to water, and he was forced to one knee. Gasping, Marianne staggered back and fell to her knees as the king's spell broke. Across the battlefield, the soldiers did the same.

Looking to the king, Caledan wondered what new power Braidon had unleashed. But the man seemed similarly perplexed. Caledan's sword had shattered as it struck Braidon's outstretched hands, but the king's attention was already elsewhere, his eyes on the distant city. A frown marked the king's forehead, while on the ground nearby Marianne gulped in great mouthfuls of air, momentarily forgotten by her enemy.

Following Braidon's gaze, Caledan gaped as the walls of Chole seemed to come alive, the stone warping and twisting, becoming a shimmering, boiling cacophony of colour. Another *boom* followed, as of a door blowing open, and the light exploded outwards. A blazing spiral spun over heads of the gathered armies and came to land not far from where Marianne and Braidon had been fighting. Men and women leapt aside as it crashed to the earth, still spinning and swirling, mesmerising in its brilliance. If Caledan had been able to stand, he might have gone to it, such was its call, but all he could do was watch as the silhouette of two humans took shape within the vortex.

Now the brilliance began to fade. Caledan could not begin to comprehend what was happening, but he knew in his heart one thing—this was true magic, unlike anything that had been seen in the last thirty years.

With one final flash, the light vanished. A young man and woman were left standing in its place, the earth scorched beneath their feet. The man sported short brown hair and hazel eyes that seemed equal parts terrified and amazed by what had just happened, while the woman... recognition shot down Caledan's spine, but before he could call her name, another voice cried over the heads of the army, a cry filled with joy and terror and love.

"Pela!"

"**P**ela!"

The cry had left Kryssa's lips before she could think better of it. She stared across the battlefield, the sword heavy in her hand, unable to believe what she was seeing. Surely this was some dream. She must be still lying in her bed back in Chole, enfolded in Genevieve's embrace. This could not be real…

Yet here she was, Genevieve at her side and the king nearby, surrounded by death and destruction, the very earth scorched by the ferocity of the battle.

And there was her daughter, standing with the strange boy, midway between the opposing forces. She guessed the boy was the overseer Genevieve had spoken of. He looked almost as shocked as Kryssa felt. Horror appeared on his face as he saw the destruction, the burnt bodies lying amidst the rubble nearby. He blanched and turned away, dry retching.

In contrast, Pela stood straight, her sapphire eyes shining

as she surveyed her surroundings. They took in the ranks of soldiers, lingering on the king and then flickering to the queen. Marianne was just getting to her feet, and fast as lightning, Pela swept up a fallen blade and stepped between the young man and the woman.

A smile touched Kryssa's lips at her daughter's fierceness. She cast a glance at Braidon, but the king was as shocked as anyone. All across the battlefield, the soldiers of both sides stood staring at the newcomers. No one spoke, and heart beating hard in her chest, Kryssa started towards them.

Pela spun at the sound of approaching footsteps, her sword coming up. Her eyes widened as they settled on Kryssa, her mouth falling open.

"*Mum!*" she screamed.

Then they were both running, and Kryssa was throwing open her arms, drawing Pela into her embrace. A sob tore from her chest as they clung to each other. Hardly daring to believe this was real, she drew in a breath, savouring the scent of her daughter's hair, the feel of her arms around her waist.

"Mum, what are you doing here?" Pela gasped finally. Tears streaked her cheek as she pulled away.

Kryssa offered a faint smile. "I could ask you the same thing, missie."

The hint of a grin touched her daughter's cheeks. "That's…a very long story." Her eyes drifted away, then widened in surprise. In an instant she had released Kryssa and dodged around her. "Gen!" she cried, her voice lifted in joy.

Genevieve's laughter carried over the plains as Pela

tackled her. The huntress staggered several steps before recovering her balance and hugging Pela back. Kryssa watched the surreal moment in bemusement, the surrounding armies momentarily forgotten.

"I see you two have bonded," she said after a moment, laughing softly. Then remembering the young man still standing awkwardly nearby, she held out her hand. "Kryssa," she said in greeting. "I hear you are a friend of my daughter's?"

The boy's cheeks grew red and he coughed and spluttered in such a way that Kryssa's was left with no doubt he was more than just Pela's friend.

"Ruebyn!" he managed finally, accepting her hand.

Shaking her head, Kryssa turned back to her daughter.

"I thought you were dead," Pela was saying as she danced hand-in-hand with Genevieve. "The Knight said he'd killed you!"

Pain flickered across Genevieve's face at the memory, but she forced a smile. "He decided I was more valuable as a prisoner." She swallowed, her eyes drawn to where Marianne stood. "I…would still be a prisoner if not for the queen."

"*What?*" Pela gasped.

Glancing around, Kryssa's senses finally came rushing back. The four of them stood in the middle of a battlefield, and while the magical conflagration had brought about a temporary truce, the battle could resume at any moment. She drew herself up and stepped between her daughter and the queen.

"She is still the enemy," Braidon said as he joined them.

Genevieve said nothing and Kryssa glanced at her, remembering their midnight conversation. But Braidon was right. They had managed a great victory, but the battle was not over yet. Marianne was still a threat. After everything she'd done, all the evil she'd wrought across the Three Nations, she could not go unopposed—

"No!" Pela's voice lifted above the others.

Kryssa spun as her daughter strode forward, placing herself between the king and queen. Braidon's forehead creased into a frown, while beyond Marianne had resumed her usual self-assured smile. Kryssa could not understand the woman's confidence, not with her army in tatters, and her magic so clearly outmatched by Braidon's. But Caledan had joined her now, the slick swordsman like a second shadow; perhaps his presence gave her strength.

"Pela, what are you doing?" Genevieve asked, stepping up beside Kryssa.

"It doesn't matter," Braidon answered. Energy crackled in his hands as he faced Marianne. "She must be stopped."

"*No!*" Pela said again, holding out her hands. She looked from Braidon to the queen, her jaw hard, eyes wide with fear. "Please, you have to listen. This fighting, it has to stop, before you destroy us all!"

"I say we listen to the girl, sweet husband," Marianne chuckled. She strode forward and halted a few paces from Pela. "Unless you're too afraid of losing your advantage?"

Braidon bared his teeth. "I'll not fall for your tricks, woman," he snapped, raising a hand.

"*Enough!*" Pela screamed, and now her voice was thunder, ringing out to crash upon the walls of Chole.

Kryssa staggered, shocked to realise her daughter had learned how to tap into her life force. Neither Pela nor Ruebyn seemed surprised by the effect, but Braidon's eyes also showed his amazement at her use of power. It gave him pause, and Pela spoke into the silence.

"I know you hate one another," Pela continued, her voice low now, though it still carried to the ears of every soldier on the battlefield. "But whatever our grievances, whatever our allegiances, they no longer matter. We have been to Trola. There is a darkness there, a demon that will consume us all if we do not stand together."

"What nonsense are you talking about?" Braidon snapped. "No one is allowed to enter Trola."

"We took refuge there, fleeing *her* Knights," Pela replied, swinging on Marianne. "We escaped from your mines and entered Trola through the mountains. We expected to find salvation, but there is only death there now."

"What are you saying, Pela?" Marianne whispered, her eyes shimmering. "What death do you talk of?"

"They said it was a plague." A shiver went through Kryssa at the mention, but her daughter went on: "Perhaps it *was* a plague of sorts, but it came from no disease. The creature needed to feed, to sate its hunger with the life force of innocents. Trola is a dead place now. Only a few remain, slaves to the demon's magic, their lives preserved so that it might feed."

Silence fell as Pela finished. Kryssa watched on, wondering what madness had overcome her daughter. How could a demon have taken Trola without anyone being the wiser? It couldn't be possible…but then, there had been no communication with the western nation in more than a decade…

Her eyes fell on Braidon, seeing the doubt in his face, the sudden indecision. If the demon truly existed, then Pela was right—this petty war meant nothing, and every death was only another soul lost to the fight against the darkness.

But only if Pela spoke the truth.

"You are exhausted, child," Marianne said softly, approaching Pela. "Whatever magic you used to come to this place was powerful. Perhaps you saw a vision of this demon, but I do not believe it to be a true one. Ardath received communication from Trola only recently, speaking of a reopening…"

"Lies!" Pela shrieked. "The king is a puppet to the demon's will. It has an army, soldiers loyal only to its strength, and power enough to destroy us all. You cannot fight them alone, cannot fight *it*. We only stand a chance together."

"I will *never* work with her," Braidon snarled, stepping past Kryssa and approaching Pela. "Maybe what you say is true, Pela, but Marianne is as bad as any demon. We cannot trust her. The second she sees an advantage, she will betray us."

"But—"

"I'm sorry, young Pela," Marianne murmured. She no longer looked at the girl, but stood staring at Braidon. "My dear husband is right in one thing at least—we can never work together." She raised a fist and light spilled between her clenched fingers.

A rainbow swirled around Braidon. "Get away, Pela," he growled. "If there truly is a demon, I will stand against it— once I have dealt with *her!*" He pointed a finger, and the light strengthened to the point of blinding…

"*No!*" Pela screamed, and now it was her turn to throw out her arms.

A shimmering yellow glow rushed from Pela, encasing

all who stood nearby—Braidon and Marianne and Caledan, Kryssa and Genevieve and Ruebyn. The king cried out, throwing up his arms to defend himself, while the queen staggered, her eyes widening in surprise. But neither could be harmed by the light, not by the power of only a single life.

But they could be shown.

A scream sounded in Kryssa's mind, of a thousand voices crying out as one, and suddenly she was in another place, another time. She watched as darkness swept from the walls of a great city, spreading across the land, swallowing all in its path. Then she was on the streets of a town, watching a figure stride the cobbled paths. Men and women fell dying before it, their skin shrivelling to wrinkled husks, their screams falling silent.

In desperation, parents told their children to flee before turning to face the demon. With swords and bows and rocks, they attacked the creature with all they had, but nothing could slow the monster. One by one they fell, their lives sucked away, and still the darkness came on. Horror tore from Kryssa's throat as the children were overtaken and their lives were sucked away by the demon's greed.

Finally the image faded, and Kryssa found herself again on the battlefield. She staggered as her eyes caught on the blackened body of a man. Bile burned her throat as she saw the death all around with fresh eyes, as she realised the atrocities her own people had committed upon one another.

So much pain, so much waste, and for what? So a king and queen could decide which would rule them? What did it matter? Life was so short, so precious; how could they have thrown it away so wilfully? What did any of it matter, when such a darkness approached, if they were all to be enslaved by the demon?

Shivering, she looked at Braidon and Marianne, and knew they had seen the same as her. She held her breath, waiting for what would come next.

The spell had taken the strength from Pela, and now she crouched on one knee, her face pale and panting, her eyes on the monarchs. Ruebyn moved to her side and knelt beside her, offering his reassurance. Kryssa shivered and searched for Genevieve. Finding the huntress nearby, she reached out and entwined her fingers with those of her lover.

Braidon's face was pale, his hands trembling. The queen was in a similar state, and as Kryssa watched, a single tear streaked her cheek. She swallowed visibly, then with one trembling hand, reached up and wiped the tear away.

"Well, that was something," Marianne murmured.

A tremor shook the king as he scrunched his eyes closed, as though he were fighting some great internal battle. His hands opened and closed, and Kryssa could sense the power radiating from him.

Finally his eyes snapped open. "We have to stop it," he whispered. Another convulsion shook, his eyes shimmering. "But how can I trust you, Marianne?"

The queen stared back at him, her jaw clenched hard. She said nothing, but at her side Caledan took a tentative step forward.

"That was truly Trola, Pela?" he whispered.

Pela nodded. "He will come for us next."

Caledan swung back to the others. "Then you must find a way, Braidon, or all is lost."

"If only it were so simple!" Braidon shouted, turning on

the sellsword. "You I would trust, Caledan. Though you are my enemy, you have never pretended to be anything different. But her…" He faced Marianne now, pointing one trembling finger at her chest. "*Her*…" His voice cracked. "She spent years pretending to love me…fathered my son, and still she betrayed me!"

"Calybe is safe," Marianne whispered. "Servo wanted him dead, but Caledan defended him. *That* is why I served the Elders, why I destroyed them when it was finally within my power."

Braidon laughed, and the sound was filled with anger and self-loathing. "Ay, and I suppose that explains as well why you pretended to love me."

Marianne could not meet his eyes. "I…" Her voice faded and she swallowed. "I convinced myself you knew my feelings, that you didn't care. I grew to loathe you for it, and then…then anything could be justified, if only it meant I could have my revenge for the years that you took from me."

"That *I* took from *you?*" Braidon snarled. "All that time I loved you, wasted, and for what? So you could steal the throne out from under me, so you could murder my Guards, my *friends*, so you could rule us all?"

Marianne's eyes flashed. "I did what I had to do to protect myself," she snapped, but her fury faded as quickly as it had appeared. "To protect my son."

"Oh yes, I'm sure that's what you tell yourself, how you sleep at night. But I see through you, Marianne, even if no one else does. You did it for the power, and nothing else. You were raised to rule, and when they sought to take that from you, you did whatever was necessary to steal it back."

"Are you any different, Braidon?" she whispered. "Were

you not raised to rule as well? Were you not destined to be king?"

"Perhaps," Braidon whispered, "but I did not commit murder for my crown."

Marianne chuckled. "No one but your own father."

Braidon said nothing, only stared at her, his eyes hard. The smile slipped from Marianne's lips and she let out a sigh.

"So what are we to do, my dear husband?" she asked, extending her arms. "Darkness threatens the Three Nations, one far greater than our own petty grievances. You saw that creature, felt its power. Alone, we will fail. Will you stand with me against it?"

A strained silence fell as Kryssa looked from the queen to the king. She knew Braidon hated Marianne more than anything else. He had spent the last months nursing that hatred, feeding his rage, all with the goal of destroying her. But now, surely, Braidon must do his duty for his people, must—

"I can't," Braidon croaked, and tears streaked his cheeks. Kryssa's heart lurched in her chest as he continued: "After everything you've done, after all your betrayals, I cannot do it. Perhaps your offer is sincere, but I cannot know, cannot believe you will not stab me in the back the first chance you have."

Marianne's face twisted as she stared back at him, and for a moment Kryssa thought she might lash out at the king, might try to destroy him then and there. Instead, her eyes slid closed and she let out a long sigh.

"My mistakes have returned to punish me," she whispered, "and yet I cannot stand by while this creature takes our world. For my son, for my people, I will not let it destroy us." She paused, her eyes flickering open. She looked at Braidon through her eyelashes as Kryssa and the world stood waiting.

"Promise to spare my life, Braidon," she whispered, "and I will give you my power."

❧ 25 ❧

Braidon stood gaping at Marianne, frozen to the spot. He half-expected the queen to throw back her head and laugh in his face at her own joke. Instead, she only waited before him, arms hanging at her side, shoulders slumped in defeat.

This had to be a trick. After all they'd been through, all the death and battling for power, she could not simply be giving up. It was not in Marianne's character to surrender, to give in or allow herself to be dominated…and yet there she was...

"What are you doing?" he croaked.

"I will not let this creature destroy our world. It has to be stopped. If you cannot trust me, then…I must trust you." She lifted her hand to him, where a silver bracelet shone. Sliding it from her wrist, she tossed it to the ground between them. "That is the source of my power. It channels the lives of Lonia's slaves to the wielder."

Frowning, Braidon stared down at the device. He sensed no traps about the thing, no power at all, in fact. But Marianne's words made sense, given all he knew of the woman's ingenuity, and the engineers at Lonia's disposal. After a moment's hesitation, he picked it up and slipped it onto his wrist, but felt no change.

"There's nothing," he murmured, glaring at Marianne. "Is this some trick?"

She lowered her head. "No, Braidon," she sighed, "no more tricks."

"Then where is your power?"

Her eyes came back up and she lifted a hand to her breast. "The bracelet does not store power, only channels it. The life forces of those that have already departed lie within me."

"Then you *are* trying to trick me," he snarled. "You are holding back your power, to strike me down when I turn my back."

"No, Braidon," she whispered, "I would not, not with Calybe's life—"

"Do not say his name," Braidon roared, his heart pounding with sudden anger. "Not after hiding him from me, not after trying to murder his father."

"I did everything I could to keep him safe," Marianne replied. "And for what it's worth, I am sorry for taking him from you."

"Enough of your lies," Braidon snapped, clenching his fists. "What trick are you playing, woman? I'm done talking."

Stones crunched as Marianne took a step toward him. He started to retreat, but she only shook her head. "No tricks, Braidon," she whispered, falling to her knees. She spread her arms in supplication. "My power is yours."

Braidon could only stare in disbelief. This was the

woman he had loved, who had betrayed him, had stolen everything from him. Now she was on kneeling before him, offering the world. And all he had to do was reach out and take it.

Yet still he hesitated. Braidon knew in his heart it could not be this easy. Around him the others watched on—Caledan and Pela and Genevieve and Kryssa and the strange young man. None of them made any move to intervene.

Braidon swallowed, returning his gaze to Marianne. He had already proven he was the stronger, that the lives he'd accumulated were greater than her power. But she might still do him harm, might still defeat him with some under-handed blow.

Gathering his power, Braidon drew it about himself in a brilliant suit of armour, a shield against any attack she might hurl. He sensed the tension growing in Caledan as the sellsword took a step closer, but a look from Marianne sent him back. The others wavered, unsure of Braidon's inten-tions, but no one else moved to intervene.

"Do it," Marianne whispered.

Sapphire eyes stared up at him, eyes he had loved, eyes he had loathed. Gritting his teeth, Braidon did as she said. His power whipped out, catching her in its swirling rainbow light. She stiffened against the magic, but made no move to defend herself, and after a second Braidon sensed her barriers retreating. Silently he left his body, soaring out in spirit to look upon his wife.

Power danced within Marianne, more brilliant than he had ever expected, and suddenly he wondered whether her earlier distress had been an act, if she'd been holding back in their brief battle. Fear shook his spirit, that perhaps this was a trap after all, that she might still lash out at him. But she still appeared unguarded, unprotected. If Braidon wished it, he might have reached out and stopped her heart.

No, this was no trap. Finally convinced, Braidon latched his power to the swirling light at Marianne's core. A whimper slipped from the queen's lips, but he could not be stopped now, and slowly Braidon drew the energies to him. Feeling the queen tense, he readied himself for resistance, but instead her eyes slid closed as she relinquished control to him.

Braidon smiled and drew more power from the queen's frail body. A gasp of his own escaped as the energy touched him, a burning, swirling cacophony of light that set his blood to boiling. His whole body shook, as though it were true fire burning within him. In that instant, he felt as though he might leap the walls of Chole itself, that he had the power to fly and soar, to face any enemy, to conquer the world if he wished it.

His breath came in ragged gasps as the raw power continued to flow, the glow within the queen dwindling by the second, even as his own strength redoubled. Braidon clenched his fists, his teeth rattling as his entire being shook.

Finally the last of Marianne's power dwindled, the multicoloured light fading to a single candle of blue—her own life force. It flickered alone at her core, its glow radiating throughout her body. Such a tiny, feeble thing, the difference between life and death. He could snuff it out with a pinch of his fingers.

A shudder ran through Braidon at the thought. Withdrawing, he looked at Marianne with his spirit eyes. She had given him everything, and all she'd asked in exchange was her life. And yet…

Marianne's will was unquenchable. So long as she lived, she would not give up her claim to the throne. Whatever setbacks she suffered, she would recover, and her wrath would return the pain a thousand-fold. She might have surrendered her magic, but that could be regathered. Then one day, she would come for him. He would never stop looking over his shoulder.

Unless…

Braidon swallowed, staring at the woman who had lain beside him all these years, who had born his son. Shadows now haunted her face, and her skin was pale beneath the blazing sun. Her eyes were closed, but as he watched they flickered open.

Now he saw not his lost love, but the woman he loathed, who had betrayed him. And he realised his love was long dead, that it had been burned away by her betrayal, and his compassion lost with it. After everything Marianne had done, after the murders and devastation she'd wrought, why should he leave her with her life? She did not deserve a second chance, did not deserve to go free.

Silently, Braidon reached out again with his mind, and wrapped his power around the flickering blue candle. Marianne's eyes widened as she felt his touch and her lips parted as though to cry out, but it was already too late. Braidon had possession of her body, her soul, and there was nothing she could do to protect herself now.

Nothing but stare at him with those crystal blue eyes.

A smile touched Braidon's lips as he saw her fear. Slowly he began to draw her life away, savouring in her pain, in this final retribution for all the hurt she had caused him. Once she had held him in her power, and done her best to destroy him. Now he would do the same.

Only he would not fail.

"Braidon!" a voice called, though it was faint, as though spoken from a great distance. He looked up to see Caledan approaching, a sword clenched in his fist. "Marianne, are you okay?"

Braidon made a gesture and a wave of power caught the sellsword in the chest. The blow sent Caledan tumbling backwards across the plain, only coming to a stop several yards away. He did not lie still, but instead pushed himself back to his hands and knees. Anger touched Braidon at the man's defiance, and he raised his hand, preparing to strike the traitor down.

"Braidon!"

Irritated, the king swung in search of the fresh disturbance. Marianne was still held in his thrall, her life his to do with as he pleased. She could not escape him now, no matter who tried to intervene, but still the interruption had enraged him. He collected his power, ready to strike this new enemy down.

He paused as his gaze found Genevieve. The huntress had her bow drawn, an arrow pointed at Braidon's chest. Her eyes were wide, her fingers shaking on the drawstring. Kryssa stood nearby, hand on her sword hilt, though Braidon could not tell whether it was to defend her king, or her lover.

"Please, Braidon. Stop this," Genevieve begged, her voice taut with pain.

"You would betray me, huntress, after I saved your life?" Braidon asked.

"*She* saved me," Genevieve whispered. Her voice cracked and the arrow dropped half an inch before she restored her aim. "I won't let you kill her, not like this."

"You don't understand," Braidon hissed. "She is too treacherous to live. I am sorry, huntress. I only do what I must."

He turned and lifted his hand, ready to draw the last flickers of life from the queen. A sharp *twang* came from behind him, and lighting fast, Braidon spun back in time to see the arrow flash from Genevieve's bow.

Rage boiled through Braidon as he watched the arrow come. Were they all so blind? Could none of them see the truth, that Marianne was playing them all like puppets, turning them upon each other? But they could not stop him, not now, not when he was so close to his victory. With a roar, Braidon threw out his hand.

A wave of energy surged from him, more than he could ever need to deal with mere mortals. It raced to meet the arrow, catching it mid-air and turning it aside, hurling it backwards...

...until Genevieve's breast brought it to an abrupt halt.

For a second, no one seemed to realise what had happened—not even the huntress. She stared at Braidon, eyes wide and mouth open, as though unsure why her arrow had not found its mark. Slowly, she lowered her bow, and her gaze was drawn downwards. A frown marked her forehead as she found the arrow lodged there.

Staggering, Genevieve looked back at Braidon, and now there was panic in the woman's eyes. Her mouth opened as though to speak, but instead blood burst from her lips. The fear grew on her face as the strength left her legs and she crumpled to the ground.

"*Gen!*" Screaming, Kryssa threw herself down beside her partner. "Gen, no!"

She grabbed the fallen huntress and turned her over.

The fall had driven the arrow deeper and now blood stained Genevieve's red and gold tunic. Her head lolled as Kryssa cradled her.

"Kryssa?" Genevieve whispered, her eyelids fluttering but unable to open.

"It's okay, I'm here," Kryssa whispered, before her head whipped up, her eyes fixing on Braidon. "Help her!" she screamed.

Movement came from alongside Braidon. He glanced around as Marianne staggered back from him, only now realising she had broken free while he'd been distracted. There was open fear in her eyes, and it was clear that she could barely hold herself up. He smiled and would have finished her then had Caledan not pulled her into his arms.

"Braidon, please!"

Kryssa's screams drew him back to the dying huntress. He frowned as he looked at the two, then let out a sigh and strode across to where they lay. A quick glimpse through the eyes of his spirit confirmed what he already knew. The arrow had sliced open the arteries in the huntress's heart. Even as he watched, her life force dwindled to nothing.

"I am sorry, Kryssa," he murmured. "She is already gone. She should not have gotten in my way."

An awful sob tore from his King's Guard as Genevieve's eyes closed a final time, the dull rattle of her last breath whispering from her lips.

"No, no, no," Kryssa gasped, burying her head in her lover's chest. "Not like this, not again."

Braidon watched them for a moment, feeling he should be sad but not quite sure why. Genevieve had gone against him, had betrayed him as he stood on the verge of victory.

Now she had paid the price. Shaking his head, he searched again for Marianne.

Boom!

Braidon staggered as the strange light in which Pela had arrived exploded once more from the walls of Chole. Ice took hold of his heart as the whirlwind of colours billowed across the plains, rushing over the head so the splintered armies, flickering here and there as though in search of a place to land.

This time it settled much further out on the plains, far beyond either army. There it slammed into the earth with a clap of thunder. Colours rushed out in all directions, then back inwards as though sucked into a vacuum.

In its wake, an army was revealed, thousands of men and women garbed in dark blue armour. They stood row upon row in perfect unison, spears held in one hand, shields in the other, swords sheathed at their waists. Black gems shone from their armour and weapons, leaving no doubt about where this army had appeared from, who they served.

Death.

❧ 26 ❧

Pela watched as the swirling light flickered, listened to the dying *booms* of thunder, smelt the distant decay as The Way faded, revealing the army now standing on the plains. She couldn't move, couldn't think, only stare as the last trace of magic vanished and the world finally saw what had come.

Ten thousand soldiers in shining armour, no raw recruits but professionals in the practice of death, well-trained and armed with deadly steel. It only took a glimpse to know they outnumbered the combined forces of the king and queen. They would cut through the ragtag armies of Lonia and Plorsea like a wave against the sand, sweeping all away before them.

And every death, every life stolen, would feed the demon's power.

Pela shuddered, scanned the ranks of blue-armoured soldiers. Ice slid down her spine as movement came from the army and Rayan came striding forward. The shadows clung to his form like a cloak, billowing as though caught in a great wind. Tendrils of darkness reached out before him, sliding through the grass and twisted shrubs, bringing death to all they touched.

Coming to a stop at the fore of his army, Rayan's gaze swept his tattered collection of enemies. The black eyes lingered on Braidon and Marianne, before finally alighting on Pela. Her heart dropped into the pit of her stomach as a sickly smile crossed the demon's face.

"Pela," he said in a whisper, and while he stood some hundred yards away, his words carried to the ears of every watcher. "Thank you for leading me to The Way. To think, it lay hidden beneath my feet all these years." The demon spread his arms. "You have granted me a great gift." His grin spread, and a tingle of warning shot through Pela, a voice screaming for her to flee. "In exchange, I grant you the gift of life."

Pela stood frozen as Rayan lifted a hand. Only at the last moment did she realise what he was about to do, the significance of his words—but she found her muscles were unable to move, her whole body petrified with terror. This was her fault, her doing—if only she and Ruebyn had remained in Kalgan, the creature would never have found the secret way into Plorsea.

Darkness rushed from the demon, just as it had beneath the walls of Kalgan, a swirling cloud that at a touch would entomb Pela's soul forever, trap her in her own flesh, to be feasted upon at the demon's pleasure. Watching it come, she thought of all she still wanted to do, that she would never get to go home, to show Ruebyn her quiet town, to climb the mountains or swim the fiord.

A voice shouted out from nearby, and suddenly someone was tackling Pela, pushing her from the path of the magic.

She gasped as she struck the ground, her head whipping around to see who had hit her. She had the merest of seconds to glimpse the surprise on Ruebyn's face, as though he could hardly believe what he'd done.

Then the darkness collided with him and his mouth fell open in the beginnings of a scream. Only the shrillest of whistles emerged, like hot steam escaping a kettle. His skin hardened before Pela's eyes, taking on the shiny look of polished wax.

"*No!*" Pela screamed.

She scrambled to her feet as the darkness receded, reaching for him, but his skin was like leather beneath her hands. Only his eyes remained the same, frozen open in his face, staring out with such desperation that Pela could almost hear his silent cries.

"No, Ruebyn, why?" she gasped, clinging to his mummified figure. "Why would you do this?"

But he could not reply, could not do anything but stand fixed to the spot as the demon's voice carried across the plain.

"Your man is brave, girl," Rayan chuckled. "If foolish. He has bought you no more than a few seconds. Enjoy your last breaths."

"Enough, demon!" Braidon howled. Leaping past them, he extended a hand towards the creature. "Your darkness ends now."

"Ah, the king!" Rayan cackled as its attention turned to Braidon. "Though your kingdom looks to have fallen into disrepair. Are these here truly the best Plorsea has to offer?"

Ignoring the demon's taunts, Braidon threw out an arm. Lightning crackled between his fingers and then leapt at Rayan, crackling as it went. The demon only raised a hand.

The blue fire struck with a *boom*, but as Rayan closed his fist, it was quickly snuffed out. Braidon staggered at the sight, his face paling a shade, and the demon laughed.

"So, you too have taken the power of the living?" Rayan murmured. "Tell me, does it burn you, King?"

Panic appeared in Braidon's eyes, before his face hardened into a mask and he turned his gaze skyward. "Nidryt, to me!"

For a second, Pela thought Braidon had gone mad—then an answering roar came from the city behind them, and a red streak shot up from beyond the walls. The air *cracked* as giant wings beat down, carrying the beast overhead. The Red Dragon circled the king once and then spiralled down to land between Braidon and the demon with a crash. A dull growl rumbled from its throat as it looked from the king to Rayan.

"What have we here?" Rayan sounded almost bemused by the beast's appearance. Folding his arms, he took a few steps forward. "Do the Red Dragons now bow to mortal masters?"

The dragon threw back its head and roared at the demon's words. Warmth washed over Pela as the great jaws swung around, revealing row upon row of dagger-like teeth and the burning glow in the depths of its throat.

Your enemies spring from this earth like rabbits, King.

Braidon scowled. "The demon comes to destroy us all, Nidryt," he replied, holding out a hand. "Help me to defeat the creature, before it's too late."

A rumble came again from the dragon as it looked upon Braidon, eyes aglow, before it turned back to the demon. Rayan had not moved, only stood watching them, that sly smile on his sickly face.

"Come then, dragon," he murmured, spreading his arms. "Do your master's bidding."

A roar sounded from across the battlefield, not only from Nidryt, but also from above. Flames lit the sky and Pela found herself shrinking as more of the Red Dragons appeared. The demon's laughter rose over the cacophony of the beasts.

"Or perhaps you would return to your true purpose, to follow your noble desires, rather than obey the whims of this mortal. Perhaps you would help me to burn the scourge of humanity from these lands."

The dragon's head whipped around at the demon's words, the giant globe of its single eye aflame. Beside it, Braidon seemed ignorant to its sudden change in mood.

"False promises will not sway our alliance," Braidon said dismissively. "Come, Nidryt, let us destroy this foul creature."

Another rumble came from the dragon's throat, though this time it reminded Pela of laughter. The beast turned its head to look down at Braidon.

You have made an enemy beyond your powers, King, Nidryt's voice growled into their minds. *We are not so foolish as our extinct cousins, to throw away our lives. Our arrangement is at an end. Humanity is once again the enemy of my people!*

The dragon's mouth spread into a wicked grin, and Pela glimpsed the flames building at the back of its throat. The hackles on her neck lifted as she threw herself to the ground, dragging Ruebyn's mummified body down with her, but the demon's voice came again before the flames could emerge.

"Wait, my eager new friend," Rayan said as he stepped up beside the dragon and put a hand on its massive forearm. Still smiling, he looked at Braidon, then past the king to the gathered soldiers. "They have brought together so many lives for me, I can hardly wait to break my fast." He laughed. "But I need be prudent. The fruits of the Three Nations must be made to last, lest I find myself starving once more for sustenance."

"I...I will stand..." Braidon started, but the demon waved a hand, and words seemed to fail the king.

"People of the east!" Now Rayan's voice rang out over the heads of the broken armies. "Your world is at an end. Your beasts have abandoned you, your king stands helpless before me. But fear not, for I have come to free you from the bonds of chaos. Surrender to my rule, and you will live long and peaceful lives." His voice hardened. "Resist, and I will turn all who stand against me to dust. I give you until the morrow to decide your fate."

With that, Rayan turned his back on Braidon and the armies of Plorsea and Lonia, as though they were of no more consequence than fleas to the Feline. Indeed, with the dragon standing between them, there was nothing anyone but Braidon could have done. And the king stood defeated, his eyes locked to the ground, his courage fled in the face of the demon's power.

Finally the dragon lifted its head and unleashed a plume of flame into the sky. Pela and the others flinched back as heat washed over them, and with a single bound, the dragon leapt into the air.

Then there was only the silent army, the row upon row of blue-armoured men staring across the plains at them. The demon had vanished, but the army remained, a promise of the death that would find them come morning.

But in that moment, Pela did not care. She crouched

beside Ruebyn's helpless body. His eyes were still frozen in terror, his mouth open in that silent scream. Throwing her arms around him, she sobbed into his shoulder. But it was like hugging a mannequin, and after only a moment she drew back, her chest in agony.

"Let me help you with him."

It was her mother, her eyes red with grief. Pela swallowed the lump in her throat and nodded, and Kryssa moved forward to take a hold of Ruebyn's petrified arms. Stones crunched and Pela saw Braidon approaching.

"Here—" he started, holding out an arm.

Kryssa's head snapped up at the sound of his voice. Releasing Ruebyn, she drew her sword. "Get away from us!" she shrieked, pointing the blade at Braidon's chest.

The king threw up his hands, a frown touching his forehead. "Surely we must—"

"*I said, get away!*" Kryssa screamed, leaping at him and swinging the blade.

Braidon jumped backwards out of range, his frown turning to a scowl, but he made no move to strike at Kryssa. For a moment, they stood facing off against one another, until finally Braidon let out a sigh.

"I am so—"

"Don't you dare apologise to me," Kryssa raged, taking another step and thrusting out with her sword again. "Don't you dare say another word, or I swear by the Gods I'll kill you where you stand."

A bemused smile crossed Braidon's face and he raised his hands, though he might have been mocking her now.

"Come now, Kryssa," he murmured. "We must work together, if we are to defeat that creature."

The sword shook in Kryssa's hands as she shook her

head. "No, Braidon," she whispered. "I will never stand with you." Her voice was breaking now. "For the first time, I am glad my father is no longer here. It would have broken his heart to see the monster you have become. Now go! Leave us! You are my king no longer."

Braidon reeled back at her words, his eyes wide with shock. But a second later, his faced closed over and when he spoke his words were like ice.

"Very well, Kryssa," he grated. "I will return to Chole. But know this." His voice rose in volume, carrying now to the entire army. "Any who wish to swear their fealty to me will find shelter in the city. But all who stand against me will remain outside my walls. Now I bid you farewell."

With that he turned and disappeared into the fading light. Movement came from around them as his men followed. A minute passed, punctuated only by the crunch of boots on dirt. Then the first of Marianne's soldiers broke rank and set off for Chole—a few at first, then as though a dam broke, hundreds more followed.

By the end, only a few thousand remained on the fields outside the city, those who had seen what Braidon had done to their queen, who still held their love for her close in their hearts. They would not abandon her now, whatever darkness came against them.

And amongst them all stood Pela and Kryssa, alone now with the bodies of Genevieve and Ruebyn, alone with their love, and with their grief.

27

Caledan stalked back and forth across the campsite, his arms clasped tightly behind him. Though just over a thousand men and women remained with Marianne, the night was silent but for whispers. Not a soul had the courage to raise their voice, to rage or fight on this night—the last night.

Turning, Caledan made another loop of their campsite, studying his companions as he did so—Pela and Kryssa and his queen. Enemies not long ago, now united in their grief, in their desperation. Before the sun had set, they had started a fire from the timbers of a broken wagon, none of them wanting to face the darkness without light. Yet its glow cast his companions in shadow, so it seemed each were already halfway to death.

A shiver passed down Caledan's spine as his eyes were drawn beyond the circle of light, where Genevieve and the petrified boy lay. The first of their party to fall. They would not be the last.

Catching Marianne's eyes on him, he stalked across to

her. "We have to fight," he hissed. "I'll kill them all, Braidon and the dragons and the damned demon itself, if that's what it takes."

He knew it was an empty threat, his rage futile in the face of what would come for them on the morrow. Always before, his skill with a blade had been enough. But now magic and darkness had returned to the world, and he found himself powerless to protect his queen. The demon was too powerful, its army to great.

A smile crossed Marianne's face as she rose and took his hands in hers. "Calm yourself, my Champion," she whispered. Though Braidon had taken her powers—and almost her life—she seemed remarkably calm. "Now is not the time for anger."

Caledan shuddered, but he knew she was right. He dragged in a breath, seeking to calm his racing heart. "There must be something we can do," he whispered, looking from the queen to their companions.

Pela and Kryssa did not respond, only sat staring into the campfire, each lost in her own private grief. Marianne spoke in their stead. "You cannot feel his power. Even with the energies I gave to Braidon, it is not enough. My soul shudders at the lives the creature must have stolen, the souls that screamed out beneath his blade." Her eyes slid closed at the words, as though she could truly see all those lost innocents.

"It cannot end like this," Caledan insisted. He tried to return to his pacing, but her arms drew him back. He resisted for a moment before submitting. "What are we going to do?" he croaked.

"I have a plan for tomorrow," Marianne murmured, "though I do not know whether it can succeed. So for now, we are going to live, my Champion." With her words, Marianne took his hand in hers and drew him away. "Come, the night is beautiful, let us not waste it."

Caledan cast one last glance back at their unlikely companions, but neither seemed interested in their departure, and finally he allowed himself to be led. The stars burned overhead, and the half-moon shone down on them, lighting the way. Several times they had to detour around sleeping soldiers, but soon they left even those behind, and found themselves walking alone across the open fields.

Inevitably, Caledan's eyes were drawn back to the city. Chole was brightly lit, as though its citizens thought the light might protect them, might keep the demon from their doors. The thought brought Caledan's rage rushing back, as he recalled how the king had tricked them with his dragon, how he had tried to steal the life from the woman Caledan loved.

He shivered at the thought, glancing sidelong at Marianne. He realised in that moment it was true. They had grown close these past weeks, and he'd come to see the woman who hid behind the mask, her steely determination, her courage to do what was necessary for herself and her people.

As though reading his mind, Marianne's glanced up to catch his gaze upon her. She smiled, her sapphire eyes dancing in the moonlight.

"What are you thinking about, my Champion?" she whispered, her hand sliding into his.

"How beautiful you are," he croaked, surprised at his own boldness.

Her eyebrows lifted, but she said nothing, and they continued their midnight walk. The whispers of their loyal soldiers had fallen far behind them now, and silence ruled the night. A flash of light from nearby drew Caledan's attention, but it was only two fireflies, dancing in the dark.

Finally Marianne let out a long breath and came to a stop. Seating herself in the long grass, she bid Caledan join her. In the moonlight her face seemed softer than he had ever seen it, or perhaps that was only the loss of her power, the removal of the illusions she had used to hide herself away from the world.

"You know, as a child, I never dreamed of any of this," she murmured, then smiled wryly. "Well, that's not quite true. I knew one day I would be queen, but I thought only of Lonia, of lifting my people from the generations of poverty that had beset them since the time of the Tsar. What did I care for Plorsea?"

"But then your father led an invasion against us."

"He was desperate. His senators convinced him it was the only way, that Plorsea owed us for the crimes of their Tsar. And because of him, because of them…" She shivered, shook her head. "No, I will not hold this hatred in my heart any longer. The past is done. I refuse to let it stain this last night."

"And yet it pains you still," Caledan murmured. He took her hand in his, squeezing her fingers.

She shivered at his touch and her eyes found his once more. Her throat contracted as she swallowed.

"They were lonely years," she whispered. "Until Calybe came. And even then, to bear that man's son…" She shuddered. "In all that time, I did my duty to my father and my nation, but…it was never more than that, a task I needed to complete." The breath caught in Caledan's throat as she lifted a hand to his cheek. "I am curious to know if there is more, my Champion."

Caledan swallowed as he looked into his queen's eyes and saw her vulnerability, the fear that he would spurn her once more, that he would turn away. Thinking of her anger before, he realised now his mistake, how he had misread her. It had been Marianne's way of protecting herself, of concealing her pain at his rejection. She was a woman used to getting what she wanted, but now all she could do was wait, was hope.

Staring into the depths of her eyes, Caledan leaned down and pressed his lips to hers. A tremor shook the queen as his arms went around her waist, and for the briefest of seconds he thought he'd been wrong. Then her lips were pushing back against his and her arms were looping over his head, her fingers sliding through his hair. A moan hissed from her throat as he hugged her close, kissing her again, tasting the rosemary of their last meal on her tongue.

They broke apart for a moment, panting softly in the moonlight. There was a wicked grin on Marianne's lips now, a sly look in her eyes. Her fingers traced a pattern over Caledan's shirt, making him tremble wherever they touched.

"I have nothing left now, you know," she said softly. "No crown, no army, no magic."

"You have me," he responded.

"Ay, I have my loyal sellsword." Again the smile, that crafty glint. "But…I fear I no longer have the coin to pay you, my Champion." Her eyes travelled down as she started flicking open the buttons of his shirt, sliding down until they were playing with the hairs on his belly. "I am afraid I have nothing left to offer you," she continued, "but myself."

A growl rumbled from Caledan's throat as he took her

in his arms. He kissed her hard now, and she seemed to dissolve into him, her body clinging to his, her fingers still dancing around his midriff. Despite the burning in his chest, he drew back, sliding a hand up her leg. She still wore her scarlet dress from earlier, the silk fabric hugging her silver skin.

"That was all I ever wanted," he whispered.

Slowly, he slid his hands up her thighs, lifting the hem of her dress. She shivered at the intimacy of his touch, but made no move to stop him. His hands slipped around her thighs, raising the dress as they went. Obediently she stretched up her arms, then the dress was gone, exposing Marianne to the night's breeze.

Tossing the clothing aside, Caledan sat back on his haunches, drinking her in in the moonlight. Naked, Marianne no longer appeared a queen or Magicker, only a woman, a human with the same hopes and fears as anyone else. Her sapphire eyes stared up at him, and he saw the fear there, the sudden worry he would find her wanting.

Smiling, Caledan slowly removed his shirt and pants, until he was as naked as his queen. Then he drew her close and kissed her. His hands trailed gently over her stomach, cupping her breasts, toying with her.

A moan hissed from the back of the queen's throat and suddenly it was Marianne who was pushing him down. Now it was his turn to acquiesce, and he shivered as her hands slid across his body, as her mouth kissed and explored his flesh, touching and tasting.

Only then did Caledan realise what he was doing, who he was doing it with. It was by no means his first time, but never before had he been with someone so powerful, with a woman who could destroy him in a single word. Whatever

Marianne said, she was still queen to the thousands camped out on the plains. If he hurt her…

Laughter whispered from Marianne as she sat up. "You just realised what you're doing, didn't you?" she asked.

Caledan's eyes widened. "You can read my mind?"

"No!" Marianne cried, her face alight with amusement. "But a fool could have seen it in your eyes." Her smile grew as she leaned closer. "Do I scare you, sellsword?"

A growl rumbled from Caledan's throat as he took the queen in his arms. "Nothing scares me."

28

The fire had burned low when Kryssa finally stood. Numb from kneeling so long beside Genevieve's body, her feet were unsteady beneath her and she stumbled several steps before righting herself. Then she straightened, her hand dropping to her sword hilt.

For hours she had sat in the darkness, wondering what she could have done differently, how she might have changed things. She had been blind to Braidon's evil. His greed for power had been there for all to see. It was behind all their troubles. Marianne might have been little better, but in the end the queen had at least been willing to sacrifice her power to save the Three Nations.

A shiver shook Kryssa as she looked at Chole. The gates still lay broken, destroyed by Marianne's black powder. Without thinking, she started towards them, before uncertainty brought her up short. She glanced back to where Pela lay sleeping beside Ruebyn. She claimed the mummified boy still lived, and while Kryssa had her doubts, she was proud of her daughter's courage that day.

Her gaze fell to the sword on her belt. Derryn's sword. She should have given it to Pela long ago, but instead Devon had been the one to pass the blade to her daughter. Thinking back, Kryssa could hardly believe how naïve she'd been, how she could have ever hoped to keep Pela from this world. Darkness would always rule, and the only way to fight it was with cold, hard steel.

From tonight on, Pela would be alone. Kryssa could hardly bear the thought, yet neither could she turn away from her fate. She had helped to raise Braidon up—now she must hold him accountable for his crimes. If not for his greed, they might have stood united against the demon. Instead, their forces had been sundered, and Marianne's followers abandoned on the indefensible plains to die.

She had to put things right, but she would not leave Pela defenceless. Silently, Kryssa unstrapped her sword belt and laid it beside her daughter, returning it as she had promised to do all those months ago.

Then she rose. She retrieved a spare blade from a nearby wagon and started again towards Chole. Movement came from the shadows before she made it more than a few feet, and she dropped her hand to the hilt of her new sword.

Pela stepped from the darkness ahead to bar her path. "You can't leave," she said, her voice breaking. "Not again."

Tears stung Kryssa's eyes and her heart ached, but all she could do was shake her head. "I must, Pela," she whispered. "I have to stop him. Everyone out here is doomed unless they find shelter inside the city."

"Then we swear loyalty to him!" Pela hissed. "What does it matter, when tomorrow the demon comes for us?"

A lump lodged in Kryssa's throat, but she swallowed it

down, even as her mind replayed the king's disastrous attempt to ally with the nomads out on the plains. The woman Loyla had seen what Braidon was, even then. Her eyes slid closed.

"He has lost himself," she whispered. "We cannot stand with him, or we risk trading one monster with another. They both must be destroyed."

Pela stared up at her, eyes wide, fists clenched at her side. But despite her anger, Pela said nothing, only waited.

Kryssa smiled, placing a hand on her daughter's shoulder. "Your father would have been proud of you, you know," she whispered. "You are stronger than we ever were. You do not seek war."

Her eyes dropped to the sword Pela now wore, her father's blade. She let out a sigh and released her daughter. "But sometimes war is necessary," she continued. "I supported Braidon, lifted him up, though disaster followed wherever we went. I should have realised the truth after the Castle, but I was blinded by my hatred for Marianne." Her gaze returned to the city. "I have to put things right."

"You are still blind," Pela whispered. "Please don't do this."

"I'm sorry, Pela," Kryssa croaked.

She was already moving away, eyes fixed on the terrible gash Marianne's weapons had left in Chole's fortifications. Only as she neared the first bodies did she glance back. Illuminated by the moonlight, Pela still stood where she had left her. Kryssa's heart lurched in her chest and she almost turned back. Then she saw again Genevieve falling by Braidon's hand, and steeling herself, she walked into the awful city.

It was not hard to gain entrance to Chole now. Braidon's forces had erected a makeshift barricade beyond the rubble of the gate, but one look at her face, and the regiments guarding the entrance allowed her to pass. Apparently, the king had not thought to pass on word of her betrayal.

Threading her way through the city, Kryssa found her path drawn away from the Castle. She did not stand a chance against Braidon, not alone. First, she needed to find allies.

The Temple of the Earth was full to bursting when she stepped through the great doors into the entrance hall. Priests wearing the green robes of the Goddess rushed to and fro amidst the crowds packing their chambers, offering aid wherever it was needed. Food and water were passed out amongst the healthy, while those trained in the healing arts attended to citizens that had been injured in the explosion Marianne had unleashed upon the city.

"And so you return, my daughter."

Kryssa found the same priest she had met on her last visit standing beside her. A sigh slipped from her lips as she bowed her head.

"You were right," she whispered. "The king is consumed. He must be stopped, before he destroys us all."

The softest of chuckles came from the priest. "Perhaps I was right, perhaps wrong. I know only that tomorrow the world could end, and I am tired of our wars."

"The queen's army is outside the walls. If we stand together, we might yet repel the demon. But Braidon can no longer see reason. The power has driven him mad."

"It was always a forbidden art, even before the fall of the Gods," the priest whispered. "The taking of a life force."

His gaze alighted on her. "But none of that is why you wish to see the king's end."

Kryssa opened her mouth to argue, but instead a sob tore from her throat and suddenly her strength was gone. Sinking to her knees, she looked up at the priest, her vision blurring.

"He took her from me," she gasped. "He has to pay!"

"Oh, my daughter," the priest replied, kneeling alongside her and drawing her into his arms. "I am sorry for your loss. This is a cruel, hard world. But you must let go of your hatred."

"I can't!" Kryssa cried, pulling back from him. Angrily she wiped her eyes and clambered back to her feet. "It is all that keeps me going," she grated. "All I have left."

The priest remained on his knees, and there was sadness in his eyes as he looked at her. "I am sorry to hear that, my daughter," he whispered.

Kryssa shuddered as another wave of grief threatened to engulf her. "The king must be stopped," she said. "But I cannot do it alone. Will you help me?"

"You would use our strength to fight the king?"

"I would."

"Then you still do not understand," the priest replied. "The energy of our souls is a pure, sacred thing. I would not ask any here to use that power to kill. To commit such an act is to invite corruption, to lessen yourself, your spirit."

"Even so," Kryssa whispered, "This must be done. And you must help me to do it."

The priest stared at her for a long time, his eyes boring into hers, as though he could see through to her very soul. Knowing what was in her heart, Kryssa thought he would refuse her, that she would be forced to stand against Braidon alone.

Finally he bowed his head, the wrinkles of his face deepening. "Very well, my daughter," he said. "We will put our fate in your hands. But I pray to the Gods you find another way."

❧   29   ☙

Standing atop the walls of Chole, Braidon watched as the sun crept above the line of the horizon. His heart lifted as the darkness retreated, the shadows that had clung to his mind throughout the night falling away. The time had come and there could be no going back now. He would stand against the demon, would end it here on the plains of Chole, or he would die, and Plorsea with him.

It was almost a relief now, to see the path clear ahead of him. There would be no more doubts, no more confusion. Braidon alone had the power to stop the demon, and he would not shirk from his duty.

Slowly the daylight grew, revealing the armies aligned on the plains below. The ragtag remnants of Marianne's forces had aligned themselves near the breach in Chole's walls, as though they thought they might still retreat to the city before the demon's army came. But they had made their choice. They might have been his people once, fellow Plorseans, but they had surrendered their right to his protection when they'd pledged their loyalty to Marianne.

Braidon shivered as he fixed his attention on the true enemy. The blue-armoured soldiers had hardly moved from where the portal had deposited them. They must have possessed some supernatural resilience, to stand in perfect stillness all through the night. The thought sent ice down Braidon's spine, and he checked them again through his spirit eyes, reassuring himself they were still mortals, that they could die.

There was no sign of the demon himself, nor Nidryt and the other Red Dragons. Anger touched Braidon as he recalled their treachery. With the beasts' aid, he might have driven the demon back, but now he must wait, must bide his time and gather his strength.

Drawing himself up, Braidon took stock of his own forces. His army had swelled with the queen's defections, which he had integrated amongst his own regiments. That would ensure their loyalty, at least until the day was done. If they survived until the morrow, Braidon would have all the time in the world to judge their true allegiance.

Not that any of them could hurt him, not with his power. It burned inside him even now, setting his veins alight, feeding confidence to his soul. The demon thought him conquered, but the creature had not seen a fraction of Braidon's strength. And there was power yet to gather, once the battle outside the walls commenced.

"People of the east!" Despite himself, Braidon flinched as the demon's voice boomed down from some unknown point in the sky. "The time to decide your fate has come. Choose: life, or death."

A ripple went through the forces aligned below, and Braidon could sense the terror amidst the ranks of Marianne's soldiers, the sudden uncertainty. He smiled at their fear. With their queen's powers lost, they had no hope of victory. Even should the demon withhold its magic, those rallied beneath Marianne's banners were little more than farmhands and labourers, men and women who until a few weeks ago had not known a sword from a spear. Their ragged lines would be swept aside, their treasonous souls put to death.

But Braidon would ensure their deaths were not for nothing. With each life lost, he would be there, to gather the energies of the dying, to add to his own power. Then, when the demon finally turned its attention to Chole, Braidon would finally be strong enough to destroy it.

"Do not listen to its words, my friends." A single voice rose above the whispers of discontent as Marianne stepped to the front of her forces. She was garbed in chainmail and followed by several others, some in the silver armour of the Knights, others dressed in the attire of Elders. Braidon recognised Caledan standing at her side.

"The demon offers life, but promises only slavery," Braidon's wife continued. "I say to you, we will not submit willingly to the damned! Whatever our beliefs, whatever our loyalties, we must let go of our hatred, must stand together against the darkness." Then she glanced back, and Braidon shivered as her sapphire eyes flashed in his direction. "The king may have abandoned his people, but I will never surrender." She lifted her blade above her head. "For the Three Nations!"

A ragged cheer rose from her army, followed by the rattling of swords striking shields. The lines of the Plorsean soldiers straightened, gathering into a tight-knit square.

Silence fell once more as they stood together, waiting for the enemy's reply.

The wind howled into the quiet, raising the hackles on Braidon's neck, and for an instant he longed to be with the army below, to stand with those he had once considered friends and family, facing the darkness together.

"So be it." The demon seemed unperturbed, as though the queen's declaration mattered naught to it. Its voice rose to thunder. "Then go, my soldiers. Bring me a feast!"

The rattle of steel echoed up to the city walls as the blue armoured soldiers lowered their spears, followed by the *thump-thump* of marching boots as they advanced. A ripple went through the queen's forces at the sight, but Marianne only lifted her sword and let out a shout of defiance. Then she was charging forward to meet the enemy, her Guard and army following, and the sounds of clashing weapons filled the air.

Braidon watched on, his arms clasped tightly behind his back. What did he care if Marianne mocked him? She would soon be dead, her life thrown away for a hopeless cause. She might have saved herself, might have bowed down to him as so many of her followers had done, but instead she had chosen oblivion. As had all the others below.

Closing his eyes, Braidon let his spirit soar out across the battlefield. With the armies joined, the deaths came quickly now. Drifting overhead, he waited for the first glow of life to be released into the world. The screams of the dying rang in his ears and he drifted closer, an ache beginning in his soul in anticipation of the fresh energy.

Then he frowned as he sensed that something was wrong. He watched as one of Marianne's soldiers leapt forward, only to be cut down. The man staggered, then crumpled to the ground, his aura flickering out. But there was no sudden release of energy, no life force for Braidon to absorb.

That's not possible.

In horror, Braidon saw a flash of light race up the blade of the demon's soldier. Only then did he realise what his foe had done. The black gems had not just been embedded into the blue-stained armour—they had been set into the blades of the enemy soldiers as well, so that every life they stole would feed their demon master.

There would be no energy for Braidon to absorb, no fresh power to use against the creature. Instead, every death would only make the demon greater, would only make Braidon's defeat all the more certain.

Braidon gasped as his soul slammed back into his body, and he slumped against the crenulations. He had made a terrible mistake, had all but guaranteed the demon's victory. Something had to be done, before it was too late…

Laughter sounded in his ears as darkness coalesced in the air beyond the ramparts. Braidon shuddered and drew himself up, the power in his core leaping to his defence. The demon materialised and hung before him, a wicked smile twisting its face.

"Greetings, brother King," it cackled. "Do you still think to stand against me?"

Fire burned through Braidon's muscles as he hurled a wave of light at the creature. The brilliant white billowed outward, pressing against the demon's darkness, forcing it back from the ramparts. Yet still the cackling sounded in Braidon's ears.

"Your last allies fall, King," the demon continued, its

hand sweeping down to the battlefield. "Their power becomes mine. Ah…what a wonder it is, to feed on the living."

"Begone, demon!" Braidon bellowed.

He sent the light flashing at the creature again, but this time the beast raised a hand and the wave was cleaved in two, parting around the demon like it was a rock in the sand. Braidon fought back despair as the demon floated closer and landed on one of the crenulations. It stared down at him, the same awful smile on its face. Braidon retreated a step, while along the wall his soldiers tripped over themselves in their efforts to escape the monster.

"You cannot defeat me, brother," the demon murmured. "Your powers are naught but the playthings of a child beside mine." It bent its head to the side, as though it were inspecting him. "But of all these boorish creatures, you have at least offered some entertainment. I see the trinket on your wrist, the power you gather from across your nation. Perhaps we might learn from each other yet."

It stepped from the crenulations and landed softly on the stone ramparts. With nowhere left to go, Braidon gathered himself for one last desperate strike. But the demon only extended a hand.

"Join me, brother," it murmured. "Join me, and I will share the power of their lives. I know you long for it. I can sense the hunger growing within you, the need to feed your soul. Come; there is enough for both of us."

The demon's words struck Braidon like a physical blow. He wanted to scream and lash out at the monster, to denounce its words as the lies they were. But even as he opened his mouth to speak, he heard again the screams from below, and imagined the shimmering energies of the dying flowing into his mortal body. All he needed was a little more, a few more lives, and he would have the strength to defeat his enemy.

But the demon's instruments thwarted him, stealing the power before it ever left its owner's flesh. Now the creature offered the unthinkable, to share those energies, to stand side by side with Braidon. He shuddered at the thought of allying with such darkness, and yet…

What if he accepted, and betrayed the monster in turn? A wave of excitement swept through him, and his every hair stood on end as he faced the beast. Did he have the courage, the strength, to deceive a creature of darkness? He must, or all was lost!

Braidon drew himself up and was about to speak, when a roar came from the battlefield. The demon spun and leapt back to the crenulations.

"It seems there is some fight left in these fools yet." The demon glanced at Braidon. "Forgive me, brother. I shall return in but a moment."

Then the demon was gone, vanishing as though it had never been. Braidon staggered to the edge of the wall and searched for the source of the commotion. His heart lurched as he saw the dust cloud rising from a nearby hill, glimpsed the flashing of hooves and swords lifted high.

Screaming their fury, the cavalry force rushed down the hillside. A great crash echoed up from below as they struck the enemy flanks. Screams followed as the horsemen carved deep into the enemy ranks and then swung away.

Braidon could hardly believe his eyes. It was Loyla and her tribe. But how had they known to come?

Then he remembered that the woman had known of his power, and the lives he had absorbed. Loyla must have power of her own and had sensed the danger. But if she had come to save them, it would not be enough. The blue-garbed soldiers were already reforming, their flanks turning to face the new threat. There was still no sign of the demon or its Red Dragons, but even on horseback, Loyla's five hundred-odd riders could not turn the tides of this battle.

Instead, their deaths would only add to the demon's power. Braidon's heart beat faster as darkness materialised above the heads of the enemy, the demon reappearing. Watching the beast, Braidon longed to lash out at it with all his might, but he knew it would not be enough. Below, men and women were dying by the score, and every second the demon grew stronger. He needed to act, find some fresh source of strength…

Braidon's breath caught in his throat as an idea came to him. Swallowing, he stepped back from the edge of the ramparts, his gaze turning the city. Through the eyes of his spirit, Chole was alive with light, its streets and buildings lit by the glow of ten thousand spirits. The energies of every citizen within the city walls washed over him, alive and vibrant. Only now did he realise their potential, that the power to destroy the demon had lain within his reach all along.

A shudder rippled through Braidon as he looked upon each soul. They would all die if the demon won. It would kill them all, would walk through the streets of Chole and drain the life from them one by one. And if he did nothing, the death would not stop there. If he failed, the demon's evil would continue on through the Three Nations, would carry to every town, every city, as the demon feasted on the lives of the free.

Only he could stop it. Only he could destroy the beast.

Turning his eyes inwards, Braidon reached out with his power.

Crouching atop the walls of Chole, Kryssa crept closer to where the king stood. The demon had just vanished, but she had heard its every word, had seen the look in Braidon's eyes. Whatever happened below, Kryssa knew now what she had to do.

The energy of a hundred souls burned in her veins, making it hard to think, and she found herself wondering how Braidon had born it so long. Madness would have claimed her if she'd been forced to contain such energy for more than a few minutes. But at least she could return it, could send it back to the Earth Temple, where the priests lay in their meditative trance.

Or she could use it.

Her ears hummed as she concentrated the power into her blade, creating a deadly point that would slice through whatever defences Braidon might raise to protect himself. All she needed was to get close enough to strike. The king had retreated from the battle and now stood looking out over the city. Kryssa sent up a quick prayer to Antonia, for the Goddess's hand to guide her sword.

Then raising her blade, she charged.

For a second it seemed she would be successful. Her boots made no sound as she sprinted the last few yards, sword held out before her to drive into Braidon's back. But just as it seemed her blow must fall, the king spun. His eyes widened as they took in Kryssa and the blade, and then he thrust out his hand.

Power rushed at Kryssa, just as it had with Genevieve, and her sword grated to a stop. Enraged, she channelled more energy into the weapon, determined to avenge her fallen lover. The blade shrieked as it struck the wall of power Braidon had summoned, and a brilliant light flashed from the steel. For a second it seemed she would fail, then with a *boom*, it cut through and plunged for the king's chest.

Braidon's eyes widened in sudden fear as he realised the danger. His other hand came up, energy crackling in his palm. Kryssa's blade was mere inches away now, and with a shriek of triumph she drove it forward, sure that it must find its mark…

…Only to find herself flung backwards across the ramparts, the sword torn from her grasp. The stone crenulations brought her to an abrupt stop, driving the air from her lungs. Gasping, she slumped on her side and clutched at her stomach. With his second attack, Braidon had ignored her weapon entirely, aiming the blow for her own unprotected body.

Boots slapped against stone as the king approached. Finally managing to inhale, Kryssa dove for her fallen sword, but a gesture from Braidon sent it skittering away.

Despair swept through her as she dragged herself to her hands and knees and found the king staring down at her.

"Oh, Kryssa," Braidon murmured. "What are you doing? Can you not see past your petty rage? I am our only hope against the darkness!"

"You are the darkness," Kryssa croaked, staggering to her feet.

A scream tore from her throat as she leapt, dragging the dagger from her belt. The king did not move from where he stood, only flicked his hand. Kryssa drew on the power of the living priests once more, forming a shield around her, but Braidon's power shattered it like glass. She gasped as she found herself frozen in place, her body no longer hers to control.

"Everything I have ever done was for the good of my people," the king said calmly, as though she had not just tried to kill him. "Though they reject and betray and abandon me, though I now stand alone, still I fight for them."

"You could have stood with us!" Kryssa shrieked. "But you were too consumed by your hatred." The anger went from her in a rush and her shoulders slumped. "Instead, you stand here watching while your friends die. But what do you care? I heard you speaking with the demon. I saw your temptation. Truly, you are lost, Braidon."

"I am not lost, Kryssa," the king murmured. "I am the only one who sees the truth, the only one with the resolve to do what must be done."

An icy breath blew across Kryssa's neck with his words. "And what must be done, Braidon?"

Braidon walked past her, his eyes drifting out over the city. "I don't know why I didn't see it before," he said softly.

"Perhaps I was too afraid—but now the haze has lifted. There is power enough here to destroy the demon, if only I have the courage to take it."

Kryssa's heart lurched in her chest as she followed his gaze and realised what he meant. "Braidon, no! You cannot—"

The words died in her throat as Braidon made a gesture and her mouth snapped forcibly closed. He made to step past her, but drawing on the power of the priests, Kryssa tore loose from his spell.

"The power has corrupted you!" she shrieked. "Braidon, this is not you, please—"

Kryssa broke off as Braidon swung around. This time when his power came, it was not ice that stole the words from her, but a terrible fire. Her plea turned into a scream as every nerve in her body was suddenly lit aflame. The strength went from her legs and she collapsed against the ramparts. She clawed desperately at the cold stones, desperate to relieve the searing, to free herself of the agony.

"And where did *you* discover such power, Kryssa?" Braidon growled, his eyes burning as he stepped closer. "You speak of *my* corruption, but your resistance reveals your own desperation. Tell me, my most loyal servant, whose life did you drink to gain such strength?"

"None!" Kryssa moaned, her back arching as she writhed against the stone. "It is only borrowed!"

A frown crossed Braidon's face. Kryssa gasped as the pain vanished as quickly as it had come, and she slumped against the ground, struggling to regain her composure. The lines on Braidon's brow deepened as his eyes took on a distant look, as though his mind was far away. Kryssa had the sense that she could have struck him down in that moment, but her body was frozen once more, and this time she could not find the strength to break free.

"The priests!" Braidon bellowed suddenly, staggering back from her. Rage twisted his face as he swung towards the city. "Traitors spring like maggots from my ranks." He raised a fist, as though to strike the whole city down.

"No," Kryssa whispered, but she did not have the strength to oppose the king, not even to stand. All she could do was watch as the flames gathered in the king's fist.

———

Looking through the eyes of his spirit, Braidon stared at the threads of energy swirling about Kryssa, radiating up from the city, from the Temple of the Earth. The priest's treachery struck him like a blow, for he had given everything to save them when the Knights had come. To learn now that they had betrayed him…

A shiver passed through Braidon as the last of his doubt fell away. He knew now that his path was true. If even his most beloved subjects had turned from him, then none in Chole could be saved. The city was corrupt to its core and must be cleansed. But the lives of its citizens might at least serve the greater good, might still save the Three Nations from eternal servitude.

He raised a fist, preparing himself to snuff out the traitors huddling behind his walls. But reaching for his power, Braidon sensed a commotion from behind him, a surge of energy radiating from the battlefield. Fear touched him. The demon approached, but he was not yet ready!

His whole body shook as dark energies washed across the walls. Cursing, he spun and braced himself for the demon's attack. Light flashed in his inner eyes, coming from the battlefield. He walked past Kryssa and stepped up to the nearest crenulation. Almost absently he gestured for her to follow, and though she could not move, his power lifted her from the stones and drew her with him.

Below, Marianne's forces were being pushed back by the blue tide. The demon's darkness now hovered above the Trolan army, but it made no move to strike down its enemies. Perhaps the creature took some perverse pleasure in the chaos of battle.

If so, the entertainment would soon be at an end. Marianne's ragtag army had retreated almost to the breach in the city walls, while out on the plains, Loyla's cavalry was attempting to harry the enemy's rear. Even as Braidon watched, they spun and charged again. A great *crash* followed as the cavalry slammed into the enemy. Dozens of the blue-armoured soldiers went down, their life forces blinking out, then surging through the black gems to the demon.

Loyla's force began to retreat—but this time the demon had had enough. An awful *roar* came from above and then the Red Dragons were diving from the clouds, their jaws open wide, the flames building in the depths of their throats. Horses screamed as panic swept through Loyla's ranks, but the inferno was not for her people.

Instead, the dragons swept past them, and their flames fell upon the earth beyond the horses. For a moment, Braidon thought the beasts had changed allegiances again— until he saw what they had done. The fields all around Loyla's cavalry were burning. Smoke stained the air black as the firestorm raged, trapping the horses in a burning circle, driving them back towards the spears of the enemy.

Ice crept down Braidon's spine as he realised why the dragons had spared Loyla's people. The life forces of those killed by dragon fire would not be claimed by the black gems—so instead the Red Dragons were forcing the horsemen back onto the blades of the demon's soldiers.

Realising his time was short, Braidon was about to turn away when he saw Loyla herself. She had dragged her horse to a stop and now stood in the centre of her people, sword raised to the heavens. The flames burned all around them, and the rest of her cavalry had come to a stop as well. As one they turned their eyes to Loyla.

"My people!" Her voice carried over the gathered armies, though she had done nothing to amplify her call. "Lend me your strength."

Braidon could have laughed at her desperation, but the sound died in his throat as a violet light sprung from her blade. Then the other riders were following suit, and each of their swords was set aglow with a different colour. The combined energies of the army rose above their heads, shining with a brilliant rainbow light, and flashed like an arrow for the darkness gathered over the Trolan forces.

Taken by surprised, the demon's energies recoiled on themselves. A cry rose from the blue army and their ranks wavered, gaps opening in their formations. With a roar, Loyla's cavalry lowered their swords and charged, and now they carved deep into the Trolan army.

Only Loyla herself remained behind. Standing alone, she still held the blade above her head. The multicoloured light had not retreated, and at her direction it rend and tore at the demon's darkness, forcing it back upon itself.

Another cry came from across the battlefield. Fear touched Braidon as he saw Marianne leap upon a stone block that had fallen in the destruction of the gate. Sword raised to the sky, she sent her strength streaming up to join the conflagration. But the power was more than anything her own life force could have summoned, and looking out through his spirit eyes, Braidon saw she had done the same as Kryssa and Loyla. Cords of power streamed from her soldiers all across the battlefield, adding their strength to hers, even as they fought and died against the blue-garbed Trolans.

The darkness flinched against this new attack, and for a second Braidon's heart lifted. Perhaps the demon truly could be defeated, if only they worked together. Silently he gathered his strength, readying himself to join the fight, to add his power to that of Loyla and Marianne…

…But at the last moment he hesitated, his eyes drawn again to his wife, to the power shining from her body. It was exactly as he had predicted, as he had foreseen and tried to stop. It had not taken her even a day to regain what she had lost. His eyes slid closed as the fear raged inside him.

"Braidon!" Kryssa was screaming at his side. "This is your chance, help them! Together—"

She broke off suddenly, and Braidon's eyes snapped open, aware something had changed on the battlefield. His gaze was drawn back to the demon's darkness, and he saw now the truth. The attacks had not lessened it, only pressed it back on itself. Now a *boom* swept across the battlefield as it tightened, forming a terrible knot of utter black. Then it shot outwards, not as an arrow or blade but an awful hammer of pure darkness. It smashed upon the rainbow powers of Marianne and Loyla and burst them asunder. Streams of light flashed outwards across the battlefield in all directions, dying to nothing.

And then there was only the darkness.

On the hillside, Loyla bent in two in her saddle, while Marianne crumpled to the stone and lay still. Even from a distance, Braidon could see they were finished, their strength and that of their people done. Already the blue soldiers were reforming, their shields slamming together as though they were of one mind. Seeing their danger, Loyla's riders dragged back on their reins, seeking to retreat before the armoured men could encircle them.

The Trolans were faster still. A great rattling rose from the battlefield as the soldiers drew back their spears and hurled them into the clustered cavalry.

The effect was devastating. Without any armour and caught in the moment they'd been turning to flee, Loyla's people were exposed. Braidon watched grimly as horses crumpled and warriors went toppling from their saddles. The blue-garbed warriors offered no chance for respite. They marched forward into the chaos, blades rising and falling.

And as the demon fed upon their deaths, the dark cloud grew larger.

"I offered them a chance to survive," Braidon said sadly, "but they spurned me."

"You can still help them!" Kryssa shouted.

Her eyes were wild as she fought against his bonds, but Kryssa could not break free of them now, could not hurt him any longer, and he only shook his head.

"They made their choice," he said. "Now they are lost, but the Three Nations might yet survive."

His gaze returned to Chole, to the thousand pinpricks of light adrift amidst the twisting streets. Gathering himself, he sent his power streaming through the city, spinning the energies at his command into a thousand invisible threads. Each one he sent swirling about a single soul, wrapping it tight, so that all it would take was a thought, a tug, and all life in the city would be drawn to him.

Excitement swept through his soul at the fresh strength that would soon flow in his veins. Not even the demon could stand against him then. But he must act quickly, before it destroyed the last of his enemies and came for him. He steeled himself for what must be done.

"Braidon, don't do it!" Kryssa's voice came from far away.

A sharp *popping* sounded in Braidon's ears as something in the air gave way. He spun in time to see the forces gathering within Kryssa once more. With a scream she tore loose from his bindings and dropped to the ramparts, her breath coming in ragged gasps. Braidon sighed, weary of her distractions. Silently he reached out to snuff the life from her.

But she was already unleashing her energies, and surprised, he threw up his defences. The attack was red-hot when it came, shooting at him as a fiery cone, a sword of flaming light. But though it forced him back a step, there was no chance it could touch him, just as there had been no chance for those gathered out on the fields of death. It was the last gasp of a desperate soul, and Braidon pitied her for it.

Only at the last minute did he sense a deception. His power brought the fiery blade to a halt, but there was no force in the blow, none of the strength he had expected. But a second wave swept on, a shimmering power invisible to the eye. He did not know how it had evaded his shield until it struck him, and he realised it had not been an attack against his body at all.

Braidon gasped as his spirit was forced from his body. In a rage, he reached for his power but found himself separated from it. Kryssa's power had formed a shimmering shield around his body, keeping him from the energy within.

Fear touched Braidon as he found himself vulnerable. It faded as he saw it was taking all of Kryssa's strength to keep the power locked inside him. Already it was roiling against her barriers, seeking to reach him, to join once more with its master.

Enough, Kryssa, he said, drifting close to whisper into the woman's mind. *You cannot win.*

A spasmed passed through Kryssa's face but she hung on, her sapphire eyes finding his spirit. "Look, Braidon, please!" she gasped. "For the love my father held for you, look at what you have become!"

Braidon recoiled at the mention of Devon, his soul suddenly heavy with grief. He had not realised how much he missed the hammerman, how he longed for his calming presence. The campaign had hardly allowed him a moment to relax these past months—indeed, he'd been afraid to, lest his courage fail him. Now though, free of his body, of his power, he found his thoughts becoming melancholy.

Unconsciously, his gaze was drawn down. A shiver passed through his spirit as he saw the shining cords that crisscrossed the city, binding the fates of the unwitting citizens to his own. All there was left to do was to tug…

"You promised to protect them," Kryssa whispered, her voice choked with the strain of holding him.

Then suddenly her spirit was alongside him. Her image

flickered in and out, strained by the force it was taking to hold him. Even so, he could sense the grief radiating from her, the pain. A picture rushed into his mind, of Genevieve collapsing to the cold earth, an arrow sprouting from her breast.

Gasping, Braidon's spirit folded in two as the anguish of what he'd done washed over him. He had killed her, his friend, and for what? Because she had tried to stop him from murdering a helpless woman?

What have I done?

He turned to Kryssa, seeing her again for what she truly was—his most loyal follower, the woman who had believed in him, even when he'd given up on himself. How he had made her pay for that loyalty.

A sob tore from Kryssa and he could see her spirit was fading, the last energies of the priests burning away.

So much, she whispered. *Now you must do one last thing!*

Then she flickered out, and back on the ramparts her body crumpled. With the last of her strength consumed, the spell keeping Braidon from his body dissolved. He gasped as he found himself flesh and bone once more, and the burning of his power came rushing back.

Groaning, Braidon sank to his knees, the certainty of just a few moments before vanished. Power surged in his veins and he felt again the temptation, the need to reach out and drain the energy from his subjects. Already the resolve he had found was fading, overwhelmed by hunger.

He clenched his eyes closed and a moan dragged from his throat. Beyond the wall, the demon's power was like a hurricane, its surface flashing as each new soul was added to the creature's strength. Seeing its power, the need grew within him, the desperation to do whatever it took to match his foe. All he needed was a few more lives, and he could save Plorsea, save the whole of the Three Nations.

What's the point of saving Plorsea, if I can't save my family?

The hairs on Braidon's scalp stood on end as he recalled Devon's words from so long ago. That night seemed but a distant memory now, words spoken in a different time, to a different Braidon. Yet still they rang true in his mind, carving through the temptation, granting his thoughts clarity.

He might not have any family left, but there was still Kryssa, still her daughter, and ten thousand other souls in Chole. They were all relying on him, had put their faith in him to protect them. He could not fail them now.

Braidon forced his mind to the present, and sending his soul flying, he merged his mind with the cold stone of the wall, seeking to escape the dark desire that burned in his body. Electricity surged through him as he sensed suddenly another power amidst the ancient blocks, a strange, unknown magic...

And Braidon knew what he had to do.

※ 31 ※

Bang.

Pela cried out as an explosion erupted overhead, sending the rainbow conflagration shooting outwards in all directions. A shock wave followed, knocking Pela backwards from the blue-armoured soldiers they fought. A rough hand caught her collar before she fell and hauled her back.

"You good?" Caledan asked quickly, flashing her a glance.

Nodding, Pela swung around in search of Marianne. There was a lull in the fighting where they stood, as their allies pushed forward to confront the Trolans. The queen had been standing atop a fallen block of granite, but there was no sign of her now…

"There!" Pela shouted, glimpsing a slender arm hanging from the top of the granite block.

"With me," Caledan growled.

The clash of swords grew louder again as the Trolans surged forward. Pela hefted her father's sword and stepped up alongside Caledan, spearing out her blade to knock aside an enemy blow. The injured Lonian soldier who had been the intended target staggered back, clutching his shoulder. Their eyes met and he nodded his thanks, then retreated towards the city.

Pela drove herself into the space he'd left and blocked a second blow from her foe. Steel shrieked on steel and the soldier stepped back. She feinted for his chest, but as his sword came down, she twisted her wrist to change the attack, and her blade went crunching through her opponent's helmet. Screaming, he dropped his blade and crumpled to the ground. The black opal set into his breastplate flashed, and Pela retreated to Caledan's side.

He offered a grim nod, but she had only a second to celebrate the victory, as two more of the Trolan soldiers took their fallen comrade's place. The fighting was all around them now, their defensive line fracturing under the weight of the enemy. Pela fought desperately, her father's sword almost an extension of her now, while at her side Caledan's blade rose and fell with deadly accuracy.

And still the blue-armoured soldiers came on. As their comrades began to fall, Caledan and Pela were slowly forced back. Caledan angled their retreat towards where the queen had collapsed, though what they would do when they reached her, Pela was not sure. Beyond the rubble that had been Chole's gates, Braidon's forces lay in wait, and the king had already made it clear they would not be allowed to pass.

Another blue-armoured warrior leapt at Pela, his broadsword swinging down for her skull. She skipped sideways and the blow cut empty air. Thrown off-balance, the soldier staggered forward, bringing him within range of her short sword. Pela thrust out, driving the point of her blade hard into his groin. Steel crunched as it found a weakness between the steel plates and plunged home.

Beside her, Caledan threw himself forward as two men came at him. Their swords danced out, one high, the other low, and for a second Pela thought the sellsword would be cut in two. But he ducked and one soldier staggered past him, while his sword flashed down to block the second. Then Caledan's dagger was in his hand and he was surging back up.

Shocked by the speed of his recovery, the Trolans had no time to recover their guard. The first screamed as the sellsword's dagger punched through the joint beneath his armpit and found his heart, while the second crashed to the ground, blood pumping from his jugular where Caledan's sword had found its mark.

"To the queen!" Caledan shouted as he leapt away from the dying men.

Pela nodded, and keeping their swords to the enemy, they crept backwards, allowing others to take their place at the front. Screams came from around them as queen's army began to disintegrate. They had all lent their strength to the queen, to aid in the desperate battle that had been fought overhead. But the demon had proven its power greater than all of them, and now they had nothing left to give.

Heart racing, Pela glanced over her shoulder and saw Marianne was now crouching atop her chunk of granite. A dozen Plorseans stood in a ring around her position, but as Pela watched a unit of Trolans broke through the frontlines and rushed at her guard.

"Back!" she cried, grasping Caledan by the shoulder.

Alerted to the danger, Caledan leapt to intercept the Trolans. Pela rushed after him, and together they tackled the group of five blue-garbed soldiers. Three turned to meet their attack while the other two raced on, determined to reach the queen.

Gritting her teeth, Pela braced as her armoured opponent bore down on her. Her father's sword leapt to deflect a horizontal blow, and her whole arm vibrated as their blades came together. For a moment she was forced back, her feet moving quickly to keep her balance.

The Trolan soldier came after her but she stabbed upwards, aiming for his helmet. Steel rang out as her blow struck, but this time her blade did not find a gap in the heavy steel. Even so, her foe staggered back, his helmet twisted out of place. Roaring, he tore it loose and tossed it aside. Face twisted in rage, he started towards her once more.

Fear slipped its way into Pela's heart as the man approached, but she did not flinch from it. In her mind, she heard her uncle's words from so long ago.

Fear is a warrior's greatest weapon—and greatest weakness!

A smile touched her face as she raised her father's blade in mock salute. A snarl tore from the man as he charged her, but even in that moment of rage, Pela sensed the sudden doubt in her foe. His sword came up, but he hesitated, and she leapt into the opening with sword raised. With his helmet lost, there was nothing to stop her blade as it took him through the eye.

Dragging back her sword, she spun in search of Caledan. But the sellsword had already dispatched his foes and was making again for the queen. The remaining Trolans had been cut down by her Guard—though not without cost. Two of the Plorseans had fallen and now lay entangled with the men they had slain.

Pela raced after Caledan, and together they took their place in the ring of soldiers. Scuffing noises came from behind them, and then Marianne stepped up beside them with rapier in hand. Shadows hung beneath the queen's eyes and her face was stretched with exhaustion, but she smiled when she saw them gaping at her.

"Marianne!" Caledan gasped. "What are you doing? It's not safe…"

The queen's smile faded with his words. "Soon nowhere will be safe, my Champion," she murmured, lifting her blade. "And when there's nowhere left to hide, a woman must choose a place to stand. I choose here, Caledan, with you."

Pela gaped at the woman, stunned that she would place herself in such danger. But then she realised the truth of Marianne's words. This *was* the end. Their last gamble had failed, and now there was nothing left to do but wait for the Trolan swords to find them, for their life forces to be absorbed by the awful demon.

Sadness touched her as she looked at Marianne and Caledan together. If only her mother had not left, they might have stood together in their final moments. But instead Pela stood alone, and Kryssa lost to her hatred.

But Pela did her best to swallow her grief. At least she had escaped the fate Rayan had planned for her, to be trapped within her own body for eternity. Just the thought of Ruebyn, lying motionless in the camp behind them, his eyes staring forever into the distance…

A shudder passed through Pela—and then, as if bidden by her thoughts, the demon's laughter rang out across the battlefield. Ice slid down her spine as the dark storm descended in a swirling column. Men and women leapt back as it struck the earth near where Pela and her friends stood together. Slowly it drew inwards, coalescing into the body of Rayan.

"And so it comes to an end," he murmured. Smiling, he started towards them. "It will be a pleasure to drink the life from ones of such courage."

A scream came from Caledan as he leapt to meet the beast. But while the creature still took the form of Rayan, this was no man, no mortal to be defeated by the blade. With a gesture, the sellsword was hurled aside and the demon walked on.

Rage built in Pela as she watched Rayan approach. This was the creature that had stolen Ruebyn from her, who threatened her friends, her entire world. Pressure built within her as she drew on her life force, as she fed all her anger and hatred and grief into a whirling ball of energy. With a scream, her power came to life, becoming a burning ball of flame. Its heat seared at her flesh as she sent it hurtling at the demon.

The inferno crackled as it flashed across the space between them but Rayan strode on, unconcerned. As the flame approached him, the darkness rippled out in a great wave, extinguishing the flames of her power at a touch.

Gasping, Pela sank to her knees as the strength went from her legs. Stones crunched as Marianne stepped between them, but another gesture from the demon and she fell alongside Caledan. The Queen's Guard shrank back before its power, unmanned by their terror.

Then Pela was all alone, staring up into the eyes of the beast.

"Oh, my poor, Pela," Rayan murmured. "You have

suffered so, trying to survive in this unjust world. But fear not: the pain is almost at an end."

"Get away from me," Pela croaked.

Finding some flicker of strength within, she forced herself to her feet. Her father's blade was still in her hand, the sword her mother had carried all these months, that Devon had first gifted her. Rayan wore only a richly woven tunic and leggings. There was no armour to turn aside her blade, but surely it could not be so simple. Her strength at an end, Pela gripped the weapon tight and thrust it at the demon's chest.

A bemused expression crossed Rayan's face as he caught the blade between his thumb and forefinger. Laughter whispered from his throat as he thrust it back, propelling Pela from her feet. Rolling across the scorched earth, she came to rest against the granite block that had once formed part of Chole's walls.

"Enough, young Pela," Rayan whispered as he closed the fresh distance between them and crouched beside her. "You need fight no longer. The time for your reward has finally come."

His hand snaked out and caught Pela by the wrist. Unable to tear herself loose, she cried out as something dark crossed between them, an awful, sickly presence. A cry built in her throat, but before Pela could let it loose, she found her mind retreating. Suddenly she was in the depths of her consciousness, in that empty void where her life force burnt.

Except it was no longer empty. The dark tendrils of the demon were all around her, swirling cords of infinite black just waiting to snare her, to hold her fast and trap her in this silent space. Terror filled Pela and she reached for her life force, for the last few drops of flame to protect herself, but the darkness was faster still.

Pela's fear turned to horror as the first black vine snapped fast to her leg. Her screams echoed through the void as she thrashed, but Pela had no strength left to resist, and soon another grasped her. Her arms were pinned fast, then her other leg. Her skin crawled as the darkness crept over her, engulfing her torso, then chest, slowly creeping towards her head.

Boom.

Light flashed across the void and suddenly the vines were retreating, as though some other force had torn them loose at the root. Pela cried out as she found herself suddenly back in the real world. Her whole body screamed in pain, but there was no time to dwell on it.

A blinding rainbow light swirled all around her, tearing at her hair, lifting her up, dragging her to her feet—no, not the light, but the demon's grasp on her arm. Screaming, she brought the hilt of her sword down on its wrist, desperate to break its hold, but Rayan clung on, his fingers like a vice. Another shriek tore from Pela as she was yanked up, her arm almost tearing from its socket.

Then the ground beneath her vanished and she found herself flying, spinning, and lurching through a rainbow of light, the world disappearing around her…

32

B *oom.*

An explosion on the battlefield tore Kryssa from unconsciousness. Gasping, she pushed herself upright and then promptly slumped back to the battlements as her entire body screamed out in agony. Distantly she felt her own pain reflected in the minds of the priests whose power she had drawn on—she'd used far too much of their energies, and now they would all suffer for it.

The last rumbles of the explosion were already dying away, but the air still hummed with power, filling her with a sense of urgency. Gritting her teeth, she forced herself to her hands and knees. Scanning the ramparts, she found Braidon crumpled nearby.

For a second, Kryssa thought he was dead, but then his chest moved half an inch, and a soft groan came from the depths of his throat. Agony wrapped around Kryssa's forearms as she clawed her way across the ground to him, but she swallowed her screams. Her heart pounded in her chest, and she sensed something of significance had happened while she'd been passed out, that Braidon had done something terrible.

Her stomach swirled as she remembered his plan—to drain the life from every soul in Chole. But she had gotten through to him, had forced him to see the truth with the last of her power. Surely, surely Braidon could not have committed such an atrocity.

The king's eyelids fluttered as Kryssa slumped beside him, and then sapphire eyes were looking up at her. Kryssa's breath caught in her throat as she saw the despair there. A sudden silence fell around them, as beyond the crenulations all went still.

"Kryssa," he croaked.

"What did you do?" Kryssa whispered.

She pushed herself to her knees to look between the stone crenulations. Beyond the walls, the battle had ceased, though there was no way of telling why. The Trolan soldiers stood frozen in their rows of blue-stained steel, while opposite them the forces of the free watched them with trepidation, clearly confused by the unexpected respite.

Then steel rattled as the blue-garbed soldiers began to disengage and pull back. The thud of marching boots carried to the walls as the Trolans retreated out onto the plains and regrouped. Marianne's army watched on, mystified by their enemy's actions, while Loyla's few remaining riders trotted their horses up to join them.

"I'm so sorry, Kryssa."

The hairs on Kryssa's neck stood on end at the tone of Braidon's voice. She spun on the king.

"*What did you do, Braidon?*" she repeated.

"I should never have tried to kill Marianne," the king continued as though he had not heard her. She leaned closer, but his eyes were fixed on some distant point, and she realised his mind was somewhere else. "Genevieve was right…to stop me. How I wish…" He trailed off, and now blinking, his eyes fixed on her. "I'm so sorry."

Anger flared in Kryssa's chest and she felt a longing to drive her dagger through his heart. She fought the desire, her soul weary of the hatred, of the rage that had driven her these last months. She could see the pain in Braidon's eyes, the guilt. She could not offer him her forgiveness, but she rested a hand on his shoulder all the same, trying to comfort him.

"Thank you for stopping me," Braidon rasped, his gaze still fixed on hers. "For saving me. I…could never have forgiven myself had I…" He scrunched his eyes closed. "I should have seen the way sooner."

"What way?" Kryssa asked, leaning closer, but Braidon was rambling again, his mind lost.

"The demon needed to be separated…from its power… but I could not do it…like you did with me. Too…well protected. Ah, but that I had acted sooner…such a price…"

Kryssa's heart was starting to race again as she sensed the meaning behind Braidon's words. He had done something to the demon, but something had gone wrong. Something terrible.

"*Braidon,*" she said, gripping him by the shirt and shaking him. "Tell me what you did, or by the Gods, you'll wish the demon had killed you."

The king's head lolled on his shoulders but he did not resist her. When she released him, he slumped back to the ramparts like a ragdoll. Only his eyes moved, fixing again on her.

"It already has," he coughed.

As though bidden by his words, Braidon's face contorted and he cried out, his whole body going taut. A convulsion wracked him and for a second Kryssa though he would die without telling her a thing. But finally he slumped against the ground, his breath coming in ragged gasps. She leaned in close, straining to hear the words he spoke next.

"It…was so strong, I hardly had the strength. But I held it. I banished the demon, though it took all the energies I had stolen. If only I could have saved her as well."

"Saved who?" Kryssa barely dared to ask the question. She knew what Braidon would say before he ever spoke the name.

"Pela."

Kryssa reared back as though she had been struck by lightning. She couldn't breathe, couldn't see, couldn't think. There was a ringing in her ears, a horrible, awful burning in her heart. She clutched at her chest as her entire body shook.

"No," she gasped, as though her denial could take back Braidon's words. Leaning forward, she grabbed the king and shook him. "No, Braidon, tell me you didn't! Tell me you didn't take my daughter from me!"

But the king's eyes only fluttered closed. The tension fled his body, the last spark of his life force with it. Suddenly Kryssa was alone atop the ramparts, with only the company of the dead for comfort. A sob tore from her throat as she buried her face in Braidon's shirt.

"No, no, no," she groaned, then threw herself back from him.

Folding into herself, she slammed her fist into the stones. A sharp *crack* came from her knuckles and pain shot through her fist. She screamed and lashed out again, concentrating on the pain, the agony of her broken bones—anything but what she had lost.

Selina, Devon, Genevieve, Pela, Braidon. They were all gone, everyone she had ever loved, had ever cared for. How could this have happened?

Kryssa lurched to her feet and stumbled to the edge of the ramparts. The battlefield stretched out below, and she saw now the piles of bodies, heard the distant groans of the dying. Marianne's survivors had gathered near the gates, but they were so few now. The dead outnumbered the living.

Slowly, her gaze travelled downwards and she stepped up to the top of the crenulations. It was a sixty-foot drop to the rocks below. Pain radiated from her hand, but it was nothing to the anguish in her heart. One step, and it would all be over.

Her eyes were drawn back to the huddle of survivors. It was impossible to say who remained, if Marianne or Caledan still lived. If both had fallen, who would take command now? Movement out on the plains drew her attention to the Trolan force. The men had retreated only a short distance from the city. Even without the demon, they badly outnumbered the defenders. And these men were men who had willingly served the beast. They could still prove a threat.

Swallowing her grief, Kryssa stepped back from the ledge. She could not give up. That was not the woman Selina and Devon had raised her to be. Whatever her pain, whatever her loss, she must go on. There were people who would need her before the day was done.

Absently, she started along the ramparts, making for the stairwell. Passing from the wall to the narrow alleyways of Chole, she made her way to the gates in a daze, to the barricade Braidon's soldiers had erected to guard the city. His solders were still there, though they were scattered and disorganised, their leaders long since fled.

"Lieutenant Kryssa!" one gasped when he saw her, hope alighting in his eyes. "What news from the king?"

Kryssa paused mid-stride, casting a glance in the man's direction. "The king is dead," she murmured. "Open the barricade. Let the queen's soldiers into the city."

She walked on as shouting broke out in her wake, uncaring whether they obeyed her orders or not. She wanted only to find the survivors, to see for herself the truth of Braidon's last words. Perhaps the king had been wrong, delirious in his final moments. Perhaps Pela had survived after all.

But Kryssa couldn't bring herself to believe it.

She climbed over the barricade and started across the blackened earth. Chunks of granite rose up around her, and it was not long before she came to the first of the bodies. The men and women who had followed Caledan into the breach lay all around, blackened and broken by dragon flame.

You did this.

Kryssa shuddered and lifted her eyes, unable to face that guilt today. Ahead, Marianne's forces had gathered in a tight group around their injured, still watching the distant Trolans. It seemed they did not believe the battle was done either.

"Does the queen live?" Kryssa called as she approached.

A dozen faces spun towards her. Several reached for their blades, but a man's voice rose above the whispers before any could attack:

"Let her pass!"

The slightest of hopes touched Kryssa's heart as she recognised Caledan's voice. The soldiers parted at her approach, and she made her way through their ranks to where a single block of granite lay. There she spied Caledan and the queen. They stood atop the block, their eyes on the enemy. At Kryssa's appearance they gestured for others to take their place, then stepped down to meet her.

"I'm so sorry, Kryssa," Caledan whispered, and the last pieces of her heart shattered. "The portal...it took her before I could..." He shook his head, leaving the sentence unfinished.

"It was Braidon," Kryssa said, her vision blurring. "But...I did not see. Please...how did it happen?"

"It was The Way," Marianne answered, "Braidon must have opened it with his power and directed it at the demon. But it already had Pela in its grasp. She was dragged in with it."

"They are in The Way?" Kryssa gasped. Her head snapped up, her heart missing a beat. "Then she is not dead!"

"No," Marianne replied, but there was such sadness in her voice that Kryssa felt the hope wither in her chest, "but it matters not. The demon's power came from its subjects. It could draw on their strength at will, from all its soldiers here —and in Trola. But The Way is another world, another place entirely. By banishing it there, Braidon cut the creature off from its source of power. But if the door were opened..."

"Its power would be restored," Kryssa croaked.

"And Pela would be its first victim, if it hasn't already..." Marianne trailed off, and Kryssa could see the sadness in the queen's eyes, the pity.

Kryssa turned away, head bowed. "Your people may enter the city," she whispered, unable to face them.

She had failed. Had failed her daughter, her lover, her king. All she had left now was her duty to her people.

"Will you join us?"

It was Caledan. He moved to stand beside her as around them the army started towards Chole. Kryssa looked up at the sellsword, wondering at his words, knowing he meant so much more than just entering the city. After all Plorsea had suffered, the nation would need rebuilding. As would Trola.

Looking back at Chole, Kryssa shuddered. So much had happened inside its walls, so much darkness. She had played her part in it, helped to feed the hatred that had consumed Braidon. How could she *not* return, to offer whatever aid she could to put right her wrongs?

And yet, hadn't that been Braidon's fate? He had returned again and again, always trying to right some past wrong, to correct his mistakes. In the end, he had succeeded at least in halting the demon's darkness, but…he had almost fallen to that same fate in the process. Kryssa had no desire to walk that line. And she had no desire to ever see the inside of Chole's walls again.

"No, Caledan," she whispered, watching as the soldiers streamed past them. "They don't need me. I will find my own path."

Caledan stared down at her for a long moment, his expression unreadable. Then abruptly, he dragged Kryssa into a hug. She hugged him back, struggling to keep the tears from falling. Her dignity was the only thing she had left, the last comfort to which she could cling. She felt a touch of pride when Caledan finally drew back and her eyes remained dry.

"I don't know what happened up there," Caledan murmured, his eyes drawn to the battlements. "But I have a feeling you had a hand in what happened. Thank you, for everything."

She dropped her head in acknowledgement but did not speak, least the dam break. Then she was turning her back on him, moving through the ranks of soldiers, away from the cursed city. Still fearful of the blue-garbed army standing out on the plains, most of Marianne's soldiers were already through the breach, but several had stayed to help with the injured.

There were plenty of those after the last hour of battle, and Kryssa's mood soured further as she looked on the aftermath of the demon's plague. It might not have come from a disease, but her daughter had been right in that, at least. The violence, the hatred and greed that had beset the Three Nations these last thousand years was just as deadly as any sickness.

But Kryssa was done with sacrificing her own life, her own happiness, for the sake of others. She would not make the same mistake as Braidon.

"Kryssa?"

The hairs on her neck stood on end as a voice called her name. Kryssa's heart tumbled into her stomach as she swung around and saw the boy, Ruebyn, standing nearby. He was as pale as a ghost, as though all the blood had been drained from his veins, and he barely seemed able to keep his feet. He staggered towards her, and she darted forward to catch him before he fell.

"Easy," she whispered, holding him up, even as her heart split in two all over again.

She could not face this, could not bear to see any more

pain, any more grief. Not when it so closely reflected her own…

"Where is Pela?"

The whisper was softly spoken, but it broke her as surely as any blade. Tears poured down her face as she hugged the boy, desperate to offer him some comfort, some words of hope, but unable to find them. Wet heat soaked into her shoulder as the boy cried with her.

She didn't have to say a word for Ruebyn to know the truth.

They clung together in the silence. It was all they could do now—comfort each other in their grief. Yet recalling the moment she had stood on the edge of the ramparts and contemplated ending it all, Kryssa felt relief that she had turned away. Her family might be gone, her whole world and agony, but she at least was no longer alone.

And nor was Ruebyn. Together, they would survive, and those they had lost would live on in their memories. Their names would be carved into fresh legends, and tales of their bravery passed down to inspire a new generation of heroes, to bring hope on the darkest nights.

And perhaps then the world would become a slightly brighter place.

EPILOGUE

P ela groaned as she woke alone amidst a broken forest. Shattered tree trunks lay strewn all around her, their roots torn up and leaves withered to a sickly brown. The earth beneath her feet was churned and broken, marked by the passage of a thousand men. She drew in a breath, then retched at the scent of rotting meat, though beneath it a faint trace of life still lingered. Overhead, the sky was a swirling purple.

The Way.

But how had she come to be there? Had the ancient magic drawn her back? No, that didn't seem right. She shivered, remembering the awful battle, the screams of the dying and the scent of blood. Compared with that, The Way remained tranquil, despite the damage the demon's forces had left during their passage.

The demon.

Suddenly alert, Pela dragged herself to her feet. She might be safe here, but the demon and its soldiers remained free. Her family and friends were still in danger—she had to get back and help them, before it was too late. Closing her eyes, she reached for the power of her life force.

Before the walls of Chole, she'd had barely a spark of energy left, yet something about this other world seemed to restore her energies. Indeed, when Pela looked through the eyes of her spirit, she found a soft mist of white all around, seeming to concentrate around her and the other points of life that had survived the demon's passage.

Returning to her body, she gauged her strength. The flame of her soul remained weak, but it would be enough. She could not afford to linger in this place, not with its strange passage of time.

She was about to wake the magic of The Way when the hackles on her neck lifted in warning. Her father's sword leapt into her hand as she spun, scanning the battered undergrowth. Laugher carried to her ears as a figure appeared amidst the shadows, and then Rayan stepped into the light.

"Hello, sweet Pela."

A scream built in Pela's throat as she leapt back from him, the blade extended before her.

"Stay away from me," she gasped, though she knew there was nothing she could do to stop the demonic creature's approach.

"I must admit, your king had more power than I gave him credit for," Rayan continued. "If he survived this effort, I'll be sure to tear the life from him when I return."

"What made you so hateful, Rayan?" Pela rasped. Her vision blurred as the demon continued forward. She staggered, her feet threatening to give way beneath the weight of her terror. She was powerless before him. All she had left were her words. "Can't you see what it has cost you?" she continued. "Can't you see the truth? Look around, look at what your evil has done."

She made a gesture at the ruined forest, the broken, lifeless trees. When she had finally left this place with Ruebyn, it had no longer been the barren world they'd found upon their arrival, but a thriving jungle, its life restored by whatever magic their presence had brought.

"What do I care for this place?" Rayan spat. "It is imaginary, a construct of some ancient magic. It does not touch the real world." His head leaned to the side. "And it is you who cannot see. The Gods had it right when they ruled us, but they lacked the resolve to bring a lasting peace. They could not see it was your freedom that divided you, that drove your petty wars. I will not make the same mistake."

"You bring only death," Pela whispered. "Only hatred."

Drawing on the last ounce of her courage, she leapt at him, her father's sword flashing for his face. She put all her anger and rage into the blow, all the strength she could muster to strike the creature down—but as her blade slashed for Rayan's neck, the strength seemed to be drawn from Pela.

Crying out, Pela's knees buckled and she staggered sideways, barely able to keep her feet. Laughter sounded in her ears, rekindling her anger. Straightening, she found Rayan still standing in the centre of the clearing, the smug smile still pasted across his face. Teeth bared, Pela leapt at him again—but again the energy went from her as though sucked down a drain, and instead she found herself crashing face first into the broken earth.

"You know, my father was like you." The demon's voice seemed to circle her as she spat out a mouthful of dirt. "Always looking for the *right* way, always seeing the good in humanity.

Even at the end, when he discovered what I had become, he sought to *save me from myself.*" Rayan cackled as though this were some grand joke. "The fool might have saved himself, had he been ruthless enough. But he proved as weak as all the others."

The demon's voice was close now, just above her head. Roaring, Pela drove her blade upwards, praying for the speed to strike her foe down. This time she summoned her own power as well, funnelling it into the blade, determined to slash through whatever defences the demon raised against her.

She might as well have poured her power into the infinite depths of the ocean. It went from her in a rush and then vanished, leaving the demon standing untouched. Pela staggered to her feet and backed away, the sword slipping from her fingers as the last resistance left her.

The air seemed to darken as the creature stalked after her, as though a little more life had left the world. The stench of rot was all around her now, so thick she could barely breathe, barely think. Suddenly her legs were giving way and Pela crashed to the ground.

Despair swept through her as she watched the demon approach. What was the point in fighting anymore? She could not defeat Rayan, could not slay the demon he had become. He was toying with her, stretching out the moment of her death, if only to savour her agony when she finally succumbed.

"Surrendering so easily, young Pela?" Rayan chuckled. A sharp *thwack* came as Pela's blade slammed into the ground beside her head. "There," he continued, "I thought you could use the help. Come on, don't give up yet. There is still so much fun to have!"

Rage fed fresh energy to Pela's limbs. Snatching her blade from the earth, she scrambled backwards. A wiry bush brought her up short but she crashed through it, barely managing to keep her feet. Glancing back, she watched the plant's last leaves wither and die, but Pela was too exhausted to care. She couldn't understand where her strength had gone. Just a few minutes before this world have been restoring her—now it seemed to have reversed. Rayan stood across from her, mocking her with his calm.

"Or maybe you prefer to flee?" Rayan rumbled. "Go on, I'll give you a head start. Run!"

Pela bared her teeth in a show of defiance. But in her mind, a tiny voice screamed for her to obey, to open the portal and hurl herself back into the real world. The Way had transformed back to a place for the dead, the life she and Ruebyn had born almost consumed now. Soon it would take her too, she sensed. She needed to escape…

But the demon would only follow. He was too powerful, could snuff out her life with hardly a thought. She was surprised Rayan had not already destroyed her. Surely he wished to return to his army, to resume his destruction of Marianne's army.

A frown touched Pela's brow as she faced the beast. Why *hadn't* Rayan finished her? On the battlefield, he had been on the brink of stealing her soul, but now he had not made single attack—only rebuffed her own efforts.

Or had he?

Closing her eyes, Pela looked out again with her spirit and finally saw what had changed. The white glow that had lit the world earlier was all but vanished, reduced to mere whiffs that clung to the last patches of life. Clouds of darkness swept out in the wake of the darkness—but they did not come from the demon.

The darkness came from her.

Pela turned her gaze on Rayan. The darkness swirled about him, but there was no longer any light in his core, no glow from the thousands of souls he had stolen. And she remembered now how the demon's power had been channelled through the king—rather than stored within Rayan.

The Way had cut him off from that source.

Pela gasped as she returned to her body. Blood pounded in her ears as she looked on Rayan with fresh eyes. Without his subjects, without his soldiers, he was all but powerless here. The darkness was sustaining him as the light had done her, but it was not enough. She could see Rayan's hunger now, as though he were a Feline and she a helpless deer. Shuddering, she backed away.

"That's right, run," Rayan whispered as he stalked after her. "Flee back to your mother's skirts."

Pela staggered to a stop. Her heart hammered in her chest and she wanted desperately to obey the demon's command, but she could not. The second she opened the portal, Rayan's connection to his subjects would be restored. She would only be dooming herself and everyone else back in the real world.

The truth struck Pela like an arrow to the heart. She was trapped here, doomed to remain in this dying land, alone but for the awful demon. There was barely a glint of green left amongst the forest now, and the sky had darkened to bloodred.

Pela's whole body shook as she imagined spending the rest of her life beneath that sky. She sank to her knees, the blade slipping from her fingers.

"No," she whispered.

Tears streaked her cheeks as she grieved for the life she would never have, the friends and family she would never see again. Stones crunched as Rayan stepped closer. She could sense his hunger now, his greed. It was so strong it almost seemed real, a stench she tasted on the air, felt in her very bones.

"It doesn't have to be this way." His voice whispered in her ears. Pela shuddered but did not pull away. "You can still escape. I will spare you, spare your loved ones. You can still be together."

Temptation shot through Pela like a living thing, desperate, burning, but she fought it down. The demon spoke only lies—and even were it telling the truth, it could not offer life, only servitude. Despair rose to take its place and she fought to keep from screaming.

In, out. In, out.

Sucking in a deep breath, Pela sought to calm herself, to follow the words that had brought her through so much strife. Her heart slowed by half a beat. The hiss of Rayan's anger sounded from nearby, but he had no power here, and reaching calmly now for her life force, she erected a barrier around herself. She was almost surprised when The Way did not steal the energy, but she did not open her eyes, did not allow herself to be distracted. In each moment, there was only the cool breeze of her inhalation, the heat of each exhale.

Finally she found herself in the void of her inner mind. Only then did Pela allow other thoughts to intrude. Warmth touched her as she remembered her kindly grandmother, Selina, and her patience when Pela had first learned to meditate.

The image flickered, and now she saw Devon as he worked on their family inn, his hammer rising and falling, sealing the roof against the coming winter. Her mother stood nearby, an absent smile on her face as she watched the aging hammerman.

Pela's heart swelled as the image of her family faded. Another rose to take its place, and she saw again Genevieve and Caledan on the deck of the *Seadragon*, their practice blades flashing as they sparred. It soon changed again, and Pela watched as the huntress lifted her from the darkness of the mines, as she stood alone in the pass to hold back their enemies, as she raised her bow that final time to defend the helpless queen.

Tears stung Pela's eyes as she watched her friend fall, but there was no anger now, only love for everything Genevieve had done, for everything she had offered the world.

And finally Pela saw herself in that cave far above the Lonian planes. Her heart ached as she watched Ruebyn take her in his arms, as they made love while the storm raged outside. How losing him hurt, how she hated Rayan for sacrificing himself, and yet…

The demon could not steal these memories from her, could not take the brief moments she and Ruebyn had shared. The warmth in her chest seeped slowly outwards, filling her every limb. Within, Pela felt her strength retuning. Without, time passed unnoticed, and The Way changed.

Finally, Pela cracked open her eyes. Wonder touched her as she looked upon a new world. Gone were the rotting trees and rotten stench, the absolute stillness of death. Life had returned to the forest and now noble firs and pines grew up all around her, their emerald branches stretching for the sapphire sky.

For a long while, Pela sat staring at the beauty of the place, her heart filled with joy at the miracle. But eventually, memories of the demon drew her mind back to the present. Letting out a breath, she turned to face her foe—and recoiled.

Rayan still wore his sickly grin, but it was his only feature that had not changed. While she had meditated, the flesh had peeled from his face, exposing the yellowed bones beneath. Empty eye sockets stared down at her, while atop his scalp the skin had retreated, and now long white hair hung around his shoulders. Even his clothes had rotted, the remnants revealing the jagged points of his ribs.

Hand clasped to her mouth, Pela stifled her horror. Letting out a long breath, she sent her thanks up to the Gods. Somehow, she had won, had outlasted—

Lurching suddenly, Rayan took a step towards her, his laughter returning. Now though it was a hollow, empty sound, like the distant scream of a man falling to his death. Pela scrambled to her feet as the skeletal remnants reached for her, a scream tearing from her throat.

"You thought me dead?" the demonic skeleton rasped. "Not without you, sweet Pela!"

Panic rose in Pela's chest and she felt an irresistible urge to flee. Instead, she steeled herself to face the demon. If this was the end, she would not retreat. Like her father, she would stand against the darkness with sword in hand. This creature could not be allowed to escape, to return its evil to the Three Nations.

But as the skeleton approached, a thought came to Pela. Fighting for calm, she straightened and sheathed her sword. "I think you are powerless," she said softly, staring into the empty eyes. "I think you have nothing left, Rayan. Only the magic of this place sustains you."

"Come, girl," the skeleton rattled, and it seemed that sparks of red appeared in its eye sockets, "and I will show you my power."

Pela shook her head. "I don't think I will," she whispered.

Even as she spoke, Pela was reaching for her life force. It leapt to her summons now, restored by the magic of this strange world, by her own love. With it, she reached out for the ancient magic of The Way, ready to open the portal. Sensing what Pela was doing, Rayan staggered to a stop. His skull's grin grew wider.

"Yessss," the demon hissed. "Open the doorway."

A rush of air struck Pela as the portal burst into life. The skeleton readied itself to leap, but Pela's sword flashed up, barring its path.

"Think twice, mighty demon," she murmured. She wore a smile of her own now. "Perhaps you should look to yourself first."

Rage twisted what remained of the skeleton's features as Rayan swung on her. "You will not stop me."

Pela spread her hands. "Why would I? You must realise there is nothing for you outside this place now?" Silence answered her words, and chuckling, she went on: "Look at yourself, Rayan. There is nothing left of you, no flesh or blood or heart. The Way sustains you, but all the power in the world cannot restore your body. The second you step from this place, your bones will collapse and your soul will flee to whatever awaits us after death."

The skeleton did not respond, did not even move. It was as though Pela's words had truly struck Rayan dead. Slowly she retreated towards the portal, sword still stretched before her. The empty eye sockets followed her, and she could sense the hatred there, but now the demon made no move to follow her.

Finally she stood at the edge of the portal. Its energies buffeted Pela as she looked back at what now passed for Rayan. He would be trapped here forever, unable to escape, yet unable as well to die. She could not imagine such a fate, yet he had made his choice. He could end it now, could leap through the portal and allow death to claim him. But despite all the lives he had stolen—or perhaps because of them—that was one fate Rayan could not accept.

"Farewell then," she said.

Then the portal was swallowing Pela up, and the swirling rainbow lights of The Way were all around her. The passage only seemed to last a moment this time, and with an earth-shaking *boom*, she found herself standing in the real world.

Relief swept through Pela as the portal vanished, quickly followed by joy. She was free, she was safe! The Three Nations were safe. Slumping to her knees, she sobbed into the dirt, uncaring who might see.

All around, the world was silent but for the wind through the trees. A frown touched Pela's forehead as her thoughts turned to the present. What had become of the battle? Had the forces of the free succeeded in defeating the Trolan army? Or had the blue-armoured soldiers surrendered when their demon master failed to reappear?

Coming to her feet, Pela finally took the time to examine her surroundings. The plains were overgrown where she had landed, the scraggly trees and bushes thick around her.

Taking her father's sword, she hacked her way to a nearby tree that stood above the rest and scrambled up.

Pela's heart was hammering in her chest by the time she reached the top. But when she looked out across the land around her, the view was not what she had expected. There was forest all around her—there was nothing like it within a day's ride from Chole. What had gone wrong with the portal? It was meant to be connected to the city walls, yet the only landmark she could see was a nearby escarpment, its surface thick with vines.

Frowning, Pela stared at the cliffs. There was something wrong about them, but she could not quite tell what. Returning to the ground, she set off towards them, using her blade to carve a path through the dense undergrowth.

She was panting hard by the time she reached the escarpment, but even there she did not stop. Blood pounded in her ears as she followed the base of the cliffs, studying the strange stones. What she was seeing could not be possible, surely. Ruebyn had said that time moved differently in the way, but even so…

Pela staggered to a stop as the cliffs came to an abrupt end. Fifty yards ahead, they resumed, but between there was only empty space, as though some giant had carved through the rock with his sword. Heart in her throat, Pela staggered into the gap between the cliffs—though she knew now that was not what they were—and the earth turned to cobbles beneath her feet.

Tears streamed down Pela's face as she stood in the breach in Chole's walls. A great sob tore from her throat as she stared at the ruins, long since abandoned by the hands of men. In a rage, she swung her blade at a sapling that had taken root amidst the rubble. But it was a futile gesture—the decades had long since claimed the city. There was nothing she could do to change her fate, to turn back time. It was already done, her life lost to the abyss. Now there was nothing left.

Turning her eyes to the empty heavens, Pela mourned for the world she had lost forever.

———

THAT'S IT FOR NOW! BUT BE SURE TO CHECK OUT MY OTHER fantasy world in Warbringer, and out what happens next in, and don't forget to leave a review if you enjoyed the story.

NOTE FROM THE AUTHOR

Wow, what a ride! And if you've made it this far, thank you for joining me on the journey! This series might have been a little different from my earlier books, and even what I originally intended, but sometimes the world and our lives have other plans. I finished the first draft of Daughter of Fate on the day of the Christchurch terror attacks, and after seeing the horrible outcome of such hate, I knew I needed to write something different this year, something that rejected that hate. I hope you enjoyed it :-)

Anyway, onto other business. With Pela now an unknown number of years in the future, there's obviously the possibility of more stories in the Three Nations, but for now I'm looking at another project to refresh myself. I hope to start working on something new in the next few weeks and all going well you might be seeing something brand new from me in February! In the meantime, if you'd like to hear more from me, please remember to join to my mailing list for updates, specials, and a free copy of my novels Stormwielder and Oathbreaker! I also send out lots of free deals and specials most months, so if you love fantasy you can't go too wrong.

FOLLOW AARON HODGES

Join Aaron Hodges on his newsletter to **receive TWO FREE novels and a short story!**
https://aaronhodgesauthor.com/newsletter

Warbringer

If you've enjoyed this book, you might want to check out another of my fantasy series!

Centuries ago, the world fell. From the ashes rose a terrible new species—the Tangata. Now they wage war against the kingdoms of man. And humanity is losing.

Book 3: Age of Gods

Book 4: Dreams of Fury

The Alfurian Chronicles

Book 1: Defiant

Book 2: Guardian

Book 3: Conquest

The Swords of Heaven and Hell

Book 1: Darkstrider

The Four Circles

Book 1: Help! My Wizard Mentor Had A Heart Attack And Now I'm Being Chased By A Horde Of Giant Spiders!

The Untamed Isles

The Path Awakens